MidKnight

ANN DENTON

Le Rue
Publishing

Le Rue Publishing
320 South Boston Avenue, Suite 1030
Tulsa, OK 74103
www.LeRuePublishing.com

ISBN: 978-1-7335960-8-4

To Mar.

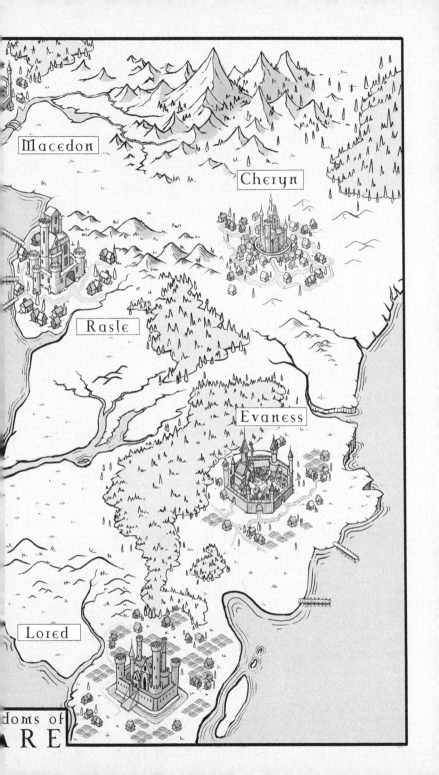

Macedon

Cheryn

Rasle

Evaness

Lored

doms of
RE

CHAPTER ONE

I had never truly hated anyone before. I realized that as black loathing bubbled in my stomach like tar. Rage ran hot in my veins as I clenched my fists to keep from throttling the man I faced.

Jorad, mother's butler—now mine—stared back at me. His wrinkled face didn't show a drop of pity. He didn't look the slightest bit cowed. He stared at me with steady brown eyes and it was all I could do not to kill him, right then and there.

"You can't go," Jorad repeated.

My cheeks grew hot. That arrogant shite. He was a butler. Not one of my knights. Not an adviser. I stood up straighter and narrowed my eyes. "I can. And I will. I am the queen—"

"Exactly."

"You can't force me to stay—"

"You can't just go off chasing dragons. People depend on you." Jorad made the mistake of moving to touch my arm.

It felt like being bitten. I backed away.

I'm not going to hit him, I told myself, though that was exactly what I felt like doing. How dare he! My sister, the only blood relative I had left in the world, had just been seized by a monster.

"Avia was just stolen by a *dragon*!" I was awed by the fact that I needed to remind him.

I faced off against Jorad in the rose parlor, a small office and sitting room my mother had used for meetings.

Somehow, my knights had marched me here. I'd been too blinded by shock to even remember exactly how we got into the castle and into the room. I might have blacked out, I wasn't certain. The last thing I was certain of was that I'd been standing on the dais, ready to give the order for the execution of a prince of Cheryn, when Avia had been snatched by a dragon. The beast had dive bombed, silent as a hawk, spreading his wings at the last moment. His taloned feet had curled around my sister's arms and with a single beat of his wings, he'd been back in the clouds.

I shook off the memory and took in my surroundings. I still held Abbas' chain in my hands, dragging the shite prince by the neck behind me like some dog. He was a dog. He was the one who'd arranged my sister's kidnapping. And he'd pay. Right after I ensured Avia's safety, Abbas would pay with his sanity. Then with his blood.

I yanked on the chain, bringing Abbas to his knees. It made me feel slightly better.

Jorad was not impressed by me. He crossed his arms. "You have no heir, have not set up an alternative arrangement for succession, and have dangers brewing both domestic and abroad," he drawled.

Abbas *tsked*, shaking his head. "Not very prepared, were you, Queen Bloss?" His words hit their mark, as deadly accurate as poisoned arrows.

I yanked his chain again. Then I kicked his ribs for good measure.

I rounded on Jorad. "Perhaps you shouldn't discuss shite like that in front of prisoners!"

"Perhaps prisoners shouldn't be brought into palace meeting rooms," Jorad's reply was steady. "I can have him sent to the dungeon."

"I'm taking him with me." I didn't believe for a second that the dragon, Abbas' shape-shifting brother, would give up Avia if I didn't provide proof of life for Abbas. I needed that greasy, sorry excuse-for-a-human being. I wasn't letting him out of my sight until I got Avia back.

"You *cannot* leave," Jorad repeated.

"Watch me," I tossed back.

Ryan, the knight in charge of my armed forces, had gone to the stables, to ready our mounts and a regiment for the pursuit. He'd already sent out scouts to scour the skies.

Declan and Connor, two of my other husbands, stood to the side, watching Jorad argue with me. Or Connor watched, his 'diplomat' face on in full force as he stroked his tan jaw.

I turned to Connor and raised my brows expectantly.

"There is an alternative arrangement for succession on file in the records," Connor told my butler.

Jorad's eyes widened, "You can't be serious!"

Connor shrugged, "Just because you don't like the current candidate doesn't invalidate the document."

I glanced between the two men, whose backs were as stiff as their starched formal tunics as they squared off. I wasn't certain what document they were talking about. I'd only recently returned to royal life in Evaness. I looked over to see if Declan knew. But he was busy scratching out calculations in a notebook.

"Declan?" I whispered, moving to touch his arm. "What are you doing?"

Dec glanced up at me, a crease at his brow. "Trying to see how much blood we'd need to stop it, Peace."

"Oh. Yes. Do that."

His mouth quirked up in a grin. "Is that an order?"

I nodded and a tiny spark came into his eyes before he bent back over his notebook and I turned back to Connor and Jorad. My sweet, blond economics adviser was right. We needed to know how much blood he'd need to multiply. He could reduce water to multiply blood. And with blood … I could make the dragon peaceful. My magic could lull it. But only temporarily. And the price of forcing peace on another creature? Blood.

The last time we'd fought the dragon, my peace magic had worn off in less than an hour. And that had taken a moat full of blood. I had no idea how long we'd have to keep the beast peaceful for our rescue. What if the dragon had dragged my sister into a cave? I left Declan to his calculations. Our lives, Avia's life, might depend on them.

I looked for the last of my four knights. Quinn, my spy master, was in the far corner of the room, facing the wall, checking in with each of his spies, to see if anyone had seen a dragon. I could see his black hair and his pointed elf ears twitch as he had silent conversations.

Quinn faced the wall so he could ignore us and concentrate. The problem with his choice was that it distracted me for a second, because it gave me a very, very nice view of his ass.

Not helping my focus, Dove.

Sorry, I thought at him. His magic allowed him to communicate via thoughts, which was incredibly useful as a spy master, and incredibly hot in the bedroom. But it was somewhat embarrassing in moments like this.

I turned back to Connor and Jorad, who were now debating.

Connor ran a hand through his messy brown curls.

"—we could re-draft a document in a few hours," Jorad said.

"Hours?" I interjected. "You think Avia has hours?"

"I think you need to do this right!" Jorad slammed his hand onto the meeting table.

"What's right is stopping that beast!" I yelled. My sixteen-year-old sister—no, seventeen, it was her birthday—could be dropped at any moment. Flamed. Eaten. The night-mares played in an endless stream in my head. Connor grabbed my left hand and drained a bit of my panic.

I met his eyes. I knew what he wanted without him having to say a word. Connor wanted me to rein it in. I took a deep, shuddering breath.

Abbas smirked from his spot on the edge of the rug. I put up my free hand and blasted the evil wrinkler with enough glowing green peace magic to knock him out. His eyes closed and he fell back onto the marble floor, smacking his skull with a dreamy smile on his face. The black-haired, black-hearted prince of Cheryn could stay passed out until we had Avia back. It was worth the fresh wound on my forearm. I dabbed at the blood with my sleeve as I looked back up at Jorad.

"I'm going to rescue my sister."

"What do your people need more, the other princess or their *queen*?" he snapped.

I decked him. I couldn't help myself. I dropped Connor's hand and just swung. The rage took over in a blur of heat and red-tinged vision. I punched that sarding dunderhead in the jaw.

Avia was everything. She was an innocent. She was one of my people. I had a duty to protect her. And she was hurt because of me. Because I'd chosen to tango with a madman. And I hadn't anticipated he'd go this far.

Of course, he would.

He wanted Evaness.

I was a fool. This was my fault. And I had to be the one to fix it.

Connor's hand stopped my arm from launching a second hit, a hit Jorad didn't deserve. I was so furious at myself that I could hardly see straight.

Connor, sensing my agitation with his magic, tried to soothe me. He rubbed my back gently, gliding his fingers over my shoulder blades, letting the soft velvet of my hem brush my spine. When my fists unclenched, Connor moved closer, lending me strength. He stood next to me, shoulder to shoulder. Together, we stared down Jorad.

My butler cupped his face as he spoke, spittle dripping onto his split lip. "If you go now and leave the current document your mother had in place, then Duke Aiden will be the regent."

My eyes widened. I dropped Abbas' chain in shock. "What?" I recalled seeing Duke Aiden at Kylee's gambling hall on more than one occasion. I recalled the duke losing round after round of poker, and then comforting himself

7

with one of the prostitutes who worked there. "That's who my mother appointed to rule in her absence? Not his wife?" Evaness was matriarchal. It was highly unusual for my mother to have picked a man as her regent.

"Not his wife," Jorad confirmed.

"A gambling whoremonger?" I bit out, grabbing onto one of the chairs surrounding the meeting table. I squeezed the chair back, willing it to absorb my distress. If I'd have been Ryan, the chair would have splintered under my fingers. It had zero reaction to my abuse, which only made me squeeze harder in frustration.

Jorad's face twisted into a bitter grin. "It was her way of deterring the other nobles from assassination. Their choices became her or him."

"Sard. Well, it did its job then." I felt like yanking at my hair. But my mother's voice sounded in my head. 'That wouldn't be seemly for a queen.' Her voice was a bit late. I'd already struck her butler. I clenched my skirts in my fists and paced.

What the hell am I gonna do? First day as queen, and sarding up all over the place. Well done, Bloss, I grumbled internally as I walked.

Jorad asked, "The question is, do you want to leave your people subjected to the whims of that man while you leave?"

It was a good question. My heart tightened at the thought. No wonder Jorad didn't want me to leave.

I turned to Connor. "Who else? We could assign someone from your family, right?"

Jorad shook his head. "The laws of Evaness say no extended family member of the royal family can be the regent."

"What the hell?" I gritted my teeth. I should have known that. If I'd been at the palace the last four years, I would have. Hellfire, there was so much I didn't remember.

Jorad cleared his throat in a clear sign of disapproval. "Your Majesty, you're more likely to all be assassinated at a family gathering."

I hated when idiotic rules actually made sense.

I turned to look at Connor even as I kept pacing. "Who can we put—"

His brow furrowed as he thought. He opened his mouth once, but then shook his head and closed it. My eyes traced the handsome lines of his face, silently willing him to know something about the nobles I didn't. To know someone trustworthy enough to—

A knock at the door interrupted us. My hands clenched into fists. "Not now!" I yelled.

Shite, Bloss. Not queenly. Not queenly, I scolded myself.

Part of me didn't care. But another part of me argued with that part, stating I had to care. My life was all scrutiny all the time now.

Jorad ignored my glare and primly walked over to the door.

"Don't—" I started.

He opened the door. "Yes?"

A nervous messenger shuffled from foot to foot as he handed Jorad a sealed scroll. Jorad thanked the lad, took the scroll, and turned to me. With a defiant glare, he broke the seal, stating, "It's from the royal house of Rasle."

His eyes scanned the scroll and his lips thinned. He glanced up at me. "Her Majesty, Queen Isla and her entourage are already airborne on a sleuth of winged bears, on their way to congratulate you on your coronation. Ready to reinforce ties and discuss treaty terms." Jorad handed the unfurled parchment toward me.

It felt as if I were reaching for my own death certificate. Or Avia's. My hazel eyes scanned the document.

Sard.

Mother's greatest ally. The country that stood to the west, between us and Sedara, the bully of the seas.

Isla was a salty, crusty old queen if there ever was one. And a clever bitch. Right now, she was a walking typhoon, heading this way to blow me down with terms and conditions that would exploit my ignorance.

My eyes flashed to Connor's. My best friend since childhood, he'd cowered with me under tables and behind curtains whenever Rasle's queen had come calling.

But my sweetheart just stared placidly back at me, his blue-green eyes an undisturbed pool of calm.

"What the hell am I gonna do?" I whispered.

Avia, my heart clawed at my chest. The need to find her, to protect her was a living thing inside me, writhing, demanding I chase after the dragon.

Connor could feel that. He strode to me and grabbed my hand. He linked our fingers. His thumb stroked the side of my wrist.

"We'll find a way."

I swallowed and nodded. I hoped like hell he was right. But fear swirled in my chest. I had a feeling this nightmare had only begun.

§

*J*orad left to prepare rooms for Rasle's royal visitors. And feasts. And parades. And whatever the hell else he muttered about that I didn't listen to because I felt like I was drowning.

Mother's voice rang in my ears. 'Needs before wants.' It was essentially what Jorad had said. He'd dismissed my rescue of Avia as a want. As something I shouldn't do because I was a queen.

Are they right? I wondered.

My gut twisted. Connor squeezed my hand, draining some of my agony.

11

A moment later, Quinn came over and touched my shoulder. His grey eyes stared solemnly at mine. *He doesn't mean she's just a want, Dove. He doesn't think you personally have to go.*

Who's gonna take out the dragon?

There are ways. In the Fire Wars, countries all had different means of taking them out.

How?

He shrugged. *I'm not the scholar. Declan might know. We might have to research. We'll find a way. I promise.*

I gave a stiff nod, trying to hold it together. *Did your people—*

They haven't found anything yet, Dove. But they're looking. All of them.

I nodded as my vision got glassy. I let Quinn pull me into a soft hug even as Connor held my hand. Connor released my hand and came up behind me and pressed against my spine. Together, the two of them enveloped me in warmth and comfort. I soaked in their care, reveled in their strength.

I knew they would do everything they could to help me. I wasn't in this alone. I took a deep breath, trying to release the tension. Another. Another. They waited patiently, just content to be there for me. Eventually, I placed a hand on Quinn's chest, and pushed lightly.

He stepped back. Then Connor did the same.

"Thank you," I swiped at the tears that had gathered at the base of my eyes, tears I hadn't allowed to fall. "I needed that."

Anytime, Dove.

"Of course, Bloss Boss," Connor gave a little smile and my heart skipped. His smiles were like sun rays.

The door behind us opened and Ryan stomped into the room. My half-giant had a hard time doing anything other than stomping, he was so huge and stacked with muscle. I gave him a weak grin in greeting. My eyes trailed over the armor he'd strapped over the formal wear he'd donned for the morning's execution. He was ready to leave.

Ryan stood at attention, "Everything's being loaded, Your Majesty. We're ready, whenever you are."

Connor went to close the door behind Ryan as Quinn hauled Abbas into a sitting position.

What are you doing? I thought at Quinn.

He needs to be locked back up while we figure this out, Quinn responded. *And I don't want him overhearing our plans. I'll take him via the royal passageways to a secure room I have.*

I nodded.

Ryan waited expectantly.

I nodded at Connor, who shut the door to the hallway. Then I told Ryan, "Actually, there's been a complication."

Ryan swore when I told him about the visit from Rasle.

"Shite! Well, I'm going to have to rearrange my forces. I'll have to pull back the very men I just had suit up. They're the best. I need them to protect you."

"I haven't decided if I'm staying—" I said.

Ryan shook his head. "Queen Isla's always been a vulture. You don't want to leave her alone here. She'll take every scrap she can. You're staying."

I crossed my arms and narrowed my eyes. "Excuse me, good knight, I must have misheard. It sounded like you were giving me orders."

Ryan stepped into my personal space, completely unintimidated by the fact that I was his queen. He dragged his index finger slowly over my jaw and gently pushed my chin until my head was tilted back enough to meet his eyes. "Oh, I'll make you stay. I'll make you do many, many things."

"Queen." I tried to trump him.

It didn't work. His finger trailed down my neck, sending shivers down my spine and making my toes curl. The finger started to dip below the collar of my dress. But he teased me, playing with just the edge. "I'm sorry. What was that? I couldn't hear."

"I said …"

He chuckled as he pinched a nipple through my dress and I lost my trail of thought again.

"Dammit!" I smacked his hand away and took a step back.

He went to the bell pull and yanked it. "I'll get a messenger sent down to one of my marshals."

I shook my head. I was angry. But not at him. I was angry at the situation. And anger was better than all the other shite emotions running through me. So, I ran with it. "Well, you wouldn't be the first to tell me what to do this morning. Jorad doesn't want me to leave either." My ire might spare Ryan, but it left no quarter for Jorad or Queen Isla. Or for the villain who'd started all of this. My eyes flew to Abbas. Quinn had just slung the sorry sack of skin over his shoulders.

I clenched my teeth. I couldn't wait for the moment I could smash in the scoundrel's face.

Ryan's tone grew gentle as he watched me scowl at Abbas. "We'll find Avia. One of my scouts said he saw something in the sky to the south. He wasn't sure what it was, it was too far away, but possibly the dragon."

"The south?" I exchanged a confused look with Connor, who leaned against the wall near the door. "But, wouldn't they take her into Cheryn? To the north?"

Ryan gave a shrug.

"Isla's arriving on flying bears," I added. "Could that be what they saw?"

"Rasle's west. So, unlikely. And this thing was headed away, not toward the capital."

I opened my mouth to ask more about what exactly Ryan's scouts had seen, but before I could get out a word, the door swung open, nearly smacking Connor in the face.

"I figured it out!" Cerena limped in, carrying a giant leather-bound book. Her hair was a wild silver dandelion, a frizzed halo around her head. It didn't look like my new castle mage had slept. Her black dress was covered in grime. She looked nearly as bad as Abbas, who'd been in the dungeons.

Cerena slammed the book on the table, startling Declan out of his calculations. A bluebird swooped into the room behind her and settled on a chair back. I hadn't realized she'd had a familiar. Then again, I'd only ever visited her cottage briefly before.

Connor closed the door again and we all turned to face Cerena.

"He shouldn't have been able to order that dragon to attack you!" she rasped.

My eyes automatically went to Abbas. Quinn had stopped walking toward the spelled passageway the second Cerena had smashed through the door. Abbas drooped limply over my knight's shoulder. The chain on the prisoner's neck trailed onto the floor.

"I've checked that damn parchment and that damn spell six times," Cerena said. I could tell she was about to start a rant, but a cough interrupted her, and her shoulders shook as she covered her mouth. Connor got her a glass of water, which she downed, before clearing her throat and continuing, "Sorry. That engagement document was done right. That betrayal spell works. I tested it."

I didn't ask how. I wasn't sure I wanted to know. The spell made those who betrayed Evaness explode. I kept my eyes on her face and off her dress, suddenly suspicious of the grime on it.

Declan took a step forward, head tilted in interest, notebook in his hand forgotten. "Well, if the spell wasn't faulty, how did Abbas get around it?"

Cerena's eyes gleamed. She pointed a gnarled finger at the man Quinn carried. "That *isn't* Abbas."

CHAPTER TWO

My mind was a shipwreck. Cerena's words were monster waves. They smashed apart everything I'd thought I'd known. I couldn't breathe. I lost all sense of direction. I felt dizzy. I staggered backward a step. Ryan was there in an instant. He caught me before I could fall, wrapping his thick arms securely around me. He noticed my cuts and used his pink healing magic to seal the wounds caused by my peace magic.

I hardly noticed what he did. I was still stuck on what Cerena had said. "What?" my voice was breathless as I looked at my mage.

"He signed that engagement document with the name Abbas," Cerena said. "The document binds the names of those who sign. The loophole? It assumes you sign your own name." She smacked her book open to a marked page and pointed at the spell. "There! See?"

Declan stepped closer and bent to examine the spell.

Cerena continued speaking to the rest of us. "That clever shite. He bound Abbas to you. But not himself. It's the only way he could have gotten around my spell work. Abbas couldn't betray you. Can't betray you, wherever the hell he is. Whoever this interloper is ... could."

I turned in Ryan's arms to stare at Abbas as Quinn set him back on the floor and strode over to the rest of us. I stared at the prince's body and literally repeated Cerena's words in my head. The sneaking parasite passed out on my floor wasn't Abbas. I pulled away from Ryan and walked toward the body on the floor. I crouched down next to him. I grabbed a hank of his jet-black hair and pulled, lifting his head off the ground. I studied his full lips. His thick brows. His beard, which stuck out at all angles.

My mind whirled: If he's not Abbas, who the sarding hell is he?

What she says ... it's impossible, Quinn thought-projected to the group, to those of us who wore his magic beads and could hear his voice inside our heads.

We all cringed, except for Cerena. When Quinn projected his thoughts to multiple people, it was horribly loud. And it echoed.

I saw his thoughts. His people's thoughts. No one thought about deception. No one pictured him as anything other than Abbas. I saw him talking to the rebels as Abbas, arranging for the dragon—

"Okay," Connor held up his hand to stop Quinn. He waited a moment, so our ears could recover before he spoke. "I agree that it seems odd. But you have to admit, the way he was able to shuffle his thoughts and emotions, that's not natural. I've never seen anyone pull off something like that."

Quinn gave a brisk nod.

"He wouldn't be able to wear a disguise potion and come through the front gate," Ryan pondered. "So, if it's not Abbas, how'd he get through the gate?"

I turned where I crouched and met Cerena's eyes. She held my gaze, unfazed even as every single one of my knights turned his attention on her.

She lifted her head as she spoke, "The gate accounts for human magic. But no hedge witch and no mage has enough magic to fully counter … non-human magics."

My heart dropped. My hands flew back from Abbas, as if he'd burnt me.

"Meaning?" Connor asked Cerena, not quite sure of her implications.

"Whatever he is … whoever he is … he's not human."

I stared down at the body below me. Whatever hid under the shell that was Abbas, it was cruel; it was evil. It had schemed and taken my sister.

A knife flayed me at that thought.

The words slipped out of my lips soft and breathy, "So … we don't even know who has Avia."

"No. And we don't know who it is that's working against Evaness," Cerena said.

My stomach crumpled.

Declan cut off my panic attack with logic. "All those servants were from Cheryn. How could that have worked? It has to be them."

Cerena shook her head. "Elven chains could do the trick, too. I haven't looked into all the fae weapons, but djinn wishes are also pretty expansive. Mermaids can manipulate memory. There are a lot of magical possibilities. Just non-human ones."

"Sard!" I slammed my fist into the table, scaring Cerena's bluebird, which fluttered over to a nearby curtain rod, to peer at me from a safer distance.

Screw queenly. I was furious. I wanted answers.

I walked over to Abbas. I bent and smacked him hard across the face. "Wake up!"

He merely groaned. I'd hit him with too much peace earlier. His eyelids only fluttered when I punched him.

Whoa, Dove! Slow down. You don't want it to be too hard for him to talk when he wakes. Quinn grabbed my hand as I reared back for another blow. *Body shots, darling. Stick to body shots.*

I love you, I thought as I started pummeling.

Jorad walked in as I smashed Abbas in the ribs.

"Torturing prisoners in our main rooms now, are we?" he asked dryly. "Should I have the room redecorated in shackles for you, Your Majesty?"

I whirled on Jorad, that smug shite. "Where are all the servants that came with Abbas?"

"As of right now, they are packing to leave. They had been detained for questioning, but it was determined they knew nothing of—"

"Put them back in their wing. Lock them in. Guards on all entrances, exits, windows."

"We have a royal entourage about to arrive and those rooms are needed."

"Open another wing!"

Jorad's eyes shut and his face contorted in anger. "We don't have time—"

"Then move the people from Cheryn to the unopened wing. Or the dungeon."

"Do you intend to go to war with the sultan?" Jorad sniped.

I sat back next to Abbas prone body. I stared at the prince, at the monster without a name. I was at a loss. I didn't know what to do.

Declan crouched beside me and offered me a hand. He pulled me to my feet. "Quinn could always send one of his people with them, have them take someone's place with a disguise spell. Dig around to see if their stories change once they're outside the palace."

I nodded.

Done, Dove. I'm going to go find my guy now. Don't kill Abbas without me.

I wouldn't deprive you.

Good.

Ryan muttered, "If Isla's coming on flying bears, she'll be here soon, and I need to rearrange my troops. I'll still send out a search party. But it's going to be smaller. We'll need numbers here."

I agreed.

Ryan left. Cerena followed, taking her book, her message delivered.

Connor turned to me and gave a tiny smile. "I need to go with Jorad. I'll need to make announcements to the nobles in residence, prepare the heralds, write a speech to welcome Isla."

He and Jorad shut the door behind them; they left Declan and I staring down at Abbas.

"Well, I suppose we can't just leave the shitepile there," Declan kissed the top of my head before releasing my hand. "I'll grab a few guards in the hallway to go lock him up."

Declan left, and I pulled out a chair and sank into it. I had no idea what I was going to do. No idea how to save my sister. No idea who was after me. I was lost.

I covered my face with my hands, leaning on the table. I tried to tamp down on the anger I felt at myself.

I was so sarding screwed.

A bird shrilled and I saw Cerena's bluebird swoop past me. She must have forgotten it—

A hand closed over my ankle and yanked. I tipped backward in the chair. My head smacked the wooden chair back and then the ground so quickly I didn't even have time to scream. Black flecks filled my vision and I was dazed. When my eyes cleared, I saw that Abbas leaned over me. The whites of his eyes glowed as he stared down at me. He covered my mouth with one hand. His other hand wrapped around my neck.

I pushed frantically against him, but he was too strong. He flexed his fingers, cutting off my airflow. My kicks slowed and my hands clawed at him. Cerena's bluebird dive-bombed Abbas.

He didn't react. Not to the bird's attacks or mine. Not even when I drew blood.

Instead, he pressed his body into mine, using his strength to pin me down and keep me immobile.

Abbas spoke and his voice had an odd, metallic echo to it. He didn't sound human. "Originally, I wanted to take your kingdom." He leaned closer, a crazed smile on his face.

"Now, I'm going to take everything from you." The fingers that had been gagging me started to move. He dragged his hand over the edge of my crown, which was tangled in my dark brown locks. Then his fingers trailed over my cheek and down my neck.

I couldn't suppress the chill that crept down my spine.

The hand that choked me let up slightly. I gasped, gulping air as quickly as I could.

I heard footsteps. Declan and the guards were almost back. I just needed to make it a few more seconds. I didn't want him to realize they were coming. I didn't want him to try to get away. I struggled to make as much noise as possible, trying to punch Abbas in the face, kicking my feet against the floor, squealing against his fingers as they clenched once more around my neck.

Abbas merely laughed and ran his nose along my neck, like a lover might. "Just wait, Bloss. I have so much in store for you. The most beautiful nightmare."

His face seemed to shimmer before my eyes. His mouth morphed and stretched until he had a sharp row of dagger-like teeth. And then he sank his teeth into my neck, biting down so hard I screamed.

CHAPTER THREE

I woke up in my chamber, stripped to my chemise, laying on top of my covers. I was desperately thirsty. But at least my neck didn't hurt. I ran a finger over the healed skin.

Declan was perched at my side on the bed. Connor was just behind him. Quinn and Ryan stood on the other side of the bed, watching over me. When I coughed, Connor handed me a tumbler of water, which I gulped down.

"Are you…" he trailed off, worried.

I rolled my eyes. "Don't baby me. Just tell me that asswipe's been beaten within an inch of his life and healed so I can beat him myself."

Declan grinned at me. "Of course, Peace," he used his nickname for me, "Ryan and Quinn both beat him."

I winked at my knights across the bed and Ryan lifted his chin.

Declan grabbed my hand, "You know, I really love the irony of your power."

I smiled at him. "Me, too. Now help me to my feet."

Declan helped me up. Because attitude or not, magical healing or not, an attack still had some physical aftermath. I had to shake off tremors from the adrenaline. I was still slightly light-headed from the blood loss. But I stared at myself in the looking glass and didn't see a hint of a scar.

"Your work?" I asked Ryan.

He nodded. "The healer and I worked together."

Ryan and the other guys followed me into my dressing room. "I'm nearly out of time to get ready, aren't I?" I asked.

"Take whatever time you need to recover, Bloss Boss," Connor said. "I'll delay Isla if we need to."

I shook my head. "I don't want to look weak during our first meeting."

Connor reached for my hand. He felt my pulse. "You sure?"

"I'm fine," I told him.

Declan spoke up. "Abbas shape-shifted. His face when I came in—"

"That proves Cerena right, doesn't it?" I said. "The real Abbas can't shape-shift, can he?"

Declan shook his head. "No. The real one's supposedly got superhuman speed. And the three wishes all half djinn get. But that's it. I believe Cerena. My question is … I didn't recognize *what* he was. Did you?"

I ran a hand self-consciously over my neck. The healer had removed the scar, but a phantom pain sent my pulse racing. "We'll make him tell us."

We certainly will, Quinn came up and pulled my hand away from my neck and kissed me gently there.

Connor came to my right side and stroked my arm. "I'm glad you're okay."

I gave him a small smile and grabbed his hands, pulling them around me. I needed a hug. I needed more than a hug. I wanted to be wrapped up in reassurances and soft crooning like an infant. But I didn't have time for any more comfort than the hug. So, I simply latched onto Connor and let him drain a little of my fear. "Thanks."

Declan paced in front of me. "Abbas is an impostor. He's capable of shape shifting. Controlling a dragon. Which now we can't even be sure is his brother. We made that assumption thinking we were fighting Abbas. But whoever he *is* … he's unstable enough or desperate enough to attack you in your own palace …"

I raised an eyebrow. "Okay. Does your pacing mean you know who he is?"

Declan bit his lip. "No. It means I'm worried about Avia. Desperation isn't good."

29

My heart dropped. I was scared for her, too. "We need to find her quickly."

Ryan nodded. "I'm going to follow my man to the south and see what I can pick up, right after the state dinner tonight with Isla. I'll fly through the night but be back early morning or so, that way I can be here for the rest of the state visit."

Quinn spoke to all of us. *After I question Abbas, I'm going to meet with some of my agents near Cheryn. And I'll send out scouts to nearby mountains to look for signs of dragons.*

"I'm going to the library. Maybe I'll find some kind of for clue as to who the hell this shitehole is," Declan said.

Connor shrugged. "Tell me if any of you need anything. But, Bloss and I will be occupied with this visit. Rasle always wants to discuss borders. They've been itching to take back some hills they lost a century ago. I'm guessing Isla thinks this is her chance."

Everyone nodded, me included. It felt better, having a plan.

Ryan scooped me up and held me eye to eye, my feet dangling two feet off the ground. "You alright?" he asked.

"Of course. He was trying to scare me," I shrugged. I didn't bother mentioning that Abbas had succeeded. I'd felt vulnerable. And he'd nearly ripped my throat out. I couldn't think about things like that. I had to block it out and focus, like mother taught me.

"My idiot guards won't leave you alone again," Ryan growled as he set me down.

My heart swelled at the protective tone in his voice. I loved it when he turned into a caveman about me. I stroked his shoulder. "I won't turn my back like an idiot again, either. It will make their jobs easier."

Ryan growled and shoved something small into my hand. "You'll wear this at your wrist from now on, too."

There was a little leather strap, made to fit my wrist. It held a sheath for a hair pin. When I pulled the pin out, it gleamed like a miniature sword.

Ryan set me down and pointed at his ribs. "Stab me, right here. Shove up under the ribs."

I nodded. "Got it."

He grabbed my wrist. "No. I mean, do it. You practice on me."

My jaw dropped. "I can't hurt you."

"I can heal myself."

"Yeah, then you'll tear the room apart."

"Better the room than you getting attacked and torn apart again."

Connor stepped forward, "He's right, Bloss. We don't want to see you get hurt again." I noticed his hands were stained. Like he'd only washed them haphazardly. It was a moment before I realized his hands were stained with blood.

"Is that … mine?" I asked.

He shoved his hands behind his back, as if he couldn't bear to look at them. "Yes, and I'd rather not have to see that again. So, stab the sarding shite out of Ryan. Okay?"

I looked questioningly back at Ryan.

He nodded. "I'm part giant. You won't be able to hit my heart. But you shove until I tell you to stop. I'm gonna make sure you can hit the heart of any other sarding dizzard who touches you."

I took a deep breath. I held eye contact with Ryan. And then I launched forward, shoving that hair pin as hard as I could.

It hit his ribs and glanced off.

"Again. Lower. Thrust upward."

That's what the maiden said, Quinn couldn't keep his smartass comments to himself.

I shook my head. "Shouldn't we be getting ready for Isla?"

Ryan shrugged. "They're dismounting. Unpacking. Need to freshen up."

So, I ran at him again. This time, my pin ran right through his flesh and I felt the sickening sensation of pressing through someone's innards.

Ryan grunted and held up a hand. "Stop," he gasped. He yanked the hair pin out and pink light flooded the room.

"Once more."

I did it again, and my aim was good.

Ryan healed himself and then strapped the pin to my arm. His rage was hardly contained. His hands shook as he snapped the leather band in place. "You wear that even in your sleep."

"Yes, sir."

He growled and grabbed my hair in his fist. "Dammit." He smashed his face into mine, biting my lip cruelly. But I loved it. His rough touch erased anything Abbas had done. When he released me, he was shaking even harder. "I have a few guards to go punish and security checks to complete. Then I'll be off south."

"Too bad."

Ryan's eyes closed and I admired how his curled lashes softened the hard planes of his face. "Yeah, too bad. I was hoping to stay here for girl talk while your maid did your hair."

My tough alpha-giant made me belly laugh. He swatted my ass. "Be good and be safe."

"Sir, yes, sir."

He swatted me one more time and then strode out, leaving me staring after him.

I turned to my other husbands. But Declan was already across the room, talking to my maid and picking out a dress.

Connor gave me a brief wave and said, "I'm going to grab the royal state visit handbook and I'll be right back." Then he disappeared into a secret passage.

Declan sat back and watched as my maid, Ginnifer, plaited my hair in a heavy braid. She had hardly gotten me into the navy blue and gold dress she'd chosen for the occasion when Quinn moved from his spot on the wall and grabbed my hand. *Incoming in ten. Isla's bears are snacking on some berries we left for them in the field in front of the castle.*

I nodded. *Thank you. Is Connor on his way back here yet? I need to know all the useless trite crap I need to say.*

Quinn grinned. *Well, if you forget anything, just lean forward a bit. Your breasts in that dress are delightful. You'll be instantly forgiven.*

Too bad Isla's visiting and not one of her husbands. I doubt she'll appreciate the eyeful.

I dunno, Dove. My spies say differently.

My mouth dropped open.

She's my mother's age.

He just shrugged.

Are you lying?

Quinn shrugged again but couldn't hide his grin.

You little shite! I pulled away from Ginnifer long enough to chase after him.

The coward hid behind my changing partition. *I heard she likes animals too!* He sent me a mental image of an old lady bent over, making kissy faces at her dog. The pup trotted over, and the woman lifted up her skirts, letting the dog disappear beneath them.

You sick bastard!

Declan's the bastard, he projected that thought to the both of us, causing Declan to look up.

"What?" Declan asked.

Ugh! I stomped back over to Ginnifer, who didn't yet have the backbone of a long-term maid. My old maid would have grabbed me by the arm and physically restrained me in order to get me ready on time. Of course, that had been on mother's orders, before I became queen.

I sighed, the memory of mother pulling me back to reality. Quinn sensed the change in my mood. He came over and planted a kiss on my head.

I'm going to go see what trouble I can stir up with Isla's entourage.

Not too much.

It's never too much with me, Dove.

I think your scale of 'too little to too much' is a bit skewed.

35

He just turned and waggled his tongue and crossed his eyes before walking out the door. I sighed.

When Connor walked back in, he had his guidebook and he was all business. That's when Declan left me. I supposed he'd been waiting for a hand-off, unwilling to leave me alone after what had just happened.

Connor got straight to business, "Okay, so the heralds will go first. Title. Title. Boring traditional first monarch visit speech from me. She'll approach, you'll come down from the throne … same level. Mutual respect, blah, blah. You'll grasp her hands and say, 'Well, met, Your Majesty.'"

I stared at him, waiting for my next line. "Is that it?"

"For you, yes."

"My mother always spoke for several minutes with visiting royals."

Connor's eyes sparkled, and he leaned forward to confide, "Queen Gela always liked to make the nobles wonder what exactly might have been said. It kept them on their toes."

My eyes widened. "I might actually like that strategy."

My knight ran a hand through his curly hair. "She was quite clever about it. Just do be careful. Isla's a sharp old bat. And her timing with this visit is …"

"Unfortunate?" I asked. Typically, new monarchs did receive or go on state visits within the first month of their reign from the surrounding kingdoms.

"Incredibly quick," Connor concluded. "She did keep in regular correspondence with your mother. But still, the day after your coronation seems … abrupt." He was searching for his court-appropriate words, already practicing for the evening.

"I will try to keep my tongue under control."

Connor rolled his eyes with a smile. "I think I know better than to hope for that."

"What?" I said with mock indignation.

"Bloss Boss, since you've returned you've shot off your mouth to nearly everyone."

I sighed. "That's true. How about I'll just keep you by my side all evening then?"

"That," Connor leaned closer, "is the one part of the evening I'm looking forward to."

He gave me a crooked little grin and then held out his hand. I grabbed it. To my surprise, he led me through our secret handshake, one we'd invented when we were eight-years-old. One we hadn't done since I'd returned home. As he smacked his knuckles against mine to end the shake, Connor turned to Ginnifer, who was waiting to put my jewelry on.

Very sternly he said, "Ginnifer, you're the only living soul who's seen that handshake. If it gets out, I'll know it was you."

Ginnifer's eyes widened. "Oh, My Lord, I'd never tell anyone!"

He wagged a finger at her and then winked. "Now you know a state secret."

He kissed my hand. The way the light danced in his eyes and his sweet grin made my heart beat quicker. Of all my knights, Connor was still the one who made me feel the most nervous, the most uncertain since I came back. But sharing our secret handshake gave me hope.

"My Lady," Connor bowed over my hand like some ridiculous noble fop.

"My Lord," I made my voice nasal in response.

"Would you do me the honor of sneaking into the kitchen with me later tonight?" his pompous tone and his words were so ill-matched that it took a moment before I burst into surprised laughter.

"Secret dessert date?" I asked.

"'Secret dessert date," he responded.

My chest swelled with excitement. It was something we'd done as teenagers, sneaking down at midnight, when most the palace inhabitants were sleeping. "I'd be honored."

Connor's grin was infectious. He turned to Ginnifer and said, "As her maid, your job is to help her sneak out, without any of the other knights noticing."

Timid little Ginnifer had a gleam in her eye as she saluted Connor, my sapphire necklace flopping in her hand. "Challenge accepted, My Lord."

Queen Isla knew the power of appearances. She rode the black winged bear all the way to the throne room. Her huge blue velvet cape (blue being the royal color of her house) trailed on the ground behind her.

Quinn sent me a very unhelpful image of her bear shitting as he walked, causing that cape to drag through a steaming pile of bear scat. It kind of ruined the effect of the pomp for me since I had to focus on containing my laughter.

The bear spread his huge black wings, making several of my nobles duck, before Isla was helped down. Her cloak was removed, and the bear was led away. Then Queen Isla slowly walked up the burnt orange carpet that was lined on either side by Evaness nobility. There were no hushed whispers in her wake. There was only a sense of awe, intimidation, and maybe even a ripple of tension in the room. Isla held her head high, appearing unaffected as she reached the middle of the carpet and waited for me to come greet her.

When our musicians began playing Rasle's most popular ballad, I left the throne and went down the steps, flanked by my knights, Connor on my right side, holding my arm.

When I stood before Isla, I realized she was taller than me by several inches. She had cheekbones sharp enough to cut. A circlet covered her head, a plain one suited to travel. But that didn't lower the amount of power the woman seemed to exude. She had no magic that I knew of, nor did the daughter she trained, but the woman's personality was sharp as an axe.

Finally, it came time for me to clasp Isla's hand.

"Well met, Your Majesty."

"Well met, and my congratulations to you on your coronation," Isla's eyes roamed over my crown.

My mind blanked. Absolutely and completely blanked. I wasn't ready for this moment. What the hell was I supposed to say? Hi, I'm queen and my mother's dead and sister stolen. And by the way, no you can't have your hills back? Shite. I was shite at this royalty business.

I opened my mouth, and nothing came out. I tried again. This time, words just spilled out. I wasn't even certain exactly what they were until I replayed them in my mind. "What happens when you cross a grizzly and a harp?"

Isla didn't answer my question. She simply tilted her head, her small court-smile pasted on her face.

I started to sweat. I couldn't look at Connor, who was squeezing my arm tightly, trying to signal me to change the subject. Or stop. Or something. But my mouth—my stupid mouth just kept talking. "You get a bear-faced lyre."

A corner of Isla's lip curled up. That was the only response I got. "Well, you're the first monarch who's ever greeted me with a joke. Was there an insinuation in there?"

I nearly face-palmed. Shite! "No, absolutely not. I just wanted to start things off light-hearted and when I heard I only had one official line, I …"

Isla grabbed my forearm gently. "I'm only teasing, Bloss. I've known you since you were born."

"Oh." Relief flooded my system. "I'm sorry." Gods be damned. Now I looked like a sarding idiot.

Isla's smile was slightly wider. Like a crocodile's before it eats its prey. She definitely thought I'd be easy pickings. She linked her arm with mine. "Now, if you want to exchange jokes with a fellow monarch, I'd suggest you choose something more like the following: What's the scariest kind of bear?"

I pressed my lips together in thought, but Isla didn't give me much time.

"My husband's bare bum."

It was very difficult not to snort. But that would have echoed throughout the throne room, so I resisted. Instead I gave a half nod, to hide just how huge my grin was. "Well done, Your Majesty." Dammit. I'd made myself look stupid. And she'd just made me look stupider by having a better joke than me. This visit was off to a shite start.

Isla nodded demurely. "I am sorry to hear about your mother."

"Thank you." Pain lanced my side. The loss was still too fresh. "I'm sorry for your loss as well. I know you were great friends and allies."

Isla patted my hand. "She was a very astute queen."

"Astute. Yes." Not kind, it would have been a lie for Isla to say my mother was kind or compassionate. I wondered for a second, if the same dull, lifeless comment might be made about me one day.

"She always worked hard for Evaness," I added lamely.

"Yes. Queens must work to shape the world they want. It's a never-ending battle," Isla inclined her head.

I smiled up at her, "I like that." I'd always thought of Isla as a shark, a predator. But never as a warrior. She was fighting for her kingdom. I had to admire that, even if it made her a bit of a thorn in my side.

"How's your daughter?" I asked.

"She's well. Keeping up the castle as I travel." We both knew that was a euphemism. Isla's daughter was soft. I might be struggling through this first meeting, but Corinna would never have made it. She was delicate. The crown would be difficult for her to take up.

After a short pause, the queen asked, "Would you like to meet my companions? I've brought a new ambassador to Evaness as Graham is getting on in years."

Connor didn't react that she could see, but his finger trailed over the back of my arm, signaling me with one of our old codes. Isla hadn't announced this. Her former ambassador was a mild-mannered man, just the opposite of the Sedarian ambassador, Meeker. I kept my face neutral as I inwardly groaned. I did not need another pot-stirrer here.

Isla led me toward the neat lines of companions she'd brought. They were as orderly and disciplined as soldiers. I scanned their smiles, disappointed I didn't see a single real one on any face, until a younger woman came forward at Isla's request.

The girl was a fairy, with black wings that trailed the ground and fluttered slightly as she walked toward me. Her hair was navy blue and matched the tiny tufts of hair on her pointed ears. Her eyes were lavender, wide and smirking, as she looked at me. She wore a long grey court gown and a black ring. I recognized her instantly.

"Ember!" I had to work to keep my 'court face.' I wanted to squeal. Mother had taken me to visit Rasle a number of times when I was younger. Ember had been my partner in crime when I visited.

Ember's mother was a fairy and a minor noble in Rasle. Her family were traders. They had several ships and ran a caravan between our two countries.

We were the same age and had met when we'd been forced into tapestry weaving together. It had started as a horrid experience for me because I'd had no eye for it. She

43

had gotten us out of it with her magic. Ember had been wonderfully persuasive. She didn't have Connor's ability to see emotions, but her parents were both fairies, so I suppose enchanting humans wasn't terribly hard for her. In any case, she'd facilitated our escapes to the gardens where we'd sung and skipped and made flower crowns. She'd been my hero.

Ember bowed and took my hand.

"Are you the new ambassador?" I asked, quite hopeful.

She grinned. "No, my father is. My husbands and I will take over the caravan. It's time Father settled a bit."

She didn't say more, but I wondered what had happened to her family. She didn't mention her mother or her other fathers. I couldn't address it in public, so I simply said what I felt, "I'm delighted to have your family represent Rasle. I'm certain this will be the start of a wonderful relationship for our countries."

Ember smiled and brought her father, Donovon, forward so I could shake his hand. He smiled shyly at me and kept his greying wings politely closed behind his back. He'd always been a quiet man, the one who stayed home and kept the books, if I remembered correctly.

"I look forward to working with you, Your Majesty."

I shook his hand.

Thankfully, Connor swept in before I had to say much else. "Well, now that formalities are out of the way, who's ready to gorge on roast pig?" He offered an arm to Queen

Isla, complimenting the train she'd worn as he escorted her toward the dining hall.

I followed behind, allowing Ember and her father to walk beside me. Declan served as my escort, since Ryan stepped aside to speak with some soldiers and Quinn blended back into the shadows.

"We heard about your sister when we landed," Ember said, peering over at me. A sad smile crossed her face. "Any news?"

I took a deep breath and schooled my features.

Declan jumped in before I had to answer and said, "Interesting. Which servants spoke about that? I'll have to have a chat with them."

Ember's face reddened. "I didn't mean to get anyone in trouble."

Declan handed me off to Ember's father and took the fairy's arm. "Well, you know it doesn't do to have servants with loose lips. You and I can go for a stroll and you can point them out to me." He deftly steered Ember out of the room.

Ember's father led me to the head of the table, where Jorad had already pulled out my chair. As he helped me into my seat, Donovon said, "I'm sorry about your sister."

I smiled fakely up at him as I settled into my seat. I wished everyone would stop talking about it.

I turned to grab my wine glass only to realize that Lady Agatha was right next to me. Jorad must have decided to punish me for hitting him earlier.

Agatha's hair was a big billowing poof of white, strung with pearls. It was so large, I couldn't see who sat on her other side.

She gave a toothy grin and leaned forward. "Look on the bright side, Your Majesty. The dragon didn't *immediately* kill the princess."

I pushed away the brutal image her words brought to mind and focused on a tingling in my gut. My intuition was roused. Something she said made sense. Somehow. I tilted my head and stared at Agatha. "What do you mean?"

Lady Agatha picked up her own wine glass and gave a shrug before downing the entire thing. She dabbed her mouth with her napkin as she said, "Well, if that dragon didn't just kill her, he or his master must want her for something."

CHAPTER FOUR

*L*ady Agatha's words stuck with me throughout the dinner and the jesters that came to entertain us.

I was still rolling them around in my head as Ginnifer helped me out of my evening gown near midnight.

"Um, Your Majesty?"

"Just Bloss, when we're alone, please."

"My Lady, I couldn't—"

I sighed. "Really, you could. But that's not important right now. What did you need?"

Ginnifer bit her lower lip. "Um, your bird?"

"My bird?"

"The bluebird."

"Oh, Cerena's bird! Yes?"

"It's still here."

I furrowed my brow. Ginnifer pointed. Sure enough, the bluebird was in my dressing room, perched on top of a rack of dresses, tilting his head and studying me.

"He'll ruin your clothes!" Ginnifer wrung her hands. "I've tried everything to get him to leave and he won't!"

I bit my lip to keep from laughing.

What's so funny, Dove?

Of course, Quinn couldn't let me laugh without trying to find out why.

You know how you always like to tease me about enchanted animals?

Yes?

I sent him the mental image of Cerena's bird.

Quinn laughed in my mind, which felt almost like being tickled.

I was right! See, animals are magically attracted to princesses.

Well, this one is Cerena's. I'll have to make sure to return him in the morning. It was sweet of her to have him watch over me, though.

No letting him see you naked.

He's a bird.

He's a he.

You're ridiculous.

Just you wait. He'll go tweeting to all his bird friends and next thing you know a whole flock will be following you around ...

He sent me a mental image of a dozen birds perched on my head, my shoulders, the sides of my dress. Naturally, Quinn pictured me covered in shite.

I rolled my eyes.

"Sorry, Your Majesty, I didn't mean to offend—" Ginnifer jumped in, thinking I was rolling my eyes at her.

"Shite. No, I'm sorry. Quinn's being ridiculous in my head. That's all."

Go away.

Fine. But I'm warning you, if you give that bird a show, he'll bring back friends.

Any word on Avia? I changed the subject.

Still working on that. We do think whatever Ryan's man spotted to the south has potential. He will be working late on that.

Keep me updated.

Will do.

Quinn faded from my head as I changed into a much more informal gown.

"I'll get the bird back to his owner in the morning, Ginnifer."

"Your Majesty, your dresses!"

I turned to the bird and narrowed my eyes. "If you shite on my clothes, I'll have Cerena lock you in a cage."

As if he could understand my threat, the bluebird swooped out of the dressing room and back into my chamber. Ginnifer rushed to shut the door behind him.

"Thank you," she sighed, holding her chest.

"No problem." I yawned. "Don't tell Quinn. He'll think that bird actually listened to me, instead of just getting scared off by the sound of my voice."

She nodded briskly and then lowered her voice to stage whisper dramatically at me. "Your Majesty, you have your *secret meeting* tonight." Ginnifer went over to the corner of the dressing room and pulled out a hidden pot of tea and a tea cup. "Why don't you sit down and drink some tea? It'll perk you up. I'll go make certain you're alone before you sneak off."

In all the pomp and circumstance, I'd forgotten about meeting Connor. My heart jumped nervously at the thought. The very fact that I was nervous made me sad. Once, I'd only have felt anticipation. But Connor and I were still getting reacquainted after four years apart.

When Ginnifer gave me the all clear, I stood and realized my palms were slightly sweaty. I ran them down the sides of my dress before taking the candle she handed me and walking into the secret passage hidden behind the wall of the queen's chamber.

I saw Connor around the first corner of the passage. He smiled and I smiled, and we turned toward the kitchen.

I stumbled and Connor caught me, saving my face but also saving me from setting my hair afire with my candle. "I suppose the sneaking isn't technically necessary," I said.

Connor shrugged. "But it's fun."

"Yes. I love tripping."

He laughed and took my hand, tucking it into the crook of his elbow. "Here. Problem solved. I like the royal passageways."

"Why?"

"Because if your guards were around, I couldn't do this," he stopped and stepped in front of me, threading our legs so that his thigh rubbed my core, even through our clothing. I sucked in a ragged breath as I stared up at him, watching his eyes grow serious and hooded in the tiny flicker of candlelight. Connor traced his fingers over my cheek. I studied his face, his tanned skin, sharp jaw, and the curls that I loved. I couldn't help myself. I reached up with my free hand and let my fingers run through those curls.

Connor leaned down and my eyes fluttered closed. He kissed each of my eyelids, the tip of my nose, my cheeks … until finally his lips brushed mine. It was so sweet my heart hurt. So perfectly bittersweet. Because at one point, there would have been no hesitation on his part. No light kisses. Only eagerness. Only joy that was so big it bubbled over and couldn't be contained. I'd broken that.

It was my job to fix it.

When Connor's lips pulled away, I leaned toward him on tiptoe and said, "I've dreamt about kissing you since I was eleven years old."

He quirked a grin. "Eleven?"

I nodded. "It was my birthday wish that year."

"I don't think you ever told me that." He interlaced his fingers with mine.

I shrugged. "I thought at that time that you might have had a crush on that princess from Lored."

"Gildera!" Connor snorted. "She was taller than me!"

I shrugged. "She rode a horse better than you, too."

"And swung a sword. Ugh, don't remind me."

"Well, those all seemed to be things you liked to do, so I was worried—"

"You didn't need to be," Connor bumped my shoulder playfully.

I shrugged. "I didn't know that."

He grinned. "What else don't I know about you?"

"Um … I now know how to milk a cow."

"Why?"

I blushed. "When I left, I didn't really consider ... money. I ran out quickly. I couldn't steal. I just couldn't. So, I had to take odd jobs as I searched for a wizard."

Connor shook his head in bemusement, "And how was that cow-milking experience?"

"After I figured out how not to get kicked ... it was still pretty awful."

Connor laughed and led me around one last corner before he took my candle and blew it out. We slipped out of the secret passage and into the hall that led to the kitchens.

The night staff simply smiled when we arrived hand in hand and the head cook, Meralda, waddled over, rubbing her hands on her apron.

"Marzipan cakes?" she asked.

That had been our go-to for years. It had been my absolute favorite late-night dessert. Until I'd left the palace.

I shook my head. "Can we have bread with quince jelly and farmer's cheese, please?"

The cook raised her eyebrows but gave a sharp nod.

"Quince jelly?" Connor asked.

"Like a cross between apple and pear," I winked. "You'll love it."

Connor led me to a seat at one of the servants' dining tables. He sat next to me and grabbed my hand. He immediately went for an arm-wrestling match. I pushed back the heavy sleeve of my gown and freed my elbow. Then I set my arm up on the table and wiggled my fingers.

"Prepare to be owned," I threatened playfully.

"Oh, I'm owned, Bloss Boss. You know it. But you'd better prepare to lose. And when you lose, I'm gonna collect," he raised his eyebrows suggestively as his hand clasped mine.

"Collect what?"

He leaned forward and whispered, "Something that isn't acceptable to say in public." His eyes glittered.

My breath caught and my nipples tightened. Connor looked so naughty that I had to press my thighs together to ease the ache.

He'd never teased me like this before. Not this explicitly. Everything we'd done was covert. Stolen kisses, stolen moments. Even after he'd been officially announced as one of my knights, we'd had to maintain a sense of propriety in public. We'd tested boundaries, as teenagers do. But not like he was doing now. Not like the suggestive way his tongue traced his upper lip. Nothing remotely close to the way he rubbed his lips together as he leaned toward me and whispered, "What I have in mind is gonna taste even more delicious than dessert."

I was sure he felt the pulse of desire that surged up my spine and made me light-headed. His cat-ate-the-cream grin assured me he did.

Of course, he took advantage of my distraction to slam my hand into the table.

"Rematch!" I cried.

He gave a nonchalant shrug and held his hand up, waiting for me to straighten my own.

I narrowed my eyes as I clasped palms with him.

"Go," he murmured.

I pushed. I did. But his sarding hand didn't move an inch. He'd gotten stronger in four years.

I cheated. I put my other hand on the back of his and pulled. I put both hands on the same side and pushed, but I couldn't even get him halfway down. "What the hell?" I'd never lost this badly before. I'd lost, sure. But he'd at least had the good grace to pretend I was strong enough to make it a struggle.

When I stood up to push on his arm he laughed and let his arm flop backward onto the table.

"You let me win," I sat back in my seat and folded my arms over my chest, pouting.

"Yup," Connor leaned back. "Now you know something about me you never knew. Your turn."

My jaw dropped. "You used to *let* me win?" Fury and admiration rose in me at once. I'd never suspected.

"All the time."

He was so sweet and so patronizing at the same time. I wasn't certain which of my emotions would win out against him, the anger or the respect. I narrowed my eyes. "At what?" We'd played countless games growing up.

He shook his head, "Your turn."

I glared at him. "I don't like that a bit, Connor Doyle … Hale, I mean. Connor Hale."

His eyes darkened, pupils dilating. Both of us stared intensely at one another. It was the first time I'd said his married name aloud. He'd always belonged to me. We'd always belonged to each other. But hearing it … I blinked, before I started to get emotional in front of the servants.

"I hate mosquitoes," I admitted, changing the subject.

He laughed, "Who doesn't?"

"You don't understand. If I could make them cease to exist, I would. Every night, *every night*, they bit me. And I'd scratch in my sleep. I'd wake up with welts the size of your fist."

Connor leaned toward me and asked in a low voice, "What were you doing out late at night?"

I faked a laugh, "Well, there aren't a lot of inns in the wilds of Cheryn and Macedon. I spent a lot of nights sleeping under the stars. That turned out to be much less romantic than the poets pretend."

A servant walked within earshot, so I added a little more for that man's benefit. "I mean, when you're *dragon-hunting* you don't get cozy castles every day." I hadn't been dragon hunting. I'd been wizard hunting, for a cure for my powers. Of course, the mention of dragons made me think of Avia.

Connor's lips thinned. He leaned closer and brushed my hair back as he whispered, "First of all, we'll find her." He knew what I was thinking without me having to say a single word. "Second of all, you're an idiot for ever leaving and not telling me everything. Every one of those mosquito bites was your own fault. Third, I'll kill every mosquito I can from now on, in your honor."

I laughed. "You're so brave."

"You know it."

His hand came to rest on my cheek. "I feel like I'm getting to know a new you. And yet, you're the same. Does that make sense?" A slight blush crept over his cheeks.

I put my hand on top of his. "I feel the same. I still love you, Cee. It's just … now, I get to have the fun of falling in love with you all over again."

He smiled.

The things his smile did to me—my heart grew warm and fuzzy. My thoughts sparkled. He'd always had this effect on me. He'd always been able to make the world around him recede. So that nothing mattered but the two of us. I sighed and grinned, content for the moment just to bask in his attention.

We were back together. Circling one another like binary stars. Shining. The connection between us felt like a living thing. It pulsed and pulled me toward him. I couldn't resist those sea-foam eyes. I leaned over and was about to kiss Connor again.

But Meralda, our cook, cleared her throat. "Your Majesty, normally I might clear the kitchen for a moment for you. But with Rasle here we're working all hours—"

I laughed, unlacing my fingers from Connor's so I could pat her shoulder. "You're fine, Meralda. I'll behave. And if you need more help, send someone down to the capital to round up a few extra hands. I'll tell Jorad it's approved."

Meralda ducked her head and bowed, nearly forgetting to give us the platter of food in her hands. "Thank you, Your Majesty."

I nodded and smiled as she set the plate down between us.

Connor stared down at the meal suspiciously. "You'd rather eat this than marzipan cakes?" He touched the dark brown bread suspiciously, as if it'd bite him.

I grinned and shrugged, suddenly feeling a little uncertain about my choice. "I wanted to show you something else you didn't know about me."

"Your taste buds have died?" he teased.

I pretended to smack his arm, but he captured my hand and kissed the back of it.

"Thank you," his voice was low and breathy, so he couldn't be overheard by the kitchen staff who were trying to work inconspicuously at the edges of the room. "Thank you for sharing this part of you with me."

I nodded. My throat was too tight to speak.

"So," Connor continued lightly, aware of our audience, "this is what you ate when you were on the road?"

"It became my favorite. A midday meal after a hard morning of … searching."

"Well then—" Connor scooped up the bread and a bit of cheese. He took large bites of both. His eyes went wide as he chewed. His entire face worked, stretching and scrunching.

I rolled my eyes. "It's not that hard." I kicked at him from my chair.

He grinned playfully. "I think I cracked a tooth." He opened his mouth and pointed, the big ball of mush still quite visible.

"Gross!"

He swallowed and pouted. "I'm not joking. It hwerts," he made little-boy eyes at me.

"Alright three-year-old, let me see," I leaned closer.

Connor snuck a quick closed-mouth kiss before sweeping me up onto his lap. He wrapped his arms around my waist and leaned his head against my side. "I love that you're my wife."

I wrapped my arms around his neck and let my fingers play with his curls. "I love it, too."

He pulled me in for a kiss and then stood, sweeping his arms under my legs. "I think I'm full."

"You only had a bite."

"Still," he shrugged, his eyes glittering with mischief, "I think I'd rather be done with my first dessert and move on to the next."

He carried me out of the kitchen, nodding his chin toward a couple dishwashers who catcalled at us.

When we made it to the hall, a few of my guards discreetly began to follow us.

"Uh-oh, we've been spotted."

Connor shrugged. "It was bound to happen. At least they're keeping their distance."

He led me toward his office, which was on the first floor of the palace, so that visiting nobles could easily find it. He whispered in my ear as he carried me, "I'm going to lay you out on my desk. Naked. In the moonlight. And then—"

We passed a darkened hallway and I saw a flash of color where there shouldn't have been one.

Instantly, I yanked Connor to a stop and dropped my legs from his hold. Some instinct told me that whoever was there in the dark shouldn't be. I ran into the shadows.

"Don't!" Connor yelled. I didn't listen as I scanned the blackness for my target.

My eyes barely had time to adjust before the window creaked open to my left. I turned and darted toward it. I yanked on person's jacket as they tried to climb outside. A rotund man fell at my feet just as I was surrounded.

"Bloss!" Connor scolded as my guards scooped up whomever I'd captured.

"Don't ever do that again," Connor shoved between me and the escape artist, who struggled to break free. Whoever it was, it wasn't someone particularly strong. Two guards held the man easily. Another brought a torch.

The flame revealed the pudgy face of the noble I reviled most.

Willard had worn a fake beard that was black and curly.

It looks like he glued pubes to his face, Quinn's voice sounded off in my head. *Declan's been searching for him with some of the guards. He'll be right there. One of my people thought they saw his fat ass—*

I yanked the beard off and scanned the face of the noble who'd talked to Sedara about replacing me.

"Lord Willard. What might you be doing, in disguise, in my castle, this late at night?"

I saw the pits of his shirt grow stained as the fat little rat sweated before me. "I just—I was—meeting a lover!"

A smile stretched across my face. "Oh, really? And who might that be?"

"It's—it's—" Willard's cheeks colored and his face paled as he couldn't come up with a lie quickly enough.

It was almost sad. To be undermined by a man so stupid.

"Guards, bring him to the mage's tower. I think it's time Willard and I had another heart to heart."

Willard's bulging fish eyes widened.

I grinned. "Oh, yes, Willard. It's time for another mage spell. This one, I'm afraid, won't be for your benefit."

Declan and another set of guards scrambled into the room just as my guards hauled the protesting pile of flesh off.

"We missed it! Damn. I was sure that fathole would come in through the larder!" Declan grimaced. He hated being wrong.

"You didn't miss anything," I ran my hand over my knight's ink-stained palm and linked our fingers in an attempt to ease his disappointment. "We're about to question him."

"Well, you don't need me for that, then," Declan backed out of the room. "I was just filling in since Ryan's out." My scholar wasn't interested in all that *questioning* might entail.

On the other hand, Quinn smirked in my head. *Oh, Dove. That's my favorite part.*

CHAPTER FIVE

*C*erena's tower room was a disaster. In her search to find the loophole in the engagement contract, it looked like my castle mage had torn through every book she owned.

She was asleep, her head drooped over an open book, drool puddled on the page, when we walked in.

She snorted when she woke. "Wha—what?"

"Sorry, to wake you. But we found an intruder and wanted to see what we could do about a mage spell or some kind of truth serum."

Cerena's eyes widened. "Oh … um …" she swiped at her mouth when she realized a line of drool hung from it. She shuffled toward me and spoke in a stage whisper that completely defeated the purpose of whispering, "I … um … used up a lot of ingredients in here, testing out that last issue. I'm dead out."

I sighed. "Fine. I suppose we'll have to chain him up for a bit until you can get more. Tell Jorad what you need."

Cerena bobbed her head. "Yes'm. I mean Your Highness. Your Majesty?" The poor woman didn't know anything about court etiquette, and I loved that.

"Just Bloss."

I waved to Connor and the guards. "I suppose we can visit the dungeons."

Willard started to tremble, like the coward he was. "I'll talk! I'll talk!"

I narrowed my eyes at him. "How can I trust you? You were sneaking around my grounds—"

"Just meeting a lover! My mother couldn't know! Please, it was nothing! I'll tell you anything! Ask me anything!" Willard visibly shook and I worried he might be about to piss himself.

I glanced at Connor, unsure what my mother would do. He gave a head nod toward Willard. I assumed that meant I should ask something. "What did Meeker tell you when you met with him in the forest?"

Willard's eyes nearly bugged out of his head. "I—he—"

"You were discussing treason, weren't you?"

The foul stench of piss met my nostrils.

"It's not what you think!" Willard insisted. "We were desperate! There was a dragon in our lands!"

"And you turned to Sedara. To a foreign country. Not to me."

"And I lied!" Willard's jowls trembled. His face turned tomato red. "We don't have a sarding port on our land, do we?"

"You would if you tried to overthrow me."

Willard laughed bitterly. "You think anyone would follow me? A man? The fat dolt? You think I'm so stupid I don't know what I'm called?"

"I think you're stupid enough to believe I'd fall for your pity party." I looked at Connor and raised my brows.

Connor walked closer and whispered, "He feels somewhat truthful. I don't sense a lie. But his fear is the overriding emotion."

I turned to Willard. "I won't kill you."

Willard fell to his fat knees. "Thank you, Your Majesty. I promise, I can prove my loyalty. I'll do whatever you want—"

"I wasn't finished. I won't kill you, and I might not even publicly strip your title, or have you flogged—"

"I can get you information!" Willard spit out. "Anything you want! Nobles, servants. I don't care."

I pressed my lips together. "You think you'd be more effective than my spies?"

Willard nodded his head vigorously, his chubby cheeks flapping. "Spies can only overhear things. I can go in and start conversations. They all know that mother's furious about the dragon. And no one takes me seriously," he spit that last statement out bitterly. "They don't mind running their mouths around me because they think I'm daft. I'm not. I figured out the dragon, you know."

I paused and let the silence grow uncomfortably long. I watched Willard. I looked to Connor, who leaned over and whispered in my ear, "He's earnest."

I waited until I was certain Willard hung on my every word. Then I said, "Perhaps a trial. If you provide unique information to me about the other nobles and their current positions, I might consider this. If you dig up our traitor, you might even get to retain your title."

Willard's eyes gleamed at that. He wanted to keep his title. Wanted it badly.

I continued, "Someone helped bring that dragon into our country. Our country, Willard. Your land. My kingdom. Both were nearly destroyed. I want you to stumble into every private conversation you can. I want you to annoy your way into invitations and find out who has been plotting against Evaness."

Willard nodded, getting up from his knees. He gave me a bow, before pulling a bright red handkerchief from his vest and mopping his sweaty face.

Quinn, are you listening? I thought.

Hmm?

I just recruited Willard into your group of spies.

Did you say Dullard?

Willard.

Dullard?

Alright. Haha. I get it. But honestly, I'd like you to assign someone invisible to shadow him. I'm going to let him stumble around and play spy in the hope it will draw attention away from your people. Or maybe even get the nobles to drop their guard, thinking I'm an idiot.

Do you really want people to think you're an idiot?

I sighed. *No. But I pretty much screwed that up today with Isla. Might as well take advantage of my stupid status until I have the chance to prove them wrong.*

You can always be an idiot with me, Dove. I won't judge you.

Shut up and send someone up here.

Will do. Just let me punch Abbas one more time.

You're beating Abbas?

Yes.

And I wasn't invited?

You were on your 'date.' Quinn's voice faded with a grunt, which I assumed meant he'd landed a hit on the imposter prince.

I looked back at Willard.

He was still mopping the back of his neck. I could see massive armpit stains. The man's body was as slippery and slimy as an eel. I only hoped his mind wasn't as well.

Connor pulled me aside and whispered, "Are you sure?"

I shrugged. "If I'd been in his position, with a dragon on my lands, I'd have done the same. I don't entirely trust him. But, he's right about the perception of him. He's the least threatening of the nobles."

Connor chewed his lip in a rare show of nervous contemplation. "I just don't want this to reflect badly on you."

I shrugged and whispered, "Quinn's sending an invisible shadow. They'll verify anything he does or says."

Connor visibly relaxed at that statement.

I punched his shoulder. "Honestly, I know I'm rusty at this court business. But I'm not a complete dunce."

He grinned.

I turned back and glared at Willard, who twisted the handkerchief nervously in his hands. "Connor will go over a few details with you. I'm needed elsewhere."

Connor pulled Willard to one of Cerena's work benches and sat with him. He lectured the nobleman about actions that might rouse suspicion.

I briefly wondered if Willard would even last a day as a spy. I sighed.

I turned to my mage, "Cerena, I'm sorry to have barged in when you worked so hard last night. But I have one last favor."

"Yes, Bloss?" she asked.

"You forgot your bird. He's in my chambers. If you'd collect him, I'd appreciate it."

"What bird?"

"Your bluebird."

Cerena's eyebrows drew up. "I don't have a bird."

My chest contracted. "What?"

"I don't know how else to say it. I don't own a bird."

I walked back toward Cerena. A strange sensation filled my limbs. It felt like the weightlessness that happened when I took a bottle of Flight and jumped into the air. "You have to have a bird. He followed you into the room downstairs."

"Why do I have to have a bird?"

"Because … because he followed you and stayed with me. He attacked Abbas when the shite bit me."

I shared a look with Connor. I was at a loss.

Cerena sighed. "You'd better show me this bird. And by the way, I think your old castle mage must have been shite. Or on someone else's payroll. I can't believe the things that got through here. A sarding full-on magical creature got in here unknown? A dragon pranced across the county? I mean ... that's just not okay.

"If that asswipe were still alive, I'd make him drink a bottle of Revelation to see what the hell he was thinking. Of course, he was a man. So, they're naturally less devious. More of an idiotic heads-on, storm-the-castle approach.

"Do you know how many vats of oil I've got in storage? Going rancid? What a waste. I'm hiring a fairy as an assistant. We need top-grade magical defense for this shite. And maybe an elf for weapons making. Silver weapons for sure. They tend to work against everything. Shapeshifters, djinn. We have a lot of rusty iron ones for fae. I'll just have to get them cleaned up. But a disappointing lack of silver," Cerena finished her rant. She gestured at a shelf behind her that wasn't destroyed by the blast that had killed her predecessor (or her own mess-making mayhem). A few silver trinkets sat on it: a tankard, a knife, a shield.

"Anything you need," I ran a hand over my face. Court-yard repairs from a dragon attack. Mage's tower in shambles. My reign was full of expensive, unpleasant surprises thus far. "This damn bird better be a bird."

Cerena's first words inside my chambers were, "That's *not* a bird."

I punched the wall. That was a very stupid thing to do, considering I didn't have Ryan at my side. "Sard!" I cursed at the bird, my hand, my life.

"What the hell is it then?" Connor had followed behind us after letting Willard walk off with an invisible spy tailing him.

The bird twittered aggressively.

Connor grabbed a silver tray and chucked it at the blue-bird, trying to get the thing to come down so we could catch it. The bird was off and across the room before the tray reached him.

Cerena looked at me and sighed. "You've dragged me into one hell of a mess, Bloss. I might need a raise. *That* is a person. A spelled person."

"How can you tell?" I watched the bluebird land on the canopy above my bed.

"I can sense the human. Or part human in him with this," Cerena held up a glowing stone in her hands. "Once I thought about what had happened with that shite trick-ster prince, I figured I'd need a little spell to check things out, until I get some back up."

"How does it work?" Connor asked.

"Light, human. No light, not human," she shrugged and handed Connor the stone. "I can't tell the partials. But it was a quick fix."

I narrowed my eyes at the bird. "Are you a spy? Huh?"

The bird very deliberately made eye contact with me and shook his blue head.

"Why are you here?"

The bird tilted his head and blinked at me.

"I think that might be bird sarcasm," Cerena stated.

"What?"

Connor spoke softly, "Yes and no questions, Bloss Boss. Stick to yes and no questions."

I smacked his arm. "Don't patronize me. My sister was stolen. I was attacked. And I've got a foreign queen, a fat-ass lying noble, and some douchey bird intruder to deal with. Excuse me for not asking the right kind of questions."

Connor held up his hands and slowly backed away from me.

Ass.

I glared at the bird. "Are you working for another monarch?"

The bird shook his head no.

"Well then, are you just passing through?" Connor asked the bird, as if he was at a damn court function and this bird was a guest.

The bird shook his head no.

"Why the sard are you here?" I asked.

"Yes and no…"

"YES! I know! I know!" I closed my eyes and took a deep breath through my nose. "I cannot deal with this right now. You figure out why he's here. I'm going to find Quinn. I need to punch someone."

I strode away, leaving my husband and my new castle mage to deal with the bluebird.

But I did yell out over my shoulder to the bird, "Since you're a person, if you shite on a single one of my things, I will *end you!*"

I was over this day.

Over it.

CHAPTER SIX

I was interrupted on my way to the dungeon because I was too sarding tired and stupid to take the secret passageways. As I crossed one of the main halls, a figure came barreling toward me. Immediately, the guards following me took up position in front of me and unsheathed their swords.

Mateo skidded to a stop just shy of their weapons. "Your Majesty!" he bowed.

When he looked up, I could see his brown eyes were rimmed in red from crying. His wavy bronze hair was unkempt. His shirt was untucked. He did not look well.

I hadn't even thought of him once since Avia had been stolen. But, of course, he would have been affected.

I cursed myself for being so thoughtless. I raised a hand so my guards could lower their weapons.

"Mateo, how can I help you?"

When he glanced up, the look in his eyes was earnest. "Please. I want to look for her. That's all I want."

My heart just about broke seeing his expression. Mateo looked like a lost child. Like a lost soul. If one of my knights were taken … I couldn't even dare to imagine that. I knew Mateo and Avia were young, but love was love. I'd loved Connor at that age. Younger, even.

I held out a hand and squeezed Mateo's fingers briefly, the only appropriate sign of affection I could give. "Of course, you may look for her. I'll let Ryan know so his men are aware."

Mateo coughed uncomfortably. "There's only one problem. I don't own a horse."

I nodded. An ambassador's son wasn't wealthy. And Macedon wasn't a wealthy nation to start.

I nodded to one of my guards. "Escort him to Jace at the stables. Tell Jace I've authorized a horse for him."

Mateo squeezed my hand and said, "Thank you, Your Majesty."

I just shook my head. "Thank you for caring so much for Avia."

"I do. I really do," his words became choked with emotion.

I had to turn away before I was overcome myself. Instead, I forced my mind to focus on the person who'd caused all this heartache. The monster who'd come into my home and ripped it apart.

I flexed my fingers as I descended to the dungeon. I hoped Quinn hadn't beaten him too badly. I desperately needed to unleash my fury.

Abbas was strung up on chains and suspended from the ceiling like a puppet. His face and chest were a mottled black and blue and a single line of blood trailed down his chest.

The walls and ceiling of his cell were a moldy, damp stone and it looked like Quinn had positioned the asshole to ensure that brackish filth dripped down on the prisoner.

"Are we in the chamber below the cesspit?" I asked.

Yes. The latrines all dump just above us.

Got it. I'll keep my face back as I hit him. Can he be lowered a little, so I don't have to strain?

Anything for you, Dove. Quinn quirked a grin and used a lever on the wall to lower Abbas, who moaned, looking worse for the wear.

"Has he talked yet?" I asked before balling up my fist.

I hadn't gotten around to asking, Quinn leaned back against the wall, casually.

Why not?

He hurt you. A shadow flashed in Quinn's eyes. The kind of darkness that occurs when storm clouds turn black, just before they unleash their fury. His look made my heart jump, but not in fear. I'd never seen this side of

Quinn before. This violent anger. But, clearly, it was a part of him. A spy master's hands were always stained.

I took a step closer to Quinn, letting the crackling force of his anger buzz along my skin. It was like static electricity. It set my nerves alight. He was darkness. And he was mine.

I sarding love you. I kissed his lips lightly before I turned back toward the prisoner and pulled my elbow back for a right hook.

I swung and connected. I didn't even feel the pain leaching up my arm because the sense of satisfaction was so intense. My hit made Abbas swing on his chains and I had to back up so he wouldn't knock me down when he swung back toward me.

"What are you?" I asked the scum licker.

Abbas merely smiled, then let his head shift to a boar's, complete with tusks. The dungeons allowed shifting. Because what the prisoners didn't know was that their chains would shift with them.

I grinned at Abbas when he realized he couldn't reach me. I took a moment to enjoy his frustration before I turned to Quinn.

Think he's a fairy? I asked Quinn.

Possible. Phouka are known to shapeshift. But dragons and phouka aren't known to work together.

Abbas changed his head to a black-horned dragon's head.

I was so emotionally wrung out, I didn't really process the threat. Too much had happened too quickly.

My only thought on seeing the dragon was this: death might be a nice change.

I didn't have time to think more than that before Quinn had eliminated the threat. He swung his sword and sliced off a bit of the dragon's nose.

Abbas roared and his head changed to human form once more. His human nose bled, a tiny sliver at the end removed.

I continued my conversation with Quinn as if we hadn't nearly been roasted alive.

Phouka come from Gitmore. Gitmore was the one country in the seven kingdoms that truly hated Evaness. The country was Sedara's northern neighbor and we'd been in a feud with them for ages. Over something stupid, I was sure. But that didn't matter. What mattered was that they might have sent a phouka to my doorstep.

Quinn didn't agree. *They've withdrawn since the last Fire War. They have that huge haunted desert between them and the sea. And it would have taken a shiteload of magic to convince all those servants from Cheryn that this bastard was Abbas.*

The bastard transformed into a troll, straining at his chains, growing larger and larger; the spelled chains grew with him and held, unlike all the other magic of Wyle's that had gone to shite.

Quinn simply leaned back against the wall again and watched as Abbas grew so large the chains started to choke him out and he was forced to return to human form.

Then my spy master continued our mental conversation. *I don't know that any one fairy has that kind of power.*

A group?

Maybe. His thoughts haven't gone to anyone specific yet. And that's another thing. Fairies like to gloat. I'd have expected to hear his thoughts. Hear some smug sort of shite. But other than when I had those elven chains on, he's shuffling—constantly shuffling his thoughts. Who can control their mind that well?

But the shapeshifting—

Djinn can shift, too. And at least a djinni would know the customs of Cheryn. It would be easier to fit in, Quinn argued.

I thought djinn could shapeshift, but that most of their power came from wishes.

Declan's researching it right now. And you're correct.

So, he can't be a djinni, I pointed at Abbas.

Not necessarily. At least, Dec doesn't think so.

Why not?

Dec thinks it depends on the wish. Djinn are slaves to wishes. Any wish short of death is fair game. If a djinni grants you a wish, he has to fulfill it. He has to do anything to see it fulfilled.

You think that's what's going on?

Quinn shrugged. *I just punch people, Dove.*

Well, you haven't punched any information out of him.

Quinn glared at me. *I haven't really tried yet.*

Abbas interrupted our silent argument. He transformed into a giant spider, his limbs growing thinner. The magic in the chains held and transformed with him. But that didn't stop me from shuddering as a brown spider with black spots stared at me with six beady eyes.

Sard!

Quinn tugged me to the side just as the spider spit. A white mass of web and smoking venom landed on the wall.

What in the sarding hell—

Abbas' spider form clicked its pincers and turned his head to try again.

Quinn's sword sliced off two of Abbas' legs in one fell swoop.

Abbas transformed back into a human, screaming and gnashing his teeth. His left hand was nothing more than a stump. A human hand lay on the ground, a ring on each finger. Next to it, several toes rolled. The prisoner roared and then his body dissolved into black smoke. The chains couldn't hold smoke.

My heart beat out of my chest. Fear and adrenaline swamped me, and the smoke whirled in front of my face.

Only one magical race could dissolve into black smoke. Not a shapeshifter. Not a fairy. They all had to maintain their bodies somehow. Only one creature could become an element.

Pure djinn.

Declan was right.

There were only about eight pure djinn left in the world. Sultan Raj had most of his competition killed.

I watched the black smoke condense and start to solidify into an entirely new form, one that wasn't Abbas.

Before the smoke could turn completely, I saw Quinn swing his sword, forcing the djinni to dissolve again.

What are you doing?

Waiting for Declan.

Declan?

Backup, Quinn's mental voice was breathless as he swung the sword a third time, making sure to slice the smoke in half. The smoke attempted to breach the cracks of the room, to crawl down the gutter, but didn't go for the bars of the door. I wasn't certain why until I looked at the door. Or where it had been. Now, all that appeared was a wall.

The door looked to be on the other side of the room, where there was actually only stone. Quinn was disguising the door and the real gutter with his illusions.

Quinn tried to keep up both his magic and the sword fight. But he was quickly tiring. His expertise wasn't in fighting, particularly fighting smoke, where he couldn't judge how hard his swings needed to be.

I shot pulses of green light at the smoke, trying to slow it down. I don't know if it did any good. But it felt better than standing there.

Suddenly, I heard a metallic clatter on the stone floor.

I looked down to see a beer stein rolling on the ground, near the actual door to the cell.

The real cell door slammed shut. The black smoke bolted toward the door, following the sound.

Shite!

Blast him with peace, Dove!

I lit the room with green light and moaned as my arms ripped open. My magic changed the smoke to a sickly grey-green color.

Quinn scooped up the cup and held it out in the middle of the room. *Get in the cup!* His mental shout echoed and made my ears ring.

But the smoke continued to swirl. Slower, now that it was infused with peace magic.

"Dec, what's the opposite of smoke?" I called out.

The smoke in front of us turned to ash. A small, rolling ball of grey dust, like a tiny planet attempting to form, floated in midair. I shot another blast of peace at it, turning the ash green.

"Ash is dust. Opposite of dust!" I yelled.

Quinn stretched out the stein underneath the green ball of ash just as Declan transformed the dust into water.

The green water sloshed down into the beer stein. Quinn slammed the lid down.

"We're good!" I called out.

A second later Declan burst into the prison chamber.

"What the sard—"

Quinn held out the stein and Declan took it from him. Quinn grabbed the hand that lay on the floor and yanked the jeweled rings off it.

"What are you doing?" I asked.

I took all his jewelry off when we first captured him. These rings here only appeared when I severed that hand. They're probably spelled or something. Which means they're important, Quinn said to both of us.

Declan nodded his approval. "Djinn are controlled by rings."

Quinn poured the four sparkling rings into his pocket. Then he scooped me up and his thoughts projected to both of us again. *We need to get her to Ryan. She's gonna pass out.*

He strode out of the dungeon, Declan trailing behind with the beer stein that rattled and steamed and even screamed.

"If Abbas was a full djinni," Declan whispered as we ascended, "you know what that means?" My knight didn't wait for an answer, "He isn't the bad guy."

Quinn whirled to glare at him.

Declan jerked backward. "I mean, obviously he's *a* bad guy. But not *the* bad guy. Djinn are powerful pawns. But that's it. Someone wished he'd come here. They wished he wouldn't be able to reveal his master or their plan."

"Wouldn't they run out of wishes?" I asked.

Declan shook his head. "That's only half-djinn. They have three wishes to grant during their lifetime. A full djinni is a slave, so long as you control the ring that controls him. The wishes are endless. And it makes sense. How he was able to shuffle his thoughts and emotions? Whoever sent him wished he wouldn't be able to reveal his true purpose."

The beer stein echoed with a tiny shriek and Declan looked down at it thoughtfully.

"From what I read tonight, djinn hate giving out wishes. They don't do it. Because they hate to be trapped. So, whoever sent Abbas was powerful enough to trick and control a djinni."

Quinn's face grew dark, even darker than I'd seen it before. His thoughts projected to both of us. *When I was beating him, Abbas merely took it. It was almost as if he was waiting.*

"For what?" I asked.

Quinn's grip on me tightened as he turned to continue up the stairs. *You. That's when he attacked. Whatever this mystery asshole has wished, I'm pretty sure he wants you dead.*

CHAPTER SEVEN

$\mathcal{R}$yan had already left on a gargoyle, to chase whatever his men had seen to the south.

So, the castle healer was brought to patch me up for the second time that day. He healed me in my chambers, without saying a word, as I stared at the bluebird perched in a golden cage in the corner.

I opened my mouth to curse the bird and ask what the hell Connor was up to, and why the sard he hadn't removed the thing … person … whatever he was … but the healing tonics made me drowsy.

Quinn took the beer stein back from Declan and stalked off to who knows where to 'contain the problem.'

Declan stayed with me, stroking my hair as I dozed.

My dreams were dark. A shadow chased me and morphed into a snake and bit me, which turned into Abbas, teeth clenched on my neck. I jerked awake with a scream. My heart raced.

"Sard!" Declan cursed and sat up beside me. He threw an arm out in front of me as he got to his knees on the bed. He glanced around the room, in the grey light of early dawn. His eyes hunted until he realized there was no one there.

"I'm sorry. Just a nightmare," I whispered.

Declan's eyes softened and he held his arms open for me. I snuggled into him, inhaling the soft scent of paper and ink and leather that he carried around.

Declan kissed the top of my head and whispered, "I've got you, Peace. I've got you."

"Yes, she's fine. I've got her," I heard Declan mutter to no one.

Why is he talking to thin air? I wondered.

Then I heard Quinn say, *You alright, Dovey?*

Mm-hmm. Dec's got me.

Okay, well, I'm still finishing up. I'm pretty sure the others are, too. We'll be there as soon as we can.

I yawned and wrapped my arms tighter around Declan.

Declan soothed me, rubbing my back. "Tell me about it."

I started to talk, but somehow, that just made the image of Abbas sinking his teeth into my neck much more vivid. My chest contracted and I started shaking. Goosebumps sprang up all over my body, even though I was under the covers and in Declan's arms. I squeezed my eyes shut as Declan pulled me into a sitting position.

"I'm sorry. I've never felt like this before. I don't know what's wrong with me."

Declan sat me in his lap and his hands closed over mine. He interlaced our fingers. It didn't stop the shaking.

"I might … I feel like I might throw up," I warned.

"My sweet, Peace. You're just reacting to the attack earlier. You don't need to apologize."

"I shouldn't have turned my back on him," I was still bitter about how stupid I'd been.

Declan just lifted my hand to his lips and kissed it. He watched how it shook for a moment before he said, "I'm going to help you calm down, okay?"

"Yes." The urge to vomit grew stronger. Abbas' voice sounded again in my head.

"Let's get your gown off," Declan dropped my hands and reached for my chemise.

Just having his hands drag up my body sent my anxiety spiraling from one direction to another. My knights had only taken me together. Declan and I had never …

"Do you seriously want our first time—" I backed away from him. I didn't. I didn't want a nightmare to be the start of my first time alone with Declan. I wanted my first time with him to be sweet and innocent, somewhat bashful, the way I pictured him.

Declan shook his head and laughed as he yanked up my chemise, so it was above my waist. "Stay still. We aren't sleeping together. I'm going to take care of you," Declan breathed on my ear. "I know what an anxiety attack is like. That's what you're having."

I glanced down at my hands. They were still shaking.

"I'll be fine. Probably. Just need to puke."

Declan's lips rested against the shell of my ear. "Did you know, I used to have these a lot?"

"No." I turned to look at him. I studied his light blue eyes. He held my gaze, steady and strong. By the look on his face, I could tell he was telling me the truth. And the ache that grew in my heart at the thought of him hurting was worse than fear. I touched his bare chest. "When? Why?"

He shook his head. "I'll tell you. But first, I'm going to help your body relax a little, Peace. Trust me."

"But—"

"Do you trust me?"

I nodded weakly. He pulled me close, so that my back was against the firm muscles of his chest. He bunched my chemise in his hands again and put his lips next to my ear. The feel of his breath on my ear and neck made it hard to think.

"I want you to trust me completely," his voice was rough and emotional.

"I do."

"I won't hurt you. Ever."

"I know," I whispered.

"I'm going to take care of you. Calm you down and chase that nightmare away." He pulled my chemise over the top of my head slowly and dropped it onto the bed next to us.

"I know."

I turned into him. I needed a kiss. The things he was saying were so sweet. And that nervous energy inside needed action, not words. My mind didn't want to make love to him until it was a sweet moment scattered with rose petals. My body felt differently. My body wanted to shed the tremors. My body wanted to writhe against Declan until he was shaking as badly as me, for entirely different reasons.

Declan didn't give in to my body's wishes. He gave me one soft kiss, feathering his lips over mine.

"It's not just the nightmare," I confessed.

"I know," he whispered, dragging his fingers through my long brown mane.

"It feels overwhelming," he whispered in my ear. "It feels like nothing is going right. Like nothing will ever go right. Like the world is spiraling out of control."

ANN DENTON

"How do you know?" I mumbled into his shoulder.

"I struggle with it on a daily basis, beautiful. Now, you could dose yourself with your power…"

I hadn't even thought of doing that. It showed how affected and shaken I was. "I *can* do that," I murmured.

"A tiny dose, if it will make you feel better."

I sent a pulse of peace to my own heart, letting the green glow slip from my fingertips to my heart. My heartbeat slowed, but only partially. I needed more.

Declan stopped my hand before I could do it again. "I think you've lost enough blood today, Peace. What if I give you a massage? What if I rub out all that—

Rub out? Hell no! Quinn's voice interrupted us.

"Quinn!" Declan and I both scolded him at once. But his interruption lightened the mood and I smiled.

"Butt out," I told Quinn aloud, so Declan could hear.

As long as Declan has to stay out of your butt, too.

You are a five-year-old.

I love you.

I shook my head, tears forming in my eyes.

Don't be sad, Dove.

I'm not. I love you, too. Now leave me and Declan alone, dammit.

Fine. But no funny business without me.

I turned to Declan. "I don't know how you stood him all these years."

Declan gave me a little grin. "I just start reciting crop calculations and figures. Shuts him up and gets him out of my head real quick."

I laughed, draping my arms over Declan's shoulders. "He's worried you're going to get up to naughty things without him."

Declan kissed me. A soft kiss that traveled from my lips to my chin to my neck. "If I thought that would help, I would."

My heart jumped. "It might."

Declan chuckled, "I'll play with you, if that's what you really want."

"Playful Declan?" I couldn't resist asking, "What would that look like?"

Immediately Declan stiffened against me. His whisper was soft, so soft I could barely hear it. "Which side do you want? Dom or sub?"

It was almost as if he were scared of my answer.

"Whatever you want, darling,"

He shook his head. "Think, Bloss. Take a moment. What do you need?"

I stared at him for a second. And then I surprised myself when the word, "Dom," slipped out of my lips. But it was a piece of Declan I'd never seen. And I was curious. More than curious. I was desperate to see that side of him. Desperate to see every side of him.

Declan immediately inhaled and straightened up so he could look down at me. His gaze was hard and piercing and sarding hot.

"Lay down on the bed."

I lay down immediately and watched him. He took his hand and ran it over the front of my body, between my breasts and down my stomach. He stopped at my hip bones. He tapped my right hip. "Turn over."

I turned and lay on my stomach, letting the velvet coverlet brush my cheek. The soft scrape of the velvet hardened my nipples.

"I want you to take a deep breath. Tonight, you had a nightmare. And that might happen again for a while." Declan said.

I took a deep breath and nodded into the blankets as Declan ran his fingers down my spine and back up again.

"Now, Peace. I'm going to give you a massage—"

I pushed my head up and turned toward him, "I thought we were playing Dom!"

Smack! He slapped my ass and then pinched the bottom of the curve, where my ass met my leg. It didn't hurt, but it startled me.

Declan frowned and put his hands on my shoulders.

"We are playing Dom, darling. And I get to decide what to do to you."

Declan pushed me gently back onto my stomach. Then he straddled me and leaned down, letting his chest brush my back, letting me feel his hardness through his pants. He rubbed himself lightly against my ass and let his lips caress my ear. His teeth played with my earlobe. "You chose Dom, Peace. Now I get to choose what happens next. You aren't queen when we play Dom." Declan's hand traced down my sides. It slid over the curve of my breast, my hip. His fingers dug in briefly. "Now wait here while I get the oil."

A minute later, the top of the bed moved as Declan climbed on behind me. "It's just me," he soothed softly. The bed bounced a little as he shuffled closer.

He wrapped a cloth around the shallow cut in my arm from my magic. Then he spoke. "I'm going to pour some oil on your back. It might be cold at first. But I'll warm it with my hands. Your job is to stay still."

When the first drops of oil hit, I couldn't help my gasp, or the slight recoil of my body. But then I smelled roses and violets. Declan had gone and gotten scented oil. His hands fell onto my back and gently swirled the oil around.

I let my eyelids close. I told my pounding heart and throbbing pussy to relax. Declan was in charge. I didn't have to worry about anything. What to say. What to do about Avia. I just had to lay here. I just had to stay still.

Gradually, as Declan kneaded my shoulders and moved down my spine, he said, "I want you to breathe with me, sweetheart." And he started inhaling deeply. He held his breath a few seconds. Then he exhaled.

I took a deep, shuddering breath. At the same moment, Declan dug his fingers deep into my back, pulling the tension away from my spine and spreading it out over my ribs until his fingers lifted. Strangely, that movement seemed to pull the tension with it. As though he'd physically lifted the tension away from me.

"That," I whispered. "Do that again."

He smacked my rump. "You aren't the boss right now, Peace." But he did it again.

I grinned into the blanket. "I forgot."

Declan's mouth met my back and he whispered. "I'm gonna have to punish you for forgetting." And then he sucked at my skin, hard. So hard he made a mark. He rolled me over. And he did the same on my chest, just above the swell of my breasts. He sucked my skin in.

"Are you giving me hickeys?" I breathed.

Declan smacked my hip as he released me. "I didn't say you could talk," he pretended to growl, but his eyes were sparkling with mischief. Declan was being playful and naughty.

"Quinn's gonna kill you," I whispered.

He shrugged. "I can take Quinn."

"I can't wait to watch that."

Declan moved up the bed so he could spread out by my side, his front pressed against me, his head propped on one arm. "It looks like you're feeling better."

I nodded as I turned on my side and buried my face against Declan's neck. "Tell me about it," I said.

He knew exactly what I wanted. "My mother was always a perfectionist. Not that I saw much of her. The bastard's nursery wasn't a popular spot to visit—"

I growled and popped up out of my snuggle so I could grab his hand and drape it over me. "It should have been. You were her most adorable baby, by far."

He gave a sad little grin and I imagined what he'd looked like, staring at the door of the nursery, waiting for his mother, Queen Diamoni. Always being disappointed.

I shook him slightly, determined to help lift his sadness after he'd helped me with my fear. "You forget, I've met your brothers. They're basically blond-colored bears."

Declan chuckled.

"I'm dead serious. Brendon's snaggle tooth makes him look like he could eat children."

"Maybe he has," Declan's grin was wider now.

I stroked his hair. "I got the best one of the bunch."

"You got the one dropped on your doorstep."

I lifted my leg and draped it over him. "I beg to differ. But we're getting off-track. You were going to tell me more about your deluded mother."

Declan cleared his throat and continued, reaching his free arm across my waist so his hand could trace lazy patterns in the oil that coated my spine. "She always came in wanting my shirts more starched or criticizing how scuffed my shoes were. Maybe it was her way of chiding my nanny for not taking better care of me. But, it always kind of felt like she was critiquing me."

He fell silent for a second, lost in memory. I waited, knowing he was sharing a part of himself with me that he had to hide at court. I'd never seen Declan anxious. Never seen him break down. But he said he knew how I'd felt when I woke. I waited patiently.

He was quiet when he spoke again. "I hadn't thought about it before, but maybe my mother had the same obsession that I do. I've always been obsessed with perfection. One of my quirks. Drives my butler mad."

I gave a naughty grin. "So, you're saying I shouldn't go sneak into your room at night and rearrange all your things?"

Declan laughed and hugged me to him so he could swat my butt. "Definitely not. That would make you a bad girl."

"If I promise I won't, will you pretend I did and punish me anyway, sometime?"

His eyes grew dark with lust. "Anything you want."

I raised my eyebrows suggestively but said, "I want to hear the rest of this story. I want to know my Declan."

He bit his lip at that. At first, I thought it was because he was nervous to tell me about what made him panic.

But he said, "Yours?"

I moved my hand from playing with his hair and caressed his cheek. "Mine."

His hand came from my back and grabbed my hand as it stroked his face. He pulled my hand down and placed it over his heart, between us. There was a long moment where we were lost in each other's eyes before he continued.

"As I said, perfection became an obsession. As I got older, it got harder and harder to deal with things that weren't perfect. Every time I made a mistake, I hated myself. Grew anxious. Had this overwhelming feeling come over me. The same kind of thing I saw when you woke up. Panic." His hand stroked mine where it lay against his chest.

"How did you learn to control it?"

He pursed his lips. "I found an outlet." He blushed and didn't hold my gaze.

"What outlet?" I breathed.

"The whip," he whispered.

It took me a few seconds to process what he'd said. But then I gasped and pulled my hand away from him. I sat up in bed, pulled on his shirt, yanking it upward. "Roll over," I commanded.

"Bloss, it's not—"

I pushed him over. "You hurt yourself?" My fingers were already tracing over the faint pink scars I could see on his lower back.

"I know I'm not normal—"

He stopped talking when I bent and put my lips on one of the scars. I kissed it. And then its neighbor. I yanked at his tunic shirt, pulling it higher, kissing each little red line I saw. Some of them were thick and big, they looked like they'd been deep.

I moved to straddle Declan's back. I made sure I kissed every single scar he had. When I was done, I rested on top of him, my cheek on his spine.

"Are you ... disgusted by me?" he whispered.

I felt his body tense underneath me as he awaited my answer. "No, sweetling. I'm not." I hugged him. "After my nightmare—my physical reaction was so intense. I couldn't stop the shaking. I wouldn't have been able to stop without you."

He let out a shaky breath.

"But you are gonna have to teach me how to use the whip. Some of your scars are way too big and there's no way in hell I'm gonna let you get that hurt—"

In a single move I was somehow on my back on the bed and Declan was looming over me.

"You'd whip me?" his voice was soft.

"If that's the only thing that will snap you out of it, then yeah. I'm here to give you what you need, Dec. We take care of each other, right?"

His mouth swooped down on mine in a bruising kiss. It was desperate and fierce, and his tongue fought to dominate mine. His hands reached out and grabbed mine, pinning them to my sides as he rolled us, so I was sitting on him once more, only this time I was on his front, his erection digging into my thigh through his pants. Declan gave me one last nip and then laid back on the mattress with the largest grin I'd ever seen.

"What?" I asked.

"You love me."

"That isn't new."

He shrugged. "It kind of is."

I smiled. "Yeah, I guess it kind of is."

We basked in sweet shy smiles for a moment as dawn peeked through the window with a ray of orange light.

I was just leaning down toward Declan, thinking our sweet tender moment might be here, when Ginnifer walked through the door.

"Your Majesty—" she stopped dead, red-faced at the sight of me nude and straddling my knight. My maid turned around quick as a whip and announced in a squeaky voice, "I'll wait in your dressing room."

I turned back to Declan, naughty smile on my face. "Well, she walked in on quite a show."

"Just wait until she cleans the oil spots on the comforter."

"Oh, I dunno if I want her to clean it up."

Declan furrowed his brow. "You want to leave that mess?"

I could almost see him controlling an eye twitch. It was too good of an opportunity not to tease my perfectionist. I shrugged a shoulder. "I thought maybe we could tell the other knights that you made me squirt."

His look of disgust turned to one of mischief. "Quinn would hate that."

"I know."

"One problem. That oil smells like flowers."

I narrowed my eyes. "Spoilsport. Oh! I know, we could tell them I asked Cerena to enchant my pussy."

He rolled his eyes. "After the attack from Abbas, you insisted I take you to Cerena to enchant your—"

"Fine," I sighed. That story was rotten. No one would ever believe it. I pouted. "Quinn would have gone along with it."

Declan shook his head and pulled me into his arms. "You do have an enchanting pussy, Bloss. But I prefer not to have the other knights pissed at me. How about this … I promise I'll make you squirt so your bed is that wet later?"

I sat up enough to see him. I tucked in my lips and waggled my head back and forth as if I was considering it. "Alright, I suppose that will have to do. After you teach me about the whip." I climbed off the bed so I could get ready for day two of Queen Isla's visit.

But Declan's arm shot out and pulled me back to the side of the bed. "Peace, there won't be any whips."

"There won't?"

"A few years ago, Ryan taught me a different way to control my anxiety."

"Yeah?"

Declan sat up on the bed so he could whisper into my ear, "Sex." Then he smacked my ass and pushed me toward the dressing room.

"What!" I screeched. "You can't say that and just—"

"Time to get ready," Declan stood and straightened his shirt, marching over to my looking glass to finger comb his hair.

Cerena's bluebird fluttered backward, away from Declan.

I bit my thumb at Declan. "You bastard. That's all I'm going to think about all day, now."

His grin was so naughty that it was sarding adorable and I hated him for it. "I know," he said cockily. "I want you desperate. So that when you finally get me alone, in some dark corner, you can't help yourself."

"I hope you have a panic attack," I gritted out through my teeth as he strode to the door.

He winked before he strolled out the door. "If I do, I'll let you take care of it!"

CHAPTER EIGHT

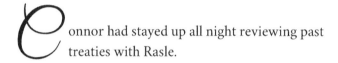onnor had stayed up all night reviewing past treaties with Rasle.

He met me in the private royal breakfast salon with a tired grin. His curls were a disaster. I loved them. I went right over and tousled them before lightly touching the bags under his sea-green eyes.

"Why didn't you tell me? I'd have stayed up with you and planned for this."

"You were attacked and needed some rest," he waved me off and poured himself some coffee imported from Lored, the tropical country to the south.

I sighed. "Well, next time, let me know at least."

He mock saluted me, and I narrowed my eyes at him. "I'm serious, Connor. Until I can find someone else to take this damn crown and—"

"Wait. Take your crown?"

I grabbed a roll and sank into a chair, yanking the bread to bits and taking a bite.

Connor came and stood beside me, "Explain. I thought you were over this whole running away phase."

"First of all, I'm awful at this job."

"You've been at it a day! Of course, you're awful!"

"Thank you," I threw a chunk of bread at him.

"I meant *anyone* would be awful."

"Secondly, I just meant I need a regent so I can help find Avia—"

"Quinn and Ryan are both working on finding her."

"But I want to help."

Connor closed his eyes and sighed. "The best way you can help is doing your job as queen. That is something none of us can do."

I put aside the rest of my bread. Connor's words had turned my stomach. Instead, I grabbed his coffee out of his hand and drank. I had to resist spitting. "Ugh. This is awful."

"No. It's the nectar of the gods, and of sleepless souls everywhere."

I made a face as I gulped more. "Tell me what I need to know for today."

"Well, this afternoon, there's to be a parade through Marscha. You and Isla will ride on a float through the main street of the capital."

"No," I groaned. Standing on a cart drawn by horses and decorated with ribbons all afternoon? Pretending to smile? I needed a regent to do those things for me.

"That was the good news," Connor shuffled slightly backward.

"Sard. What the hell is the bad news, then?" I drank the last of the coffee, ignoring the bitter aftertaste. I'd need it to stay alert during the interactions with Isla ahead.

"We get to meet with Isla all morning to discuss fun items like the border towns of Singah and Jewl, which she claims are still part of Rasle. We get to discuss trading terms and tolls, though really, we'd need to bring to trolls in to discuss all of those in detail, so hopefully—" he ducked as I grabbed the remains of my roll and chucked it at him.

I felt like stomping my foot. I wasn't ready for negotiation! Not with an experienced queen. Not even with a three-year-old, if I was honest. I was a torn-up wasteland inside. Which meant my head wasn't where it needed to be.

I rubbed my forehead. "I think I'd rather Abbas bit me again."

Connor's lips thinned, and his hands clenched as he said, "You don't mean that."

I sighed, "Of course not." I stood and grumbled, pouring myself more of Connor's foul-tasting drink. "Tell me what our positions are. What do I say?"

I sat there and listened to Connor, learning my lines and hoping like hell I didn't choke like the day prior.

It was only as we were leaving the salon that I remembered to ask, "What happened with that bird?"

Connor clapped a hand to his forehead. Then he mussed his dark curls. "Thank goodness you said something! I want that bird to come with us."

"What?" I stopped dead on the plush red rug and stared. "I thought that bird was a person under a spell. Why the sard would we want him with us during negotiations? What if he's from Gitmore or something? Sent as a spy?"

Connor grimaced. "I don't necessarily want him there the whole time. Cerena spelled a cage for him so he can't attack. I want to see Isla's reaction to him. He basically arrived when she did. So, I want to see what her reaction is."

When we went into the hall, Connor asked one of my guards to run up and put the bluebird in a cage and then bring him to us.

The young man ran off, and I whispered to Connor, "Cerena's sure this thing isn't out to attack me? It's not just another Abbas?"

"We spoke with him at length last night, it doesn't seem so."

I laughed. "You spoke at length. With a bluebird?"

Connor shrugged. "He was able to answer a lot of yes and no questions. He has a family. Didn't get to his official species yet. Not troll, giant, two dozen types of fae, or mer-person. He didn't directly see who cursed him. But he knows who it is. The specifics were a bit difficult to get at, of course."

I sat back, impressed. Connor really could talk to anyone. Even a bird. It almost made me laugh. But he was so earnest. And he hadn't slept. So, I bit down on a grin and tried to hold my face steady as I asked, "Really, and what else do you know about this bird?"

"He claims to have been on the grounds for several days, pinning down exact times made him shrug. We asked him about where he came from and when Cheryn came up he went into a tizzy."

"Could Abbas have done this to him?"

Connor shrugged. "Maybe. But djinn typically deal in wishes. Why wish for someone to be an animal?"

I shrugged. "Hatred?" If I could turn Abbas into a fat little gerbil, I might consider it. It would only be the start of his punishment.

"Well, if Abbas did this to him, then he probably came here for revenge. Though how the hell he thought he'd pull that off—"

I smiled, and my heart grew warm. Someone else might hate the sarding prince as much as I did. "I'd love to let him try sometime." I imagined letting him peck at the prince's face down in the dungeon.

"Fat chance, Quinn's locked him away in the mage's tower so no one can find—"

"Good morning," Ember bounded up to me, her black wings bouncing. She was far too excited for what was about to be a mind-numbingly boring event. "Did you hear about the parade later? Of course, you heard. This is my first official state visit. And it's all so exciting!"

"Yes, it should be great fun later," I responded, wishing I had her enthusiasm. "Did you and your father get settled into the ambassador's quarters?"

"Oh, yes. Dad loves them. They're so nice. I think he's going to really like this. Change of pace, you know?"

"Wonderful. Well, I'm happy to have him. And I hope you'll visit often," I said.

"Of course!" Ember giggled and went to grab my hand. One of my guards stopped her. "Oh, I'm sorry. I'm probably not supposed to touch." She backed up and gave a half-curtsy.

"I didn't get a chance to ask before, but how's your family?"

Ember's face fell for a moment before she pasted on a smile. "They ... they had a bit of an accident on a trade route. It's just my father, Donovon, and me now."

I pulled her into a hug, breaking protocol.

Behind me, one of my guards coughed loudly. I sighed and released Ember, stepping back so the guard wouldn't have a fit.

"I'm so sorry." I knew her pain. Losing your family was awful.

Ember's eyes teared up for a second. "All we can do is move forward and make the best of it. Learn from what happened and try not to let it happen again, right?"

I nodded.

Ember gave a small curtsy. I could tell she wasn't long from truly crying. "Well, have a wonderful morning, Your Majesty." She walked away swiftly.

"You too." I smiled sadly and turned to Connor. "I botched that. I had no idea her parents had passed."

Connor took my hand and said, "Not your fault, Bloss Boss." He waited until she rounded the corner to say more. "Her parents caught the bad side of the Sedarian navy. Accused of smuggling."

My eyes widened. "Was it true?"

He shrugged.

My bluebird arrived in a birdcage just as we reached the green salon, which Connor had chosen for negotiations. Connor took the golden cage into his hand as he allowed the guards to clear the room before we entered.

My knight turned to me and put on his 'lecture' voice. "It echoes in here, Bloss. This room is full of stone. So, no shouting or everyone will hear you for miles."

I rolled my eyes, "You chose this room on purpose."

"Yup. But you know and Isla doesn't, so if she loses control, she'll be a bit embarrassed," he shrugged.

"Manipulative little sucker, aren't you?" I grinned, swelling with pride.

"Just doing my job," he winked and led me by the arm into the room.

We got situated and waited for Isla while servants brought treats into the room. Rolls baked with cheese on them, a traditional breakfast in Rasle, arrived.

The bluebird twittered at that, fluttering in his cage.

"Do you want breakfast?" I laughed and asked the little creature.

He nodded solemnly. I grabbed a roll and broke it, placing little bites in his cage. I looked at Connor, "Did you get a name for him?"

Connor rolled his eyes, "Is that a yes or no type of question?"

I stuck my tongue out at my knight. "You're chippy this morning."

Connor poured himself more coffee. "Yup."

I turned to the little bluebird, who was scarfing up the bread. "Careful, little man, or you'll choke. You are a man, aren't you?"

The bluebird nodded.

"Good. Well, then, my I call you Mr. Blue?"

The bluebird shook his head.

"Unfortunately, since you can't talk, you don't get a choice."

The bluebird scolded me in chirps.

"Sorry, what was that? Can't hear it, you're enchanted." I made a face at the bird.

"Leave the poor man alone. You'd hate it if you were stuck as an animal."

I yawned. "That's true. Guess I'm chippy, too."

I set my finger through the bars of the cage. "Truce, Blue?"

The bird nipped my finger lightly but then rubbed his head against it. The feathers were soft and light and soothing.

"Do you know Queen Isla?" I asked softly.

Blue wobbled his head side to side. I wasn't sure if that meant he knew of her, or if he sort of knew her. And I didn't have a chance to ask. Because the door opened a moment later, and my first official royal negotiation began.

*F*our hours later I was considering gouging my eyes out with my teaspoon.

Isla had argued all morning that the hills near our river were originally entirely Rasle's land and should be returned.

"They were lost during the third Fire War," Connor sighed, repeating himself for the third time. "They've been part of Evaness for nearly a century."

"That agreement was supposed to be temporary," Isla snapped, setting her teacup down with a jolt and ignoring the way her voice echoed.

"Well, tell that to your ancestors. They failed to rectify it."

"My people ended up on the dry side of the mountain with no rain and no water. They can't grow, they can't travel easily. They can't trade what they do grow without river access. They struggle to support themselves."

Isla's people were mostly part mer-person or part-troll descendants. Human blood really diluted either of their race's magics. It made Rasle one the least magical of the seven kingdoms. Farming and goat herding were their mainstays.

Connor spoke for me. "Again, the current residents on our portion of those hills are Evaness citizens. While we're sorry for your plight—"

"Our plight is your plight! Don't they raid your villages each winter? Don't they bring their starving children here to beg?"

Connor responded with an annoying level of calm, which only set Isla and her diplomatic staff off further. The echoes started as their voices grew shrill.

I pulled Blue's cage closer and set my finger through the bars. He rubbed his head against the pad of my finger. He looked just as miserable listening to this argument on repeat as I felt.

I swallowed a sigh. I understood what Isla wanted. When people couldn't support themselves, they turned to lawlessness. It wasn't good for Rasle or Evaness.

But to just hand over entire towns was foolish. It wouldn't make Evaness safe in the long run. It would make me look weak. Make our country look vulnerable to invasion.

"What your people need is more access to water," Connor said. "I've offered before and I'll offer again, we can help magically create a lake in that area to collect rainwater."

"A lake doesn't do me any good," Isla huffed. "Let's say you help with water, and my people aren't starving. What if they actually have excess? It takes two weeks to go through those hills and get to my other townships. We need more of that land so we can reach the Gorgonite River. We need to be able to *trade*."

I chewed on my tongue, thinking. Given enough time, Declan might be able to reduce enough dirt in the area to help create a new tributary. But that would pull him away from helping Evaness. From ensuring our own people were fed. A lake was quicker. Less of an investment.

"What if we agreed to a lake for now, with the possibility of gradually building a tributary to link to the river?" I threw out as I opened Blue's cage and let him out on my finger. I petted his soft little chest.

Isla and Connor turned toward me. I was pretty sure Connor wanted to boil me alive based on the blank stare and carefully calm look he was giving me.

I was offering something we technically didn't have to offer. I was potentially offering more than Declan could take on. I was pretty sure he'd tell me I was 'giving away the castle.' But there were people going hungry. Not my people. But people. We couldn't try nothing.

"How would that work?" Isla's scribe asked.

"We'd have to discuss details, but perhaps my knight, Declan, could visit to assist over the next few years—"

"Years!" Isla shook her head, the pearls in her crown rattling slightly in their settings.

"We can't wait years. We need his help now!"

I bit my tongue from telling her that her people could always add more fishing to their repertoire if they needed more food. Her part-mer communities would never hear of it. They'd rather starve or steal than possibly kill kin.

I took a deep breath through my nose. "Isla, I just began my reign. I want to work with you, but you have to understand that Declan is—

"What if you sent him for a month? Just a month? Surely, you could spare him now that harvest is over."

I sighed, "I'm trying to compromise."

"Two days. What if you send him back with me for two days to simply work out a preliminary plan?" Isla countered. "I need to be able to tell my people something."

Connor intervened. "Perhaps we should break for the day. Give everyone time to mull over the options as they've been presented. Maybe tomorrow, we'll have time to develop more potential solutions."

I stood, not waiting for anyone to respond. I grabbed Blue's cage and put him onto my shoulder as I strode out of the room. I was halfway back to the royal wing when Connor caught up with me and my guards.

I cringed, not wanting to hear his critique, but needing to know at the same time. "How bad was it?"

"Well, you basically offered everything she wanted on a platter," Connor shook his head at me, and I shrugged.

There was nothing for me to say. He was right. I had just wanted to yell at Isla and tell her what she was doing wrong. Suppressing that impulse had made me blurt out something else.

Connor rubbed my shoulder, "At least you didn't agree to ship Declan off yet. We still have time to backpedal."

I put a hand to my forehead, forgetting about Blue. He fluttered off my shoulder and flitted down the hall. "So ... poorly is the answer. I did poorly."

Sarding idiot, Bloss, I told myself.

Connor sighed, "Try not to kill Dec by giving everyone exactly what they want, okay? She'll see you as a pushover. Word will spread. And Declan will constantly be gone, pleasing these other assholes' every whim. They have a lotta' whims."

I sighed and rubbed my forehead as I said, "Alright. Sorry."

He put an arm over my shoulders. "It's fine. And if it makes you feel any better, when your mother was younger, she nearly gave away the rights to all our minerals to a fairy from Gitmore. Part of why she hated them so much."

I gave a little grin at that, "At least I'm not the only fool, I guess."

Connor smiled and kissed the tip of my nose. "I need to go mingle and get a read on Isla's people. But you're not a fool, Bloss. You have a heart. The problem is, Isla and most of these other royal assholes don't."

That was a problem.

A big one.

And I had a feeling that it was one of those other royal assholes who was controlling Abbas.

I just didn't know who.

CHAPTER NINE

*T*he parade was as awful as I expected.

A jester, wearing a long-nosed mask that constantly poked me in the back, rode on a wagon with Isla and me. He tossed coins at the children and then shot little colorful sparks of magic into the sky. The crowd was enamored. I was annoyed. I had to stand wedged between him and Isla and wave, a fake smile plastered on my face as I tried not to fall while we bounced over ruts in the road. My knees hurt like hell.

There were half-clothed dancers in front of us who constantly made our cart start and stop because they'd pause to do some ridiculous lift that showcased the women's splits. The men in the crowd loved it. After the fifth time my ass hit the back of the wagon because we jerked to a stop, I ceased to be impressed.

Soldiers marched behind us, their trumpets and tubas blasting my ears with noise. Blue huddled close to my neck, scratching me whenever the screaming children or loud bursts of sound startled him.

"Stop that," I scolded him between my teeth. "You aren't really a bird so don't let those bird reflexes take over."

I was pecked for that.

I clenched my teeth and fists, telling myself I couldn't snap a bird's neck in front of children.

Quinn had insisted I let the bluebird ride on my shoulder, partially to see who might react to the bird and give us a clue about him, and partially to test my patience, I'm sure.

Isla didn't even bat an eye, I told him. *This is stupid.*

You're the beast-tamer, Dove. The crowds will love it.

Why I caved to him, I wasn't certain. Perhaps it was because he'd left to sneak into Cheryn and search for Avia. I missed him already. Or maybe it was the fact that Connor and Declan, who were both riding on horses behind me scanning the crowd, agreed with him. I hated when my husbands ganged up on me.

The parade lasted a gods-awful two hours.

But the afternoon festivities had only just begun.

In honor of Rasle, and the end of harvest, plow races took place next. Isla and I had to stand on a dais and watch a line of brawny men race to plow a field as quickly as they could. No horses or donkeys. Only men making asses of themselves.

Each man wore a colored ribbon on his arm, as did his cheering section in the crowd. It was amusing. More so than the parade. One large man had a white ribbon and seemed to have more fans than the rest. They were the most organized, at least, so it made his group seem more impressive. They'd even made up a cheer, "Straight lines! True hearts! Plow through! New starts!" It wasn't the best cheer. But it was better than the wolf-whistle and simple name yelling the other groups did.

Connor and Declan stood beside me and I leaned closer to Declan to ask, "What time should Ryan arrive? I thought he said he'd be back sooner?"

Declan stroked my hand, "Return trip just took a bit longer. He's been in touch with Quinn. Don't worry, Peace."

I nodded and turned back to watching the sweaty men rip off their shirts and growl like bears before leaning into their tasks once more. Their concentration and dedication to this foolishness was admirable.

But then a little lilac rabbit made a mad dash through the plows, tripping up men and causing gasps from the crowd.

"Don't hurt the bunny!" a little girl cried.

The grey-purple blur of fur doubled its speed after a plow nearly clipped its back leg. He tumbled head over heels in a furrow but somehow managed to right himself and bolt forward. Then he made a mad leap for the dais. He overshot a bit, crashing into the temporary wall erected behind Isla and myself to block the sun.

Immediately, Blue flew off my shoulder and at the rabbit, tweeting and chirping like a madman.

Connor and Declan pulled me back and got between the bunny and me. Isla's guards did the same, sheltering her.

I peered around them and watched as the rabbit batted away Blue, ignored the short sword that Connor had drawn, stood on his hind feet, and bowed directly at me.

A gasp went up around the crowd.

Wonderful. This stupid Beast-Tamer nickname was bound to stick after that bow. No chance of Bloss-the-Beautiful. No Bloss, the Dragon-Tamer—though that was clearly a false name. Sard it all.

Blue fluttered back to my shoulder, quick angry little chirps still issuing from his beak.

"Do you know this bunny?" I asked him.

Blue nodded.

"Is he here to kill me?"

Blue shook his head.

"Do you like him?"

Blue shook his head again.

I sighed.

"Is he here to harm me?"

Head shake.

"Harm anyone I know?"

Head shake.

"Is he also under a spell?"

That got a nod.

"So, he's human?"

That got a head waver from side to side.

"Part human?"

A nod. And the bunny took a hop forward at that.

I sighed and looked at Connor, who pulled a glowing stone out of his pocket and surreptitiously flashed it so I could see the bright light.

Dammit all. I couldn't just hand the bunny off to some child in the crowd.

Connor had the audacity to look a little amused.

I glared at him, "I suppose we need to get back to the palace. I think Cerena needs to spend some more time with our new animal friends."

Isla looked like she wanted to ask about the rabbit in my lap and the bird on my shoulder as we rode in a royal carriage back to the palace. But she held her tongue.

Ember, my fairy friend, was not so tactful when we trudge back into the Great Hall in the palace.

"I heard you have a whole menagerie!" she laughed, arms outstretched. "I just love animals! That winged bear I got to ride over on was just the sweetest!"

When Blue and the bunny saw Ember getting close, they both backed behind me. I couldn't blame them. Ember was loud and boisterous. And it seemed as if, even though they were spelled people, some animal instincts kicked in for Blue and his rabbit friend.

"Sorry, Ember. I think they're shy." I scooped up the rabbit and Blue and walked past her. I wasn't trying to be rude, but I was eager for Cerena to figure out a spell to change these poor people back to their original forms. There was far too much dark magic going around right now.

I left the animals with my mage, promising to pick them up at sundown.

Cerena took one look at the rabbit and Connor's glowing stone and said, "Really? What are the odds? Two people with the same spell?" She sighed and had me put the rabbit on her work table.

Declan and Connor had followed me in, Declan with his brow furrowed. He glanced up at Cerena, "What did you just say?"

"I said, what are the odds of two of the same? Got to be the same person casting this spell, same magic—"

Declan stared at her for a second, but then latched onto my arm and Connor's. "Thank you, Cerena! We'll be back to check on them in a bit."

He literally dragged Connor and I through the halls until we came to a concealed royal passage. Then he basically shoved us inside. The guards followed until we came out in the hallway leading to my chambers.

Once we were in my rooms, Connor turned to Declan and asked, "What's wrong?"

"What are the odds?" Declan asked. "What are the odds of having two girls?"

Connor laughed. "Are you thinking about kids already? We've barely been—"

"What are the odds that Queen Gela had two girls?"

I waved a hand. "Everyone knows she had magical assistance. She was older. That's the only way she could have possibly conceived—"

Declan shook his head. "No. Something feels off. I don't know what. But something feels off about all of this."

"About all of what?" I asked.

"Why would someone kidnap the second daughter?" Declan's blue eyes flicked from me to Connor and back to me. "She doesn't have magic. She isn't the heir. Even when you left, your mother never made her the heir. So, why do they want her?"

I sucked in a breath. "What are you saying?"

"I think we need to find out more about Avia and the circumstances surrounding her birth."

℟

*C*onnor had a trail of servants trickle discreetly through my sitting room, so that Isla and the other court gossips wouldn't catch on that we were fishing for information. I couldn't imagine the uproar if people heard what Declan had said. Or the fallout for Avia when she returned home. But we needed to know. In order to find Avia, we had to pursue every avenue.

And so, the servants came in and Connor questioned them, while Declan and I pretended to go over ledgers.

In reality, we were checking old war documents stuffed into the ledgers for tactics on fighting dragons in between the interviews. It looked like many countries used to use wizards. But, as my search of the countryside had shown, most of the wizards had killed one another or disappeared. I hadn't been able to find one to help me with my powers. We'd have to find another way.

I glanced over as Connor worked, smoothly asking workers about their jobs as if they were up for promotion. He slid in questions about Avia with ease. I admired his silver tongue. Declan or I would probably have just outright asked the question or two we needed and raised a shite-ton of suspicion and gossip. But all these workers would leave here thinking about was the chance at a better job.

At least eight servants confirmed they'd seen my mother pregnant. But their testimony didn't seem to sway Declan. Whenever one would leave, he insisted, "Disguise spells work for the royal family. She could have used a spell that kept her face and gave her a different body."

"How do you know that?" I asked.

He blushed but waved me off. "I research everything, Bloss. Who was in the room when Avia was born? Who was actually there? That's who we need, Connor."

I nearly told Connor to call off this search, because it seemed like Declan was a little ridiculous. Maybe even a little obsessive. But something about what he'd said tugged at my gut.

I'd always thought Avia had been more suited to be queen than I was. I'd always thought Mother should give her the crown. We'd had massive arguments about it when I was fourteen. And Declan was right, it was insanely unusual for a monarch to have two daughters. No other queen had two. Even Sultan Raj, who'd sat on his throne for nearly a thousand years, hadn't had more than one daughter in the past thirty years. She'd passed away young and he hadn't had another girl. Only his five sons.

A stone sat in the pit of my stomach, weighing me down as more servants came and proclaimed they'd seen the princess the day she'd been born.

"She was a cute, squirmy thing. A mite big for a girl, I'd say. But she had a good set of lungs on her. Screamed like a banshee!" said one old parlor maid.

We were through most of the castle servants who'd been working in the palace at the time of Avia's birth when

Connor ushered in an older woman, a midwife who said she'd been in the room. She had white hair and her lower eyelids drooped, giving her a pink rim around darting green eyes.

"Yes, I helped deliver Avia," she said, after Connor helped her into a chair by the fire and asked the same questions he'd asked countless others.

"She was … an easy baby," the woman stated. "Quick."

She opened her mouth to talk more, but Connor tilted his head and studied her. "What do you mean, quick?"

I watched Connor. He'd been quiet, reading emotions throughout the afternoon. But for some reason, this woman's slow answer had perked him up.

"Queen Gela was hardly in labor at all that night," the midwife shook her head, "I had ordered things brought up, hot water and the like, and then … there she was. Little Princess Avia."

Connor stood. "Thank you. Would you mind waiting here a moment? There's someone else I'd like to bring in to speak with you."

"Of course, My Lord," the woman nodded and rested her head on the chair.

Connor strode out of the room without another word. Declan and I exchanged a glance.

A few minutes later, Connor was back with Cerena and my animals. The bluebird rode on Connor's shoulder and the rabbit followed at his heels. He grabbed the bird and thrust it at me. "Here. This sarding thing shite on me when I tried to leave without him. And your damn bunny bites."

"Blue, you naughty boy," I took Blue as I noticed a white streak down the back of Connor's vest.

Blue puffed up in pride. I pulled the bird close to me and said, "Now, you're only supposed to do that to Quinn."

Did you say my name, Dove?

Nope.

Liar.

Just be safe and get home. And tell Ryan to do the same.

He's already flying back.

Blue settled in on my shoulder and the bunny hopped over to snuggle into my skirts where they pooled on the floor. He scratched at the silk until he'd piled it to his liking and settled in.

I sighed. Dammit. Pretty soon I'd be naming him, too. I didn't even love animals. I'd always liked the gargoyles more. The fact that these were spelled people cuddling up to me just made me twice as uncomfortable. Cerena needed an assistant to help her break this spell. Yesterday.

My eyes followed my mage as Connor led her over to the midwife. "Mrs. Borroughs, can you please repeat what you just said?"

Connor came and stood next to me while the midwife told Cerena about the day my sister was born. I leaned toward my knight and whispered, "Why did you get Cerena?"

Connor leaned closer. And Declan bent near so he could hear. "When she spoke, her emotions went blank. It was odd. She was excited about the baby and then just blank."

I stared at Cerena as she asked the older woman another question.

"Blank, how?" Declan asked.

"Blank, like she was spelled," Connor's lips thinned. "I've seen it once or twice before. People's minds have been modified by a spell."

Cerena's eyes met mine. She nodded grimly.

Shite. Connor was right.

Cerena pulled a bottle of salt out of her pocket. "Excuse me, ma'am. But we're about to …" Cerena looked to Connor.

"Promote you, Mrs. Burroughs," Connor supplied. "You've served us so well. But we need a … confidentiality spell performed."

The old woman gave a toothy grin and settled back into her chair, letting Cerena do as she wished.

My mage sprinkled the salt in a circle around the servant. She grabbed a candle from off a nearby table and asked the woman to hold it. And then Cerena took out a knife.

She sliced her own palm, letting the blood drip onto the salt. She grabbed the old woman's hand and raised it, placing her own bloody palm against the servant's. She took a vial out of another pocket and said, "I'd like you to drink this. It's called Revelation. And then I'd like you to think about the day Princess Avia was born again."

Cerena recited a spell that made the hair on my neck rise and Blue bury his face in the high collar of my dress. A blue glow filled the room. Silver sparkles rose from the midwife's head and morphed into outlines. Then the outlines filled in, as if a painting were being created midair. A moving painting. My mother's chamber appeared. Three of my fathers spoke in hushed tones. And I realized we couldn't just see, we could hear.

The view turned from the men to a fireplace with a crackling fire inside and a hand stoked the flames. We were watching things from Mrs. Borroughs' perspective. The servant's memories were on display. When the view turned back toward the room, a silver blur passed over everyone.

Cerena muttered to us, "That's the spell. We'll see if we can peer around it." She cut her other hand and added more blood.

Though the images remained mottled, as if we were watching them through a rain-splattered window, I could see a short man pull open the door and enter the room. He had wild brown hair and a pair of goggles sat on his head. Wyle set up candles near my mother and said, "Nearly time."

The window to the room flew open and the curtains rustled in the breeze. I watched as my father Gorg, our former spy master, landed on the windowsill and climbed into the room. He had a heavy cloak on, one that whipped in the wind as he shut the window.

"I came as quickly as I could," he said.

My other fathers left my mother in bed and went toward Gorg.

"Well?" Lewart, my biological father, asked.

Gorg nodded and pulled off his cloak. "We did it."

Strapped to his chest was a thick bundle of cloth. He unwound the sling from his shoulders and held out a crying baby bundled in blankets.

Lewart took the bundled baby girl and brought her to my mother.

Mother's eyes hardly glanced at the child, though she held the babe close to her chest. Her gaze stayed pinned to Gorg. "Were you followed? Does she know?"

Gorg shook his head.

Finally, my mother looked down and the tiny pink infant in her arms. "Good." She rocked the child a few seconds and then nodded to Wyle.

"Enchant her. She needs to look enough like Bloss that no one will ever suspect."

The mage nodded, stepped forward, and emptied a vial over Avia's head. Red smoke poured out.

"That was?" Mother asked.

"More permanent than a disguise spell. It was a humanity spell. I got it from a wizard years ago. He told me not to use it until I was ordered to."

"And?" Queen Gela prompted, staring down at the squirming infant.

"It will make her appear completely non-magical. Completely human."

CHAPTER TEN

For the next two days, I walked through the castle in a daze. My sister wasn't my sister. What was more … she wasn't human.

It also appeared my mother was a thief. Gorg had been our spy master and he'd flown in through the window with that baby.

She'd asked if he'd been followed.

To me, all of that screamed conspiracy, secrecy, theft.

Declan had argued that maybe my parents had simply adopted Avia. "Maybe she was an unwanted bastard like me."

I thought he gave my mother too much credit for taking him in.

"There'd be paperwork," I'd argued.

"Well, all the damned confidential paperwork that is handed down from monarch to monarch is kept with the castle mage. And since ours got blown up—" Declan shook his head.

Connor said, "Maybe her family couldn't keep her."

Quinn thought, *Maybe her family didn't want her.*

Ryan got home, a full day and a half later than he'd originally planned because he'd spotted something to the south. But whatever was flying through the sky had been so elusive that Ryan hadn't been able to get close. Each time he'd tried, a storm had come up and he'd been forced to land.

Ryan had heard everything that had happened from Quinn. He knew how distraught and distracted I was. So, when he saw me, even though I was in the middle of a public audience in the throne room, he swept up to my seat, scooped me up, and carried me off, shouting, "Newlywed privilege!" to the delight of every male courtier.

I was tomato-red when he set me down in my chambers. But when he kissed me, it wasn't with the passion and ardor I expected after his newlywed claim. It was with concern. "How are you, Little Dearling?" He sat down in a chair and pulled me onto his lap.

I sighed and leaned against him, moving my head until I could hear the strong, steady beat of his heart. Ryan's presence just made me feel safe. His hand rubbed down my back, soothing me. We sat like that for a bit.

"I can't even imagine how I'd feel about my family if I thought they were liars," Ryan broke the silence.

"It feels like … a huge hole in my life," I struggled to explain it. "Or like I'm off balance."

"We base our whole lives on the idea that our families raise us right and teach us the truth," Ryan said. "But if you look at your knights … look at Declan, cast off; Quinn and Connor were sent away like they were burdens; it's not true. Families don't always do right."

"Your family's all right," I pulled at the lapels on Ryan's vest.

"They're simple."

"Ryan!"

"It's not an insult. They like routine. They like predictability."

"But you?"

I traced a finger over his jaw, where stubble was starting to creep over his cheeks and down his neck. I nuzzled his stubble and said, "I liked the monotony of farm life when I tried it. But then, I didn't grow up with it."

"No. You didn't."

"Is that why you wanted to become a soldier?" I leaned back so I could look in his eyes.

ANN DENTON

Ryan gave a brief nod. "Didn't know I'd just be trading out activities. Plowing for sword practice, weeding for walking the ramparts."

"I'm sorry you were so bored here."

He gave a half shrug from his reclined position and leaned in to push my hair back. "There were some perks."

I raised my eyebrows and asked, "Really?"

"There was this one amazingly hot princess ... every time she came down to the yard, I could see her little nipples tighten under her dress." His hand trailed down and flicked one of my nipples through my green silk dress.

I sucked in a breath. My core tightened.

"And what did you think about when you saw her?"

"I used to dream about walking into my room to find that naughty little girl on her knees, waiting for me."

I slid backward off Ryan's lap. I stood and took a step backward until I was in the middle of the rug in front of the fireplace. Then I dropped to my knees.

My heartbeat quickened. I felt stomach-dropping anticipation. Gods, with just a few words, this man had me wet. All other thoughts flew away as I knelt in front of him. The only thing I could think about was him and what I wanted him to do to me.

Ryan smiled and stood. He kept eye contact with me as he slowly unbuttoned his vest and slid it off. When he started on the ties on his shirt, he said, "I always wanted more of a challenge out of life. I've always wanted to be the best. That's something I and the other knights have in common. We all want to be the best."

He tugged his shirt upward slowly, revealing his stacked abs one by one. I licked my lips as his pecs came into view. His nipples were already hard and tight. I wanted to bite them so badly.

He threw his shirt aside and moved casually onto his belt, smiling when he saw how quick and heavy my breathing was.

"Little Dearling, one thing you have to know is that all parents lie to their kids. My parents told me sex was a hug until I was twelve."

"You believed it?"

Ryan snapped the belt in his hands. "What are you supposed to call me?"

"Sir," I breathed, the single word making my heated pussy grow even more damp. "You believed them, sir?"

He tilted his head to the side with a smile. "It's hard to hide sex on a farm when the animals go at it."

I giggled and Ryan moaned. "Shite. You're gonna do that around my cock. I wanna feel that sweet laugh."

He dropped his pants and sat to yank off his boots. And then he came and stood in front of me, a chiseled dark masterpiece. His hand stroked my hair. "I need you, Little Dearling."

ANN DENTON

He did. He was hard and stiff, so thick and engorged it looked painful.

I grabbed his dick and licked the underside. He was so tall that I didn't even have to bend to reach it. I bladed my tongue and licked until he moaned. And then I moved and sucked one of his balls into my mouth.

"Unh, I didn't tell you to do that," Ryan's hand fisted in my hair, but he didn't pull me off.

I popped one ball out from between my lips and sucked in the other. Then I started pumping his shaft with my left hand as I sucked. His balls were so big they filled my mouth. I let my tongue stroke the center, where that sensitive ridge ran along the underside of his cock. I brought my right hand up and bent my knuckle, like the women at the brothel had shown me. And then I put my knuckle on his taint. I circled it slowly, letting him get used to the sensation before pressing a bit harder.

When he grunted, I released his ball and shot my mouth up to suction the head of his dick. My hands kept working, pumping his shaft and circling his taint until he grabbed my hair.

"Now, laugh for me, Little Dearling," Ryan commanded.

I smiled on his cock and tried to giggle, letting the vibration from my lips and throat stimulate him.

"Bloss I'm gonna—" he didn't get to finish his sentence before gobs of cum shot into my mouth. I swallowed the best I could, but Ryan's load was gigantic, and a good deal dribbled out of my mouth.

When his body finally relaxed, I sat back on my knees and wiped my chin with my sleeve.

"How was that?" I was on my feet before the sentence was finished; Ryan yanked me up into his body.

His hands clamped down on my shoulders and jerked roughly. His brute strength pulled my overdress tight over my breasts and ripped the laces. His hand reached for the center; he pulled roughly down. My dress was off three seconds later, and my chemise followed it.

Ryan stepped back for a second, his chest heaving as he stared down at me.

"You are so sarding beautiful," he rasped. He reached out slowly and traced a finger down my left breast, letting his thumbnail gently scrape my nipple.

I whimpered, "Ryan."

He groaned, "Even how you say my name … it's so much better."

"Better than what?"

He didn't answer. He knelt in front of me and rubbed his head gently against my belly, just brushing the undersides of my breasts. He kissed my stomach, the slight bumps where my ribs protruded. His tongue traced a hot wet path along the underside of each breast. And then he feathered light kisses over them, never lingering, just teasing.

My mind was full of cloudy, lusty bliss.

"Ryan," I breathed. I needed him. I was going to burst if he didn't take me soon.

He used his hands to trace up the outside of my hips. His rough, calloused hands felt so good against my skin. He grabbed my ass and pulled my cheeks apart. And then his mouth closed over a nipple. He sucked hard, holding my cheeks, leaving my ass exposed to anyone who walked into the room. It felt so good and so naughty at the same time.

Ryan released my nipple and blew a hot breath over the wet bud.

He nuzzled his face between my breasts and released my ass, moving his hands around to the inside of my thighs. I braced myself for his fingers to trace upward and touch me. But he scooped me up without warning. His forearms hooked beneath my thighs and his hands pressed against my back. He pulled me up, up, up. Until his biceps were level with his shoulders and my thighs were around his neck.

"Ride my face," Ryan growled.

"But I'll fall," Even kneeling, Ryan's shoulders were nearly five feet from the floor. And I had only his arms for a seat. I put my hands down on his short, shorn black hair for balance.

"I'd never let you fall." Ryan used his hands to shove my pussy onto his waiting tongue. He licked up my slit, keeping me perfectly balanced on the bulges of his biceps, his elbows locked against my ass, his forearms forming a seat back. He licked again and heat traveled up from my core through my spine. I couldn't stop myself from arching back into his forearms. My hands clawed at his short hair and I wished it was longer.

Ryan blew warm, hot air on my pussy and I arched again, the hood of my clit hitting the base of his nose. Pleasure shot through me and I tightened my thighs, arching again and again.

Ryan stuck his tongue back out, splitting my pussy lips and spearing me. He gave a long, hot lick up my slit.

I latched onto the back of his neck to give myself more leverage. I put my feet on his ribs and pushed up further, until his nose was directly rubbing my clit. I felt shameless, wanton, as I used my entire body to ride his face for my pleasure. I sped up, my breasts bouncing. And Ryan's huge biceps never wavered. He held me steady as heat crawled up my spine and a mindless haze clouded my thoughts. He held me steady as I turned him into my own personal sex toy. I jerked wildly against him as I saw stars and he nodded his head up and down to draw out my orgasm as I screamed, curling my toes, digging them into his sides.

A guard burst into the room but quickly shut the door when he saw what was going on.

I didn't even feel embarrassed. My orgasmic high was so good that I felt giggly and floaty.

Ryan gently lowered me to the ground. My thighs shook with the aftershocks of my orgasm and I sank to my knees on the rug. Ryan lowered himself to a seated position and pulled me sideways onto his lap. He used his arm to wipe his very wet face, a huge grin lighting up his features.

"That was a screamer."

"Who knew orgasms midair could be so intense?" I sighed and flopped into his chest. "Thank you."

"Always, Little Dearling."

Did I just hear the word orgasm? Quinn's voice popped into my head.

No, I snuggled into Ryan, unwilling to ruin this moment with Quinn's silly antics.

You better not be having orgasms without me.

We were just talking about ... chasms.

Quinn's voice faded and I thought that was the end of it.

Until he popped back a moment later, growling, *Bloss, you're a liar!* He must have read Ryan's thoughts.

Sorry.

Oh, you will be sorry. I couldn't even watch your thoughts because some damned Cheryn soldiers—

Are you safe?

Yes. But I'm pissed.

I'll give you all the orgasms when you get back.

You'd better.

Go away. It's Ryan's time now. But be safe! And I love you.

He huffed but his voice disappeared.

Ryan chuckled. "Did Quinn just yell at you?"

I nodded and shrugged. "He can't be there every time I have sex with you."

"He would if he could."

I giggled. "I know he would. He's a horny bastard."

"Who's out risking his neck for us right now. That djinni came from Cheryn. Had to. He came with Cheryn's party and was able to blend in. The Sultan did this. Now Quinn just has to figure out why."

I turned in Ryan's arms so I could better face him. "I know. And I feel like it's my fault he's out there."

Ryan jerked his head back, skepticism coloring his features. "That's his job. He's a knight."

"But he's only going to Cheryn to check on the whole Abbas thing because Abbas attacked me twice. I think he thinks someone out there wished I'd die."

"Djinn can't grant death wishes. They can't kill directly with their magic. It's one of their limitations. That, and you can't wish for something you've

147

already had. Djinn can't put things back exactly as they were."

I shook my head. "I know. I just have this feeling Quinn's right. Whoever sent Abbas is clever. They might have found a way for him to wish for my kingdom or my crown, or something that implies my death without actually stating it."

Ryan tucked me back into his chest. "Well, I'd never let that wish come true."

I shook my head against Ryan's pecs and let my hand rest against the soft rise of his abs. "You didn't see him in the dungeon. Abbas was crazy. Scary. I'm certain he wants to kill me. If I die—" I shot up straight in Ryan's lap. I scrambled off his giant knees and turned to face him, eyes wide.

"I need to dissolve the law that makes knights follow their queens into death. I need to do it now. In case—" I grabbed my chemise, but it was too ripped to throw on. I walked toward the bell pull to call for Ginnifer, but Ryan's arm stopped me.

"Don't. Don't change the law."

His answer surprised me. I met his chocolate eyes and asked, "Why not?"

He grabbed my hands and encased them in his. "Because I want you to trust me. Always trust me. And the others. We're yours. You're ours. I want us to be tied together. It's important."

I gave a little smile. "Don't be silly. I do trust you."

He shook his head. "This life. The palace. It's not like the farm I grew up on. There, everyone pitches in. Every day —work to eat. Work to eat. Again, and again."

"And?"

"And the palace is full of liars and cheats. If my life weren't tied to yours, I'd worry … that you'd start to see things that weren't there."

"Like what?"

"Like ambition. Or jealousy. Or betrayal. Or a million other things," he leaned in and planted a soft kiss on my lips.

"I don't see those things," I whispered.

"I know," he let his nose skim my jaw, sending soft tendrils of sensation over me.

When he leaned back, his eyes had an expression I'd never seen before. There were little creases by the edges of his eyes. "I'm not Declan," he stated, "but he's taught me a lot about Evaness. History and things. And one of the reasons Evaness didn't break apart like Lored and Rasle did two-hundred years ago, one of the reasons we haven't ended up with a lot of in-fighting like Gitmore, is that the bond between a queen and her knights is so strong. I'm your knight, but Evaness will never accept me as a monarch. If I betray you, I can't get more powerful than I already am. In the past, some queens and knights have even had their mages cast bonding spells. So that if one dies, they all die."

I blinked. "I don't remember that."

"Dec said it was hushed up, he found it in a scroll he snuck off his mentor. Don't want assassins getting ideas. But … again, quoting the master here—"

"I'm telling Dec you called him that," I giggled.

Ryan's grin spread ear to ear. "He knows. I'm the master in the bedroom. That's it."

"Yes, you are," I agreed, and he lifted me into his arms, looping my legs around his waist. I could feel him start to grow beneath me.

"Do you want this history lesson or not?" he bopped me on the nose.

"Yes, sir."

He groaned, "Bad girl." His fingers dug into my hip and ass, just short of painful. "Stay still and quiet while I finish."

I nodded.

"Kingdoms are too big, too much, for just one ruler. Dec likes to use Cheryn as an example a lot. The sultan there has made a lotta bad choices that have hurt his people. He doesn't do advisers. Been ruling for nearly a thousand years. That djinni has gotten arrogant. Evaness doesn't work like that. Knights were designed to be advisers. We're *trained* to be experts that help you run the kingdom. Our daughter becomes the next monarch, so we're emotionally invested in making the country as strong as possible. I guess, in the first Fire War, maybe eight hundred years ago, there was a Queen … Onica. Dec tells the story with all these details."

"Don't worry about how he tells it. Give me your version." I placed a chaste kiss over Ryan's heart.

"I told you to stay still."

"Oops," I'd forgotten. But if he wanted to punish me, there was no way I was going to make excuses for myself. The very idea had me wet again.

Ryan's eyes narrowed as he said, "This is your only warning."

I nodded, tempted to say 'yes, sir' again. But, clearly, he wanted to tell me this story. And if I said those trigger words, neither of us would hold back.

"Onica's knights were all from different provinces. And they had trouble getting along. One of them plotted to kill the others, wanting to be her only knight. Onica found out. She had the mage put a bonding spell on them all so that if any one of them died, they'd all die. Her reign ended up being one of the most peaceful and productive in all of Evaness history."

"That could be a coincidence."

Ryan smiled and shook his head. "That's what Connor told Declan, when he first brought it up."

"You all have talked about this?"

Ryan's lips pressed together, and he was silent for a second before he said, "We did more than talk about it."

My stomach fluttered like a hummingbird's wings. I was shocked—no—awed—no—confused. "Are you saying …?"

Ryan nodded. "We had Wyle put the spell on us about a week after you'd fled. It was just the four of us. We had to band together and run this country. A mute, a bastard prince, a farm boy, and a noble politician."

I gripped Ryan tighter, fear replacing my earlier emotions. My knights were vulnerable. Four times as vulnerable as I'd ever thought. "That just makes me want to recall you to the palace and never let any of you leave."

Quinn. Quinn's out there. Near Cheryn's soldiers. When a mad djinni might have been sent to kill me; my thoughts tripped over one another.

Ryan grinned. "Little Dearling, you're adorable. But you don't need to worry. Dec's a smart guy. He looked into all this before we did it. And this spell has made us stronger. We work together better. We trust each other. We're far more cautious about everything. It's a good thing."

"Why haven't any of the others told me about this?" I grumbled.

Ryan's lip quirked up. "They're afraid of you."

I pushed on his chest. "They should be. Now I wanna lock you all up in the dungeon."

"Declan might be into that," Ryan kissed my neck. "I'd rather see you wearing shackles."

I moaned.

Ryan's kisses had nearly convinced me to put off running to Cerena for a counter-spell when a knock at the door interrupted us.

"Shite."

Ryan laughed, "Come on, Little Queen. Someone needs you."

I looked down at his stiff cock. "Don't you need me?"

"Always. But we have a kingdom to protect."

I groaned, "Always with the responsibility."

"A queen's work—"

"If you quote my mother while we're naked, I'll kill you."

"Then you'll kill us all."

I hopped down and smacked Ryan on the ass. "Not funny!"

His eyes grew wide. "Did you just *spank* me?" He straightened, letting his angry dominant persona shine through.

I giggled and ran toward the dressing room. "Yup. And you can't do anything about it because you want me to be responsible!"

"Sard!"

CHAPTER ELEVEN

*I*t took a few minutes for a blushing Ginnifer to get me dressed and fix my hair. I had no doubt she'd heard everything that had happened between Ryan and me. At first, I was a bit embarrassed. But after Ryan walked into my dressing room, fully clothed, with bedroom eyes still in full force, I completely forgot about being self-conscious. I was too busy trying to keep my lady parts from soaking my skirt.

"Willard and Quinn's man are outside," Ryan watched as Ginnifer tightened the strings on my corset, pushing my breasts upward. He licked his lips and I cursed my crown. I wanted nothing more than to let him ride me over and over into glorious oblivion.

"Damn," I bit my lip.

"Did I hurt you, Your Majesty?" Ginnifer shrank back.

"No. I just don't want to deal with this idiot," I said.

ANN DENTON

"Lord Willard is a bit of a dunderhead," my maid confided as she grabbed me a new gown. It was the most I think I'd ever heard her say.

"And why do you think that?" I was curious.

Ginnifer blushed. "Oh, excuse me, it's not my place."

"No, I agree with you. I just wondered what he's done to you."

"Me! Oh, nothing to me, Your Majesty. He'd never. He's just ... a bit entitled with the servants," she rolled her eyes.

"What?" I leaned back, not allowing her to put the pale blue paisley overdress on me.

"What do you mean?"

"Well, he thinks he can walk in and just speak with us in the kitchens or the backrooms and everyone is just his new best friend," she shook her head.

"What's everyone's opinion of him?"

She shrugged, "A few of the grooms are brave enough to mess with him but most of us just try and avoid him out of respect for Jorad."

"What?" I asked.

Ginnifer cocked her head and gazed at me, "You know, he and Jorad have been an item for years."

My eyebrows shot up. I looked at Ryan. "Did you know this?"

Ryan nodded. "Of course. Quinn told us ages ago."

I shook my head. "Ugh. Well I can't think of two people who annoy me more. Look, could you please tell everyone that Willard's harmless? Maybe make things a bit easier for him? He thinks he's helping me out." I rolled my eyes. I should have just taken his title.

Ginnifer actually smiled as she slid the overdress onto me. "They're quite the opposites, aren't they? He and Jorad."

Apparently, relationship gossip was the key to unlocking my shy maid's mouth. I'd have to make sure she was never around for any arguments between my knights and me.

I sighed. "Maybe I should just call Willard off. He's too much of a bungler. And if he's seeing Jorad; that man would never violate a single rule."

"I wouldn't trust anyone that far, Your Majesty," Ginnifer yanked my skirt so it fell properly. "If one of those two was a woman, you'd be sure they'd try for the crown. Make a mess of it. But try."

I eyed Ginnifer, "Well, if you do hear of them trying anything, let me know."

She gave a curtsy. "I will."

I strode out of the room without letting her put up my hair. Screw it all. It wasn't as if Willard gave a shite what I looked like. Clearly, I wasn't his type. No wonder he hadn't wanted to get engaged. I chuckled as I took Ryan's arm.

"What?"

"I was just thinking about how terrified Willard looked when he thought I might make him a knight."

Ryan laughed quietly. "I'm pretty sure Jorad would have cut off his balls before he let that happen."

"If that's allowed in the royal rulebook, I'm certain you're right."

"Quinn wanted me to remind you his man is still invisible. Willard doesn't know he's being followed."

I nodded and took a deep breath before I pushed open the door to the hall. For all my jokes about Willard, I did want to know which of my nobles might be scheming against me.

There were six provinces in Evaness besides Agatha's. Duchess Malia was part mermaid and held a good chunk of land to the north, where a lot of our timber originated.

Connor's mother, Duchess Kycee, held a good bit of land to the south. She controlled a bay where our battle and trade ships were located. For obvious reasons, Connor's family didn't make it onto the list of suspects. Their granddaughter would be a princess. They'd have no reason to betray Connor and me.

"What do you think of Duchess Orunta?" I asked.

Ryan grunted, "Money-wasting snob, not unlike Duke Aiden. But she's bogged down right now. I heard she just lost three ships full of lace the other day."

"Three!"

"Yeah, rough waters or something. First time I've heard about a ship going down in years."

"Were they able to rescue anyone?"

"No. I think they might have been too far out. They were on their way back from Sedara."

I furrowed my brow. "Wow. I don't recall a report that bad since I was a young girl. Three ships!"

Ryan nodded. "I sent an air patrol. They're gone. Completely sunk."

"Was there a storm?"

"That far out at sea? I don't know," Ryan shrugged. "Probably."

I turned back to the mirror while Ginnifer put jewels around my neck and on my fingers.

I weighed the other nobles who might have issue with me. The other three provinces of Evaness spread out to the west.

Duke Aiden and his wife held the land just west of the capital.

The Cerulean Forest was overseen by a half-fairy named Fer.

And to the west of her, along Rasle's borders, an outspoken pixie named Sunya ran her own province, the province that Queen Isla was so eager to get her hands on.

Other than Connor's family, I felt like I could rule out Fer. I'd spent a fair amount of time in the Cerulean Forest over the past four years. It had been where I'd thought the wizard was most likely to hide. And from what I could tell, Fer's people were happy for the most part.

That still left me with quite a few nobles who made my list of potential traitors. It wasn't a good feeling. Thinking about it made my stomach swim. It felt like sickly worms tunneling through me, eating at my confidence.

I faked a calm smile as I met Willard in the hall. Unlike most days, where the slob was wandering through the castle untucked and half-shaved (I honestly had no idea how meticulous Jorad stood that), today Willard was wearing a pressed shirt and his minimal hair was neatly combed.

"Let's have tea, while we speak," I said. I led the way down the hall to the small diamond parlor. It was named that because of the carved crystal collection stored there. One of my ancestors had loved the pixie creations and had a fondness for glass unicorns, crystal castles, and the like. I had always loved the room. Partially because it had been forbidden to me as a child and partially because I thought of it as a giant prism. Connor had always hated it. It was too "rainbow-y."

I settled into a chair. Ryan stood behind me and we let Willard stand awkwardly in front of us. There was no nearby chair for him. I didn't really care about his comfort. I cared about his information.

"So, Willard, do you have any idea who might have helped get that dragon into Evaness?"

Willard shuffled on his feet. Behind him, the rainbows projected by the crystals reflected oddly. I gave a nod to Quinn's invisible spy. The rainbows dipped slightly, so I assumed that whoever was there bowed to me in return.

My eyes flicked back to scan Willard's pasty face. "Well?"

"Your Majesty, I believe it was … Duke Aiden," Willard gulped as he finished his sentence.

I kept my face neutral as I asked, "Why do you think this?" Inside, I was angry. I'd known for years Aiden was a shite human. A cheater and a gambler. But a traitor?

"He's got too much money. Last night, he wagered I couldn't—well, we made a bet."

"A bet about what?"

Willard's cheeks and neck grew rosy. "I'd rather not say."

"I'd rather you did." I placed my elbows on the arms of the chair and folded my hands in my lap, doing my best to channel my mother. He better not have done something illegal while working for me. He'd already made a fool of himself with the servants. Maybe I'd made a mistake trying him out in the first place.

I was messing up this monarchy bit by bit.

"I … we bet two hundred gold crowns on drinking a bottle of castor oil. Whoever … was ill first, lost."

"You mean whoever shite his drawers," Ryan said gruffly behind me.

"Or puked," Willard amended, staring at a rainbow that danced on the carpet. His eyes traced the rainbow to its source, a dancing tree and maiden figurine that sat on a windowsill.

"And … you lost?"

Willard glanced up. "No. I won. And that's why I think Aiden's the one betraying us all. First off, it's near winter. Who goes spending their reserves like that? Secondly …" Willard pulled a pouch from his belt. He opened it and poured coins into his open palm. Then he stepped toward me. "Secondly," he repeated, "take a look at those coins."

I plucked several from his palm. Ryan did the same. I held a coin up and studied it. But it didn't have my mother's visage.

"What's this?" I asked. The coin didn't show the profile of any of the royals from any of the seven kingdoms. Occasionally, old coins still circulated. Those from my grandmother's era popped up every now and again.

But Declan routinely gathered and traded out old coins with the annual tax collection. And I knew my grandmother's profile. This wasn't it. Was it an old coin from one of the other kingdoms? I flipped the coin over. The back was clearly stamped the burning rose, symbol of Evaness.

I glanced up at Ryan who shook his head. He didn't recognize the profile either.

"Do you recognize the face?" I asked Willard.

He shook his head, jowls bouncing. "I don't. That's the question isn't it? Is it even real money? Where'd it come from? He's got loads of them."

I studied the coin. A woman with a crooked nose peered off to the side of the gold piece, her curls flowing over a tiara that looked familiar, but I couldn't quite place it.

"He's been paying with these coins?"

Willard nodded. "All over the place. People see the burning rose and just take them."

I glanced at Ryan and clamped the coin in my palm.

"Not bad, Willard. Better than I expected."

Far better than I expected after the dismal information Ginnifer had given me about his performance with the servants. Willard had actually found something. Duke Aiden's pockets overflowed with fake coins. But what did he do to get them? Where was he getting them from? Who?

There were still so many questions.

Willard smiled wide, bowed, and turned to leave. I waited until he reached the door. Mother taught me that. Let people think they were off the hook before you gutted them.

"Now I want you to follow him," I called out just as Willard turned the knob.

Willard turned back, his eyes bulging. If his face had been red before, it was positively on fire now. "Wh-what?" he spluttered.

"I need you to follow Duke Aiden. I need you to find out where the money is coming from. Or is he minting these coins himself?"

Ryan bit one to test the gold. He looked at me and said, "It's real."

Real gold. A lot of it. Guiding a dragon through our lands might cost a lot.

"Follow him every day. Attach yourself at the hip. Whatever's necessary."

"I—Your Majesty," I watched the wheels slowly turn in Willard's brain. "Surely, I am not suited for such long-term subterfuge?"

"Nonsense. You've done so well already. Come back in a day or two and let me know what progress you've made." I nodded and waved my hand, dismissing him.

Willard stood gaping just as a maid came in with a tea cart. I grabbed Ryan's arm and pulled him toward the cart as Willard let himself out.

Once Willard was gone and the maid had left, I collapsed into the settee near the cart, tossing the coins onto it.

"Damn. How did I do?"

Ryan grinned. "Not bad. You pulled his strings well. He's a good one to practice on. Others won't break so easily."

I grabbed a biscuit and shredded it. "What the sarding hell do you suppose that dung pile Aiden is up to?"

Ryan shrugged before grabbing the teapot. "I asked Quinn to have Declan come up and take a look at these," he gestured to the coins on the cart. "I don't know if Aiden's making them or found buried treasure on his land or what."

I shook my head. "I doubt it's either of those things. I think he's taking payment for guiding that sarding dragon through my kingdom. That shite's selfish and short-sighted enough to do it."

"You think he was working with Abbas?" Ryan sat next to me on the settee, careful not to jostle a crystal knight with a tiny lance on the side table.

I nodded. "It would fit. I worked at a tavern. He started coming in to spend money a few months before I heard about the plan to send a beast after Avia. The timelines match."

Ryan grimaced. "You really think he'd turn against Evaness?"

I shrugged. "I know his reputation more than the man himself. Only spoke with him a few times. Slime, though. Most prostitutes refused to serve him twice. And that's a sign. Those women choose to make good money off the skewed birth rate and male desperation. They probably could have charged double. Most do, for repeat business. And they were turning Aiden down."

Ryan stared at me. "I'm not sure if I find it hot that you know so much about brothel business."

I quirked an eyebrow at him. "You liked what I did to your taint earlier, didn't you?" I winked. "You can thank a girl named Lera for the tip. She used to like to share stories."

Ryan belly laughed until he got tears in his eyes. Then he swiped at them and set me on his lap.

Declan arrived moments later. "I was told you all needed me? Took me awhile to figure out what 'the room with all the glass shite' was," he used air quotes to emphasize his annoyance. "I know Quinn has a palace map memorized, he could have just used that. Sometimes, I think he just likes to sard with me."

"He does," Ryan confirmed.

I scooped up a coin and held it out to Declan. "Do you recognize this?"

"It's a gold—oh," he flipped it over and saw the woman, "Interesting. I have a reference book in my rooms. I can look it up."

"Thank you."

Declan turned to go and though I'd just used this technique on Willard, I decided to use it again. Because I was still hot and bothered from my session with Ryan. And because two of my knights were in the room, the very two who had a lingering secret.

Just as Declan grabbed the door handle, I said, "Oh, one more thing. The other day you mentioned that Ryan helped you relieve your tension with sex."

Ryan grew tense beneath me. Declan froze, hand still on the handle.

"I think I might require a demonstration," I stood, desire lacing my words. "I don't know that I could adequately ever help you through your panic, without knowing exactly where to touch you." I stalked toward Declan.

He turned back to face me, his blue eyes wide. I loved seeing his throat bob as he swallowed hard. "Um…"

I reached my blond sweetling and trailed my fingers up his chest. "Come on, Declan. For me? You know I've been thinking about you for days now. About what it might look like with Ryan swallowing your—"

Declan squeezed his eyes shut as Ryan said, "It's not what you think, Little Dearling."

I turned back to my tall giant, who'd stood to defend his fellow knight.

"What do you mean?" I asked.

Declan's voice was soft but clear when he answered, "Whenever we helped each other out, one of us took a disguise spell and turned into *you*."

My fantasies of seeing the two of them, hot mouths clashing and hands tugging one another desperately, vanished. I took a step back as I gathered my thoughts.

I pictured it. Them in a room together. Declan swallowing a vial and transforming into me. Ryan reaching out and grabbing him by the hips, yanking him forward into a hot, open-mouthed kiss.

No sarding wonder Ryan had been so confident he could hold me up and have me ride him without falling. No wonder Declan had known exactly how to soothe away the tension in my body.

At first, my jealousy flared. They were mine. But I pushed that irrational emotion down. Because I'd left them. I'd left them with no options. They'd only turned to one another in desperation. In need. Could I begrudge them that? Of course not.

Was I going to make that abundantly obvious to them right away? Hell no.

My eyes narrowed as I glanced between the two of them, planting my hands on my hips.

They both shuffled nervously, worried I'd judge them. I shook my head. "Well, no sarding wonder you're so good at giving me orgasms. You're *cheaters*!" I smiled to show I was joking. Immediately, the tension fled from their bodies.

But I was on a roll, "Just look at all the orgasm training you saved me. I don't have to do all that uncomfortable 'to the left, no softer, no harder' shite that every other woman does. I should pass a new law. Grooms should all be required to take a disguise spell and practice before the wedding night. Shite. Forget every mistake I've made thus far. I'm going down in history as Bloss-the-Orgasmic."

Their laughter shook the room like thunder.

I wagged a finger at them. "Don't think this gets you out of playing together. That's still on my wish list." I turned to let myself out the door, because unfortunately, I realized that the sun was setting, and I needed to check on my animal friends. I looked back to find Ryan and Declan both frozen. I wasn't sure if it was in horror or shock.

I grinned. "I'm not opposed to playing with girls either, you know. So, you just decide which of the two of you is gonna take the disguise potion when we finally have time for that."

When I shut the door behind me, the loudest argument in the history of Evaness started.

CHAPTER TWELVE

*C*erena wasn't alone when I went to her tower. Ember stood off in the corner of the room as Cerena chased the little bunny toward a box.

"Get in there, you mangy flea-filled little—" Cerena held a carrot like a weapon more than a treat. She waved the carrot at a wooden crate lined in burlap nearby.

The rabbit dodged her and ran for her bookshelf on the far side of the room, away from her and Ember.

"Shite!"

Ember giggled, her black wings shaking in laughter.

"They giving you trouble, Cerena?" I stepped into the room, my guard holding open the door for me.

"This little bastard leaves a trail of shite wherever he goes!" Cerena jabbed an accusing finger at the bunny, who bolted toward me. I scooped him up and held in front of me, legs dangling. "That's not very nice of you, Lilac."

The shitehead pooped.

I skittered back from the pellet holding him out as far as possible. "What the hell?"

The rabbit twitched its ears meaningfully at me. As if I could understand whatever the sard that meant.

"What? Don't like your name, Lilac?"

The bunny shite again. I dropped him on Cerena's work table.

"Fine. You can be Shiter then."

The rabbit shite. I turned to Cerena. "Are you sure there's a person in there?"

She nodded. "Oh, I'm sure. And I'm sure right now that it's a man. No woman would be so disgusting."

The rabbit dropped another pellet.

"Do you think he has a disorder or something?"

She shrugged. "I dunno. I use rabbit innards. I don't typically keep them around like this."

At that, Shiter scrambled off the table and scuttled under my skirts.

"If you shite while you're under there—"

"What if he looks up while he's under there?" Ember called out. The Raslen fairy nearly doubled over in laughter, pulling at the ends of her blue hair manically, as I lifted my skirts and hopped away from the rabbit.

"Out!" I scolded the thing.

Shiter did not shite. He sat back on his haunches and crossed his bunny arms. He lowered his ears toward Ember as if he were pointing an accusing finger at her.

I narrowed my eyes at him. It made me wonder if he did look up my skirts and was angry at her for ruining his fun. I determined that Shiter was indeed an appropriate name for the dirty little bunny.

I turned back to Cerena, "Tell me how what's happened to them is different from a disguise spell."

Cerena sighed. "Well, the short of it is that a disguise spell is a potion. Specific mix of ingredients, specific expiration date but generic use for whoever holds it. It's a temporary, on-the-go type of magic. Whatever was done to these two was a curse, a spell with negative intentions. Intended specifically for them. Probably used their hair or some-thing to create bad magic. It's typically permanent unless you are able to exactly reverse spell."

In the corner Ember cocked her head, listening. "That's so interesting. And how would you do that?"

Cerena looked at Blue. The bluebird was perched on a goat skull on the far side of the room, watching the goings-on from a distance. "Well, I'd need to figure out who the spell-maker was. And who these two are. I'd need samples of their clothing or hair or something from their prior life."

My heart dropped. I pressed my lips together, suddenly not begrudging Shiter quite so much. "So, you're saying it's impossible."

Cerena gave me a sad half-smile. "Near to as it can be, I'm afraid."

I blinked back tears. I was surprised I was this emotional over a bird and rabbit I hardly knew. But, then, Blue had attacked Abbas for me. And I could imagine what it might be like to be stuck inside an animal body for the rest of my life. Probably even worse than being stuck with a crown.

"Blue, you wanna go for a walk with me?" I crooned at the bird. He spread his wings and flew gracefully across the room. Then he alighted gently on my shoulder; he didn't scratch me once.

He gave a little warble, rubbing his soft feathered head against my cheek. A bird hug. Blue was a gentleman.

"Poor man. Well, I'll give you the best birdie life you can have, okay? I can have someone dig up all the worms and spiders you can eat."

Blue bit and tugged on a piece of my hair.

"Alright, clearly bird tastes haven't won out yet," I laughed gently. "How do mutton pies sound?"

He twittered happily.

I looked back to see Shiter huddled on the floor under one of Cerena's tables. "Well, are you coming, Shiter?"

The bunny lowered its ears and narrowed its eyes.

I shrugged. "You're welcome to stay here. I'm sure Cerena would find you useful for spell ingredients. Or parts of you, at least."

Shiter begrudgingly hopped forward but kept a good two feet between himself and me.

Ember called out, "Can I go with you?"

I smiled. "That would be wonderful."

She grinned. "This looks like it will be an adventure-filled outing."

I rolled my eyes. "So long as Shiter stays to the back, it shouldn't be too unpleasant."

I led the way downstairs and out onto the castle grounds. "So, what were you doing in there with Cerena?" I asked.

"Oh," Ember waved her hand dismissively, a black ring on her finger glinting in the torchlight. "She stopped to talk to me and my father and invited us up there. It's my last day here, I leave tomorrow."

"No, don't go yet! We've hardly gotten to visit."

Ember sighed. "I know, but *work*."

I groaned. "For both of us. Work. So, you were saying about Cerena?"

Ember smiled, "My father got tired, but she was asking me if I knew any fairies in the magic business. We do see a few on our trade routes, you know."

"Good," I was relieved. Cerena did need help. "I hope you were able to give her some names."

Ember nodded. "One or two. Hopefully someone works out. Her poor tower's a bit of a mess."

"Yes. Our last mage had a bit of an accident."

Ember's eyes widened. "What happened?"

I held out my hand so Blue could perch on my finger. I stroked his belly and kept my answer deliberately vague. Not even all the nobles in Evaness knew exactly what had happened to Wyle. "You know mage towers can be dangerous," I said. "So many explosives and magical potions in one place."

Ember nodded sympathetically. "Just takes one mistake."

I led her toward the orchards to the side of the castle grounds. I figured the two animals might prefer running in the open instead of walking the evergreen maze.

"So, what have you been up to?" I asked.

Ember shrugged. "Working. It's always a struggle, you know? Tolls and protection fees and—" She gave a brief laugh. "I mean, never mind. I'm speaking to a queen. I still can't believe you're a queen!" she playfully tapped my arm. Blue twittered and flew off ahead of us.

"Yes, well, queens know about struggle, too," I said, watching the sun set. "We all live and die constrained by a million rules."

"What if we didn't have to?" Ember asked.

I gave a bitter laugh, "I tried leaving all the rules behind. And yet, somehow I ended up back here." I glanced up at the palace. The grey stone was cold and unyielding as winter. I shivered as the sun dipped lower and the air chilled around us.

"Your knights must be some consolation," Ember said. "They say you have some of the most powerful knights in history."

I shrugged. "I suppose." They were powerful. I could see how Ember would say that as an outsider. But my men were so much more. My husbands were so sweet and thoughtful. I thought of Declan's massage; I thought of Connor's silly confessions about pretending to lose to me when we were young; I thought about Ryan's hot tongue and Quinn's silly teasing. My heart swelled. "But they're wonderful, too."

"Even Declan?" Ember's face was full of innocent curiosity. "I haven't met many Sedarians who didn't think they made the moonlight."

I laughed, "Well, his family chuffed him off, ashamed of a bastard, I guess. So, I don't think he's too much like other Sedarians I've met. He's really pretty wonderful." My cheeks warmed as I thought of Declan and Ryan and how I'd left them. I couldn't wait to get the two of them alone and see what they'd decided.

My naughty thoughts were interrupted by a loud rustle in the bushes to our right. My guards, ever-present shadows, started and pulled their swords.

"Shiter?" I called. "Is that you? Are you and Blue being snots and trying to scare me?" I wouldn't put it past the stupid bunny. He seemed like the kind up for trouble.

But it wasn't Shiter who stumbled out of the bushes. It was worse.

I screamed at the top of my lungs. Ember scrambled backward. My guards ran forward with swords; one of them grabbed me and started yanking me back toward the castle.

Because a massive grizzly walked out of the bushes into the light of the setting sun.

My heart squeezed so hard I was certain it collapsed in on itself.

I watched the scene unfold and it was as if time slowed. A pimple-faced guard raised his sword and charged the beast. The bear stood on his hind legs and swatted the sword down. The kid, his bravery at an end, backed away and ran, flat out toward the castle, leaving us behind. Another guard stepped toward me and Ember. He took up position in front of me and backed me out of range while a third guard tossed a knife. The bear—ducked. My guards cursed and another drew and threw. The bear ducked again.

Realization set in.

One of my guards raised his sword.

"Wait!" I yelled.

Everyone, including the bear, froze.

I took a step forward but the guard in front of me held out an arm and blocked me.

I sighed and settled for making eye contact with the bear. "Sit."

The bear sat.

A murmur went up amongst the guards. This time, when I stepped forward, no one stopped me.

"Are you under a sarding spell? Nod if you are."

The bear nodded.

"Bescumbered bugger!" If I ever found this spellcaster ... I clenched my fist just as Shiter and Blue showed up. They settled next to the bear like they were old friends.

Great. Just wonderful.

I imagined the jokes the bards would make about me.

A bluebird, a rabbit, and a bear walked into her castle...

I shook my head. The gods hated me. Clearly, they did.

I sighed and waved my arm toward the castle. "Sard it all. Well, come on, then."

And my little menagerie followed like ducklings. Fat, shitey, blue ducklings. All the way back to the castle.

CHAPTER THIRTEEN

I had my first official meeting with my nobles the next morning.

Ginnifer put me into a lavish lace overdress before dawn. I didn't have time to appreciate the beauty of the gown; I had to read through a scroll a mile-long listing all of the minuscule details of the day.

Connor met me in the dressing room, steaming and stewing about the time as my maid did my hair.

"I'm going to have the hardest time not accusing someone of treason today, Ginnifer," I growled when I saw that Duke Aiden was representing his province. His wife was still resting after their newest child.

Ginnifer's eyes widened and she paled. "I … I don't know what to say, Your Majesty."

Connor rolled his eyes as he joined me on the bench I perched on.

"Say, Bloss Boss, control yourself. There will be six gossipy duchesses and a duke there today. Willard will also probably accompany his mommy, because he always does. And you don't need any more awkwardness just now."

"But Aiden's sold us out!"

"Proof, beautiful," Connor's blue-green eyes sparkled with amusement at me. "Willard could easily be hiding his own guilt by throwing Aiden under the horse's hooves."

Ginnifer's eyes widened again.

"You're going to have to get the shocked look under control if you're going to be my maid," I told her.

Connor turned to my maid. "Thank you, Ginnifer." He stood and took her hand and escorted her from the room. "You have outdone yourself today. Bloss looks wonderful."

Ginnifer blushed, of course she did—Connor could make a wizened old grandmother blush like a school girl. She gave a curtsy and let herself out.

Connor turned to me with a stern expression. "Bloss Boss, Ginnifer was chosen for her discretion. But you have to realize, she's new to this, just like you."

I sighed and rubbed my neck. "You're right. I'm sorry."

"I know this job is more than stressful to you."

"Honestly, Connor, it feels like I'm drowning."

"You aren't. Trust me. You aren't."

I sighed, "I feel as though anyone else would be better at this."

Connor quirked a smile. "You're the perfect queen."

I snorted, "How could you possibly say that?"

"Because you don't want the job. You're not power-hungry. Because you take it seriously. Because even with all these responsibilities weighing on your neck, you don't forget your sister."

I sighed again, "She's not technically—"

"She's still your sister. You still love her."

I pressed my lips together. It was true. I did. But I pushed the tears down, unwilling to get emotional right before I faced a roomful of snapping turtles.

Ohh, snapping turtles. That's a good one, Dove. Quinn sent me a mental picture of snapping turtles dressed in court gowns, trailing jewels and biting each other's tails. *You should bring your menagerie to the meeting.*

I could hear Quinn's mental laughter in my mind as he pictured the bear encounter from the night before. He'd made me tell him the story four times before allowing me to fall asleep. Clearly, the shine hadn't worn off that experience yet.

I couldn't help a grin as I scooped up the scroll for the meeting and turned to Connor. "Quinn's being ridiculous."

"As usual. Do you have any questions?" Connor caressed my arm.

I looked up at him, truly taking him in for the first time that morning. He looked amazing in a royal blue ensemble edged with gold. His mop of curls was brushed more to one side this morning. It was too neat. I had the urge to take him to my chamber and muss his hair, so that he walked into that meeting looking well-sexed. Looking claimed. Looking like he belonged to me. I stepped closer and bit my lip seductively.

But I was cut off at the pass.

"I know that look, Bloss Boss. We don't have time. We need to get through this introductory meeting with your nobles. I'll do the talking. You just need to sit."

"I feel like a useless fool."

Connor kissed me. "You aren't useless. You're just …"

Not tactful, Quinn cut to the point.

Shut it, or I'll set my bear on you when you get back.

It's true. You've got too much tavern wench in you now.

I rolled my eyes. "Connor, what is the point of this meeting? We aren't announcing any changes."

Connor took the scroll from me, tucking my arm into the crook of his elbow, "That *is* the point. We want to reassure them."

"Why couldn't that be done in a letter?"

"It's not how things are done. Now, we have a meeting with them this morning, while Isla's entourage packs. Tonight, is a dinner with all the duchesses. Isla's group will finish getting ready and officially leave sometime before that dinner."

"Thank goodness. We're basically at a stalemate on the hills, yes?"

Connor smiled and shook his head. He ran a hand through his brown curls and said, "You do remember offering Declan up on a platter to build them a tributary, don't you?"

"I said slowly, over time."

"We'll see. Isla's man is drawing up some documents for me to review after they depart. He and I will sort the details out from there."

I sighed. "So, the point is, keep my mouth shut."

Unless you're opening it for my cock, then yes, Dove.

Don't you have spying to do?

Doing it. Breaking into Cheryn's palace as we think.

WHAT!! My hand flew to my heart. My eyes grew wide. I turned to Connor. "Did you know Quinn's at the—"

Connor's hand clapped over my mouth. "Yes. And that's not something we speak about."

"But he could get caught. He could get hurt! He could—"

I'm glad you think so highly of my skills, Dove.

That's not it and you know it! I snarled.

I'm just checking on those so-called sick princes. And looking for where Raj might have stuffed that damned dragon and Avia. The sarding assholes haven't left a trail as pretty as I'd like.

You'd better be careful.

Gotta go, Dove. Spotted a dragon. Uh-oh! He's after me! He's—

You are not funny!

I'm hilarious. Go sit in your meeting and let me focus.

Stay safe.

Quinn didn't respond and I let Connor lead me into a morning full of polite drivel.

The polite nothings gave my thoughts a chance to spiral into worries: Who has Avia? What are they doing to her? Does she know she has magic? What kind of magic does she have? Is that dragon keeping her trapped in an underground cave or something?

Blue fluttered from my shoulder to my lap, sensing my agitation. Shiter was hopping around the room, soaking up pets and treats from the various duchesses and living up to his crappy name.

The bear, who I'd yet to name, sat off in the shadows. He'd discovered it was best not to move too much, or hysteria ensued. Poor man. I assumed he was a man. I hoped he was a man. I hadn't asked yet.

My thoughts went from Avia to my awkward magical menagerie. What about all these poor people who've ended up spelled? I wondered: Who's enchanting them and why? What could they have done to deserve it? Did they see something they shouldn't have?

I started and stared down at Blue.

I was an idiot. I was a fool.

Only a powerful magical being could control a djinni. Control a dragon. Turn people into animals permanently. How many beings that powerful were out there?

It had to be the same person. It had to.

I wanted to stand up immediately and drag my animals off for an intense and possibly annoying session of yes and no interrogation.

But I was trapped.

Duke Aiden's heavy-lidded eyes stared at me, watching me disdainfully. I petted Blue's head gently, trying to smooth my face back into the placid calm that court functions required.

Watching the duke, his smug pock-marked middle-aged face, reminded me that I needed to speak with Declan about the coins Willard had found. I gave the duke a fake little smile while I imagined Quinn locking up and punching Aiden until he revealed whoever he'd worked with to set the dragon loose.

Two leads. I had two possible means of finding out who had plotted against Evaness and stolen my sister. I had the djinni and Aiden. I needed to pursue both.

I took a deep breath and reached down for my teacup. This horrific waste of a morning was giving me time to think, to make connections.

I gave a real smile to the half-fairy who managed the Cerulean forest. Fer smiled back at me.

Connor's smooth voice trailed on about something and I'd nearly managed to get lost in thought again when Jorad arrived, interrupting us with a haughty bow.

"Why don't we all pause for a moment," Connor said, "We can resume after we've all taken some time for refreshments." He gestured toward a spread at the back of the room that would have fed an entire orphanage.

The courtiers nodded and stood. There was little else they could do. Connor followed Jorad to a small alcove, where Jorad handed over a scroll.

Only Sunya approached me. The slight pixie used Connor's distraction with the messenger to her advantage. She flew over to hover next to me.

"What's this I hear about building a tributary for Rasle?"

I sighed. "It's merely a discussion. Some of her people need more access to water."

"A lake is easier." The tiny, brown-haired woman was not the least bit intimidated by me or my position. It immediately raised my opinion of her.

"She didn't like that option."

"Of course, she didn't. She's a reacher, that one. She doesn't just want water. She wants everything. She wants my hills because of the river access."

I swallowed a sigh. The regional battles were close to the heart. Mother had always said it didn't do to get involved in those frays. You couldn't win.

I merely listened as Sunya ranted about Isla, claiming the queen wasn't satisfied with her share of the river closer to its mouth because all the diversions for farming made the mouth of the river too shallow for ships.

I didn't bother to point out that Isla had an entire coastline and the Sedarian fleet of ships were always at the ready to take trade goods to any location. That didn't matter. The only thing that mattered was the fact that Isla couldn't access the local river.

Connor rescued me just as I was growing uncomfortable, wondering how I could continue to hold a placid smile.

"Care to stretch your legs, wife?" he winked.

"Of course, excuse me," I practically leapt to my feet. Blue had to fend for himself as I latched onto Connor, eager to escape. He led Blue and I out to the gardens. Shiter and Fuzzy—I decided on the bear's name as we walked outdoors—followed.

The animals darted off to stretch and do their animal things as Connor turned to me.

He handed me the scroll that Jorad delivered.

"I need to read it? It's not just for you?" He handled most of the kingdom's official correspondence.

Connor nodded solemnly but didn't say anything.

Nervous butterflies flitted through my stomach. "What could be so important that Jorad interrupted our first meeting with the nobles?"

"Read," Connor's answer was terse and put me on edge.

I glanced down at the message and saw Queen Diamoni of Sedara's seal. I gulped. That was serious. The most powerful monarch in the seven kingdoms of Kenmare had written to me directly.

I flipped over the parchment and read the message. It was a single line.

You have seven days to find Avia. Or we will take over the search.

CHAPTER FOURTEEN

"*H*oly sard!" I nearly stumbled off the path. Connor caught my elbow and held me steady.

"What does that mean?" I whispered frantically.

Connor stared darkly at me, "I had Quinn tell Declan to pause on researching coins and dragons and everything else that kept him up last night. I told him to look at our confidential documents. Anything that might indicate what the hell Sedara has to do with this."

My chest felt tight. "They've always been a good ally. At least, they were before their ambassador and Willard met in the woods."

"I think that might have been Meeker on his own," Connor said. "None of his staff have had feelings or thoughts of disloyalty or secrecy. Quinn and I have checked. And Meeker hasn't been spotted anywhere."

191

I arched a brow. "Or Meeker could be working with those involved in whole shite dragon-djinni-kidnapping debacle."

I stared down at the parchment. The black lines looked as sharp as blades. "But this note from Sedara. Did I misread the tone?"

Connor shook his head and reached for the note. He reread it. "It reads like a threat to me."

I pressed my lips together and watched Fuzzy scare a half-dressed noble couple out of the bushes. I couldn't even laugh.

I didn't understand. Why was everything turning on its head? I didn't need another nation threatening me when it already looked like Sultan Raj had it out for me. I didn't need anything else, much less a threat from the most powerful monarch. Why would she do this? "Mother and Queen Diamoni always got along."

Connor nodded. "They seemed to, though they never visited one another.

I thought back. Connor was right. I'd been sent once or twice in my teen years. But always by myself on a gargoyle. "Yes, that's odd isn't it?"

"Mother never liked the ocean," I said. "She always refused to let Avia and I even board a ship. She'd send our fathers to do any christenings or whatnot."

"Yet, she somehow convinced Queen Diamoni to send over Declan."

I shrugged. "The way Declan speaks, the Sedarians were just happy to be rid of the embarrassing bastard prince."

Connor took my hand and turned me toward him. "She might not have loved him. But Diamoni knew how powerful Declan was."

"Well, he's powerful, of course, but—"

"No, Bloss Boss," Connor interrupted. "Why do you think Isla was so eager to get her hands on Declan? He's incredibly unique. He's the closest thing there is to a wizard left."

"What are you saying?"

"I'm wondering how two queens who never saw one another were so close. I'm wondering why the queen of the strongest nation in Kenmare, the nation with the greatest navy, would willingly hand over her most powerful son."

I studied Connor's eyes. The green was more prevalent than the blue when he was upset. Just then, his eyes looked like emeralds. "Well, what's your theory?"

"I think that Declan was sent here as protection."

Connor's words washed over me like ice water. Goosebumps formed along my spine. My entire being felt cold.

"Protection from what?"

Connor simply stared at me as the pieces fell together in my head and I said, "Gorg brought Avia. But he was our spy master. He wasn't a diplomat. Spy masters don't negotiate. They steal. Information. People."

Connor nodded, "I think Gorg stole Avia. From someone powerful."

I blinked. I felt drunk. Dizzy drunk. But I was sober. And the world around me was simply wavering, changing shape, morphing to throw me off balance. I braced myself on Connor's shoulder. I took a few breaths. What he said made sense. Too much awful sense.

Connor rubbed my arm sympathetically. "Do you want me to stop?"

"There's more?"

He led me over to a bench and helped me sit. I waved him on. If my world was collapsing, better to get it over with.

"I'm guessing Sedara knows who Gorg stole from. That's why they sent Declan."

"But why protect us? Why send him?"

Connor shrugged. "It's just a guess. But, if I had to bet on it, I'd say that Sedara helped your mother get Avia."

Just then Blue plummeted out of the sky. It felt like my heart went with him. Two countries conspired to steal a baby and keep her hidden? Did I not know my mother at all?

I watched, dazed, as Blue nabbed a beetle that had been trundling along in the garden and pecked at it until he seemed to remember he wasn't really a bird. He dropped the beetle and frantically wiped his beak on his feathers. He flew back to me, distress on his bird face.

I knew exactly how he felt. Lost. Confused. The world didn't make sense anymore. We were in the same boat.

I petted his tummy and crooned, "It's alright, Blue. I'll feed you some apple when we go inside."

He rubbed his head against my thumb.

"Did Lewart ever say anything to you about Avia?" I asked Connor, still staring off into the distance, trying to come to terms with all of this. The wind pushed the clouds quickly. In the distance, it looked like there was a storm.

"I've been thinking about that," Connor slid the letters into his vest and took my arm, helping me stand back up. "We need to walk so the nobles don't become suspicious."

He tucked my arm into the crook of his elbow and started down the stone path. After a few steps, he said, "Lewart always told me that black and white fade to grey as we grow older. He told me that time and perspective changed our view of the world. But then, he'd always follow it up with 'One day, you'll eat spinach. And instead of spitting it out, you'll swallow it down and ask for more.' I always thought he was joking about my hatred of vegetables—"

"It was pretty intense," I gave a small grin.

Connor smiled back down at me. But his face grew serious again as he continued, "I've been thinking that was his metaphor. For how things change. How something we once thought was so abhorrent becomes palatable."

"They took someone's *child*."

"First, we still don't know it wasn't an adop—"

I turned to Connor and gave him the look. "If Sedara's willing to find Avia, I'm pretty sure that she was taken. Forcefully. It's too much to hope for otherwise."

He raised a shoulder. "You're probably right. But we don't know why. Maybe she was rescued from someone who wanted to—"

"I appreciate you trying to make my parents into the heroes instead of the villains," I sighed, "But that doesn't seem realistic right now." I shook my head. "I always knew my mother had a hard heart. But—"

Ryan dropped out of the sky on the path in front of us, mounted on a gargoyle. The wind from his descent made me squint.

Blue dug his claws into my dress and buried his face in my neck as the gargoyle snorted.

Ryan dismounted and walked over to Connor and me. He held his hand out to me.

He was a little breathless when he said, "We finally found what was in the sky to the south. You're going to want to see."

My throat tightened so much I couldn't breathe. I felt frozen as I stared at Ryan.

"Did you find the dragon?" Connor asked.

Ryan shook his head and a small, crooked grin curved his lips. "We found a wizard."

My jaw dropped. Emotions sloshed through me. They were so big and bright and bold that I wasn't certain if they were joyous or fearful.

I'd searched … so long. I'd never found any hint of a wizard in Evaness. Everyone had stories. But that was all.

My eyes flickered between Connor and Ryan.

"I'm scared." It seemed silly, when I said it out loud. I wasn't scared to rescue Avia. I was furious. But to meet a wizard …

Ryan came and swept me off my feet, making Blue squawk in protest and crawl over to huddle on my chest.

Ryan cradled me in his arms. "I was deadly scared when they first asked me to be your knight. Excited. And terrified I'd fail you."

My hand brushed his chin. "You could never fail me."

"When you've thought about something for so many years … dreamed about it … being on the verge of getting it actually kinda makes you want to puke."

I laughed, "So true."

Before I knew it, Ryan had lifted me onto the gargoyle.

"I don't know that I'm ready—"

Ryan climbed up behind me. "Once you get what you've dreamed about, you'll realize your dreams were all wrong. Horribly wrong."

"Are you trying to comfort me by insulting me?"

"No. Dreams are just that. Dreams. Reality is reality. And we're going to find out what a wizard is really like."

With that, Ryan whistled, and we rushed up through the sky, Ryan's arms around my waist, the wind whipping my hair. Blue had tucked himself between my breasts despite my suggestion that he stay with Connor. He tucked his head under my collar as we flew higher and the cold chill of winter froze my bones and turned my breath into white puffs.

"Just a little further," Ryan whispered in my ear, encouraging me.

We traveled through the clouds, which were wet and unpleasant.

"Can we go around?" I whined as my dress got soaked and my toes turned into icicles.

Ryan's voice was warm on my ear, "No, Dearling. Just a warning, it's going to get slightly more intense before we get there. That's why it's taken my men and I a few days to get through."

I didn't have time to ask him what he meant before the clouds around us grew darker. The raindrops grew larger and more intense. Suddenly, a jagged streak of light flashed ten feet in front of us. The thunder that followed was a concussive force that made my ears ring. Blue scratched my chest as he scrabbled in fear. I put a hand over him, steadying him.

Ryan navigated upward; he flew us straight into the heart of a thunderstorm.

He carefully steered us through the dark clouds. The lightning bolts grew closer and more intense. The hairs on the back my neck stood up.

My jaw clenched. I wanted to yank the reins out of Ryan's hands and pull us into a dive. I wanted to scream. But any of that might just lead us straight into a lightning bolt. All I did was clutch onto Ryan's massive forearm with my left hand, keeping the other over Blue. I slammed my lips together and forced myself to keep quiet when a bolt made my hair stand out all around me. One wrong move and we'd be burnt to a crisp.

Ryan yanked back on the reins, making our gargoyle head straight up. I fell into the hard planes of his chest as we tilted back and darted vertically through the sky. The only reason Ryan and I didn't plummet to our deaths was because his giant legs were wrapped around the gargoyle's belly in a death grip. We crested the clouds, exiting the storm, and then he brought us level again.

My heart lurched in relief that we were through the storm. My body nearly rebelled the swift change in direction. But I took a moment to breathe deeply before I launched a curse at Ryan, "What the hell—" my rant died on my lips as I saw where Ryan had brought us.

Floating on top of the white puffy cloud in front of us was a quirky wooden cottage. It had wooden plank and shingle siding, and the roof was curved in a low arc. It looked to be two stories; the second story was an odd mixture of windowed jetties that jutted out beyond the first story. The curved roof was coved in red tiles.

"How?" I asked as Ryan led our gargoyle to land on top of the cloud. Ryan didn't immediately answer; he dismounted and helped me down. To my shock and amazement, the cloud's texture was soft and spongy, like a very thick layer of moss.

"This is the home of the wizard who helped Quinn," Ryan whispered.

"The thought beads?" I asked.

Ryan nodded.

Quinn's beads were some of the best magic I'd ever seen. He'd had them since he was a kid and they didn't fail over time, like most mage spells would. They didn't fade with distance. Quinn and his spies could travel across the sea to Sedara and still communicate via thought. Each of my knights and I had a bead as well. Hope blossomed. I felt certain this man could help us recover my sister.

Ryan murmured, "I showed Quinn the mental image of the wizard after I found him. He confirmed it's the same man." Ryan gestured at the little cabin. "This house must have been what we spotted flying south after the attack. The wizard's our best bet to ask about Avia. Even get help with Abbas. Or the dragon."

Blue tweeted plaintively from inside my dress. I helped him wriggle out so he could perch on my shoulder.

The door of the cabin opened and a man with an eye patch and a long golden beard trailing his knees popped out. He was dressed in a bright yellow shirt and trousers that had been mended so often with so many colors that I couldn't tell which ones belonged to the original pants. He only had one shoe on, and the shoe's toe curved up into a point. He looked like a jester fallen on hard times.

"What's the difference between a princess that's lost and the lost princess?" the wizard called out instead of greeting us.

"I don't know," I told him as I looked up at Ryan, curious.

Ryan shrugged at me. I assumed that meant he hadn't spoken to the wizard when he found him last time.

"I'm searching for one, you're searching for the other. Both will be found by a different brother." The old man gestured toward his door, waving. "Come in, come in, so we can begin."

I whispered to Ryan as we walked toward the cottage, "Are you sure this is a good idea?" This wizard was obviously incredibly powerful, if he could levitate his home. But he didn't seem all there.

Ryan nodded, "We've still got a dragon to fight, and Declan says wizards ..." he trailed off as we reached the stoop.

I reached the old man's steps and extended my hand delicately, so he could kiss it. "Thank you for inviting us in.

It's wonderful to meet you. I'm Bloss Hale, the Queen of Evaness."

He didn't take my hand, just widened his single eye and let his grin stretch ear to ear. "There is no need for royalty here, there's nothing but loyalty here in the clouds, with only crows and snows and sunset glows allowed."

I retracted my hand and pasted on my court smile, the fake one. This wizard either enjoyed speaking in riddles, in which case I was certain I'd soon have a headache, or he had lost his marbles. I hesitated, but Blue flew right into the living room.

"Oh, ho! Quite the friend you have! You like supernatural men, then? I've been called bewitching a time or two, it's true." The wizard winked at me with his good eye.

Ryan stiffened beside me. I just laughed. "I am looking for a man who can tame a dragon. Would that be you?"

"Step into the flame to earn bright fame!" he gestured to his living room. "The name is Donaloo, or it was before I went askew."

Donaloo led us to his cramped living room. Three chairs and a small round table huddled close to a brick fireplace. The fire crackled merrily, and a teapot sat steaming on the table, as if we were expected. Maybe this wizard wasn't quite as far gone as he appeared.

The wizard served us tea in tankards after we sat. The side of the cup burned my fingers when I picked it up, but I swallowed my gasp, trying to remain polite. If this wizard wasn't intimidated by the thought of facing a dragon, then I needed him.

"Ryan tells me you are the one who created beads so that my knight, Quinn, could speak to us. Thank you. He and I are quite grateful."

Donaloo waved a hand dismissively. "What is power for but to give voice to the voiceless and choice to the choiceless?"

"Your magic is astounding. The beads still work perfectly. I've never seen such a spell," I tried to take a sip of the burning hot tea. It tasted like boiling mud. My fear about the wizard's sanity increased.

Donaloo looked at me. "Spells come in all sorts. Sorting through the spelling can be quite a feat. After all, M-I-N-U-T-E can mean time or a bit, W-O-U-N-D can mean wind up or a hit. The spelling's in the details. And the details are in the spells."

His comment led me to switch topics. Maybe he didn't want to speak about magic openly. A lot of mages guarded their discoveries jealously. Wyle had. Perhaps Donaloo felt I was prodding and was being obtuse to get me to change topics.

I wasn't certain I believed my own logic, but I wasn't quite ready to give up hope and acknowledge he was completely mad. "My sister was recently stolen by a dragon. He flew off with her. I came to ask if you've seen them."

"Is it a wise man or a madman who sees only foes—no matter where he looks, no matter where he goes?"

I stopped making roundabout excuses. Clearly, Donaloo's mental state had devolved since he'd helped Quinn out. I tried to smother my frustration. I asked directly, "Have you seen Princess Avia of Evaness? I wish you would simply give me a straight answer."

"Wishful thinking never solved any problems. But every solution began as a wishful thought." The wizard winked and looked at Blue, who fluttered next to his chair. "Isn't that right?"

Blue swooped down to land on my lap as I stared at Donaloo, struck by the fact that he didn't end with a rhyme. "Wait. Did you say wish? We are having trouble with a djinni."

Ryan gave me a sharp look at revealing such a secret.

I ignored him because we'd come because we were desperate for help. If that meant giving state secrets to a wizard, I'd chance it.

"Do you know anything about djinn? Do you know the djinni that attacked me?" I leaned forward.

Donaloo tilted his head and looked at me with a sad sigh. I swear, in that moment he looked present and sane. "A wish started, and a wish will stop the curse. But only when you've seen the worst."

I felt a chill run down my spine and I instinctively grabbed onto Blue on my lap. I needed something to hold. He squawked in protest, but I didn't release him.

"What about Blue? Can you reverse the spell on him?"

"What is the most potent magic? It's stronger than death or hate, twice as strong when you reciprocate."

I gaped at him. I wondered for a moment if he'd think more clearly if I decked him.

Don't you dare hit my wizard! Quinn popped into my head.

He's just throwing riddles at me. Is that how he talked to you?

No. But he came to me when I was a kid. I wouldn't have understood that shite.

I don't understand it!

Tell it to me.

I recited the riddle to Quinn.

A moment later, I was sent back an eye-rolling image of Quinn. *It's obviously love.*

Declan told you that, didn't he?

What? Sorry. Can't hear you... Quinn faded from my thoughts.

I turned to the wizard and said, "Love. Love is the most potent magic."

Donaloo gave a bright smile and nodded. "Correct."

I waited for a rhyme. But none came. I didn't know if that meant I'd passed some test. Were those all tests?

I leaned forward in my chair, "Can you help me find who did this? Can you help me find my sister and this dragon and everything else? Please. I desperately need your help. I could offer—"

Donaloo held up his hand, and gave me a small smile, "Offer only love. The only payment worth anything in the end, is the true heart of a friend."

I nodded, completely uncertain whether he'd agreed to help me or not.

Thunder shook the house, tilting it slightly. Ryan's tankard fell to the floor. The wizard jumped up from his chair and ran to his front door.

"Trouble's brewing, the eight kingdoms are stewing!"

Shite. Eight kingdoms? Kenmare only had seven. The poor man's addled mouth was back to spewing nonsense.

The wind blew open one of the windows and the house started to spin. Donaloo stood and gestured frantically at the door, "Hurry, hurry, time to go. The war is at hand, don't you know!"

Ryan and I stood and made our way to the door. Blue flew up to perch on my finger, digging in hard as the wind ruffled his feathers.

As we walked out the door, Donaloo reached up and plucked Blue from my shoulder. "A kiss without love is

merely a kiss, but love can pull us back from the abyss."
He kissed my bird.

Ew, I thought.

I felt sorry for Blue but was hesitant to grab him away from Donaloo. I didn't want the crazy man to hurt anyone.

Mother always said to be overly polite to the crazy ones. I took her advice.

"Thank you so much for the tea," I said.

"It's never the tea, dear, always the company," Donaloo winked.

Then he grabbed my hand, pushed Blue into me, and said, "Remember, failure is the toll we pay to cross the bridge to success. You must pay the toll or forego your goal."

He pressed something small and round into my hand and then pushed me out the door.

I stumbled, falling onto the soft clouds at the base of his house. Ryan followed me out and pulled me to my feet.

Donaloo spoke as if he hadn't just shoved me down the stairs. "I'll pack my bags and be with you as soon as I can. For a bird's eye view is nice for a while, but the ground is better for a man. Tell Cerena I'll be there to set her castle square."

Ryan and I watched, frozen, as the wizard's house whipped around like a tornado had caught it. But the tornado didn't touch us. It merely turned the house in circles. Faster. Faster. The little cottage spun and spun until it was a blur of color. And then, in a blink, it disappeared.

We were left standing on a cloud.

"Well, that was a waste," Ryan grumbled.

I stared at the sky as Blue fluttered in front of me. "I'm not certain, it was, actually."

I held up a coin that glinted in the light. It had the burning rose of Evaness on one side, but the profile of the unknown woman on the other.

"If one ridiculous noble and one ridiculous wizard both hand you the same coin, it must mean something."

"Maybe carrying the coin makes you go crazy?" Ryan suggested, as he helped me mount the gargoyle.

"Could be. Or it could mean that Aiden and this dragon, and the crazy war the wizard is talking about are all tied together."

"By what?"

I held up the coin. "This."

CHAPTER FIFTEEN

*R*yan left me at the castle door, handing me into Jorad's care. Connor had returned to the meeting with the nobles. At first, I thought Jorad might force me to return to that dull affair, but he actually followed Ryan's orders to lead me to Declan's chambers.

The butler and I didn't speak to each other, both still a bit taut and angry from our prior encounters, until he held open the door.

"Your Majesty," Jorad said, bowing his head politely.

"Jorad," I gave a stiff nod. But then I decided against holding grudges. Perhaps because of the loony wizard's little lectures on love. Or perhaps because Jorad knew so much about my mother, the thief, and might be useful one day. "Willard did us proud the other day. I hope he continues to do so."

Jorad's eyebrows raised. He didn't give me any further response.

I walked into Declan's chamber, swallowing a sigh. With some people, it wasn't even worth trying. Blue twittered on my shoulder, agreeing with me.

Declan spun around in his chair when I walked in, pieces of parchment flying from the stacks on his desk. "Bloss!"

"Hey, handsome." I smiled and stooped to help him pick up the fallen pages.

I caught Declan staring down the gap at the top of my dress and I grinned. "See something you like?"

He quirked a brow. "Actually, something I don't." His hand went into my dress and pulled out a little blue feather. "I knew you were sexually adventurous, but bestiality's a bit far, isn't it?"

Blue nearly died. He started tweeting on my shoulder so hard that it turned to wheezing. He nearly fell. I had to catch him and set him down on Declan's desk. Declan and I watched his fit with amusement.

"Do you think that's laughter?" Declan asked.

"Gods, I hope so. Because contrary to whatever you think, I'm not into animals. The idiot crawled in there when Ryan took us on a gargoyle."

Declan grinned. "That better be it. If I find feathers anywhere else …"

"Wanna check?" I opened my hands wide with a smile.

"Oh no, Peace. Don't you remember what I said? Our first time, I want you desperate for me," Declan leaned in and nuzzled my nose and then gave me the world's softest kiss. His plush lips hardly touched mine and then he was gone, leaving me leaning forward into thin air.

"Argh! Unfair!" I stomped a foot.

"You're adorable when you pout. And when you bathe." Declan's eyes drifted to a tub that sat in the middle of his room.

My gaze followed. "They didn't move it."

"I wouldn't let them. It was the first time I got to see you in all your glory."

"Apparently, you saw Ryan as me hundreds of times," I grumbled.

Declan shook his head and sat back down. "Not the same."

"Why not?"

"That was transactional. Orgasm trading."

I sat on Declan's lap and snuggled in, making myself comfortable. I ran a hand through his blond hair. "What is it with me?"

"Perfect," Declan said softly, his blue eyes gazing deep into mine.

I groaned. "How can you think I'm not desperate for you when you say shite like that?" I leaned up to kiss him.

"Not desperate enough," Declan murmured, backing away from the kiss. "I want you clawing at me, I want you so needy and desperate that tears fill your eyes, I want you to not even be able to see anyone else in the room because all you see is *me*," Declan whispered.

I stared at him. Really looked. Because Declan was being vulnerable with me. He was telling me his greatest wish. He was asking me to grant it.

It filled my heart to bursting to know that he loved me that much. So, I nodded. "Okay." Somehow, I would give that to him.

He smiled softly and dragged a hand down my arm. "Now," he cleared his throat, "Ryan said you had another coin."

I reached into my cleavage, causing Declan to moan. "Really? You had to keep it there?"

I giggled, "Making you rethink your requirements?" I pushed up the girls so he could get a better view. One of my nipples popped into sight.

"Uh," Declan reverted to grunts, his eyes dilating as he reached to tweak it.

"Nope, I'm not desperate yet," I tucked myself back into the dress. Now that I knew how much he really wanted our first time alone to be special, I wasn't going to let it randomly happen. Instead, I grabbed the coin and handed it to him. It was still warm from my skin.

Declan took disappointment better than I expected, but perhaps his submissive side was used to being told 'no.' He grabbed the coin from my hand. "It's exactly like the other one."

"Yes. Donaloo, the wizard, gave it to me. And said something about failure being the price we pay for success."

"Donaloo?" Declan's eyes went wide. "He's a legend!"

"Well, he's also only half-there." I wound a finger around my head in a 'crazy' motion. "He may or may not be coming to help us with the dragon."

"This is amazing!" Declan's face lit up.

"I might be slightly offended over you getting more excited about a half-crazed wizard than sex with me," I said.

"Peace, he could help us."

"I realize that. It's why I asked for his help."

"He's nearly three-hundred-years old," Declan said, suddenly standing and dumping me off his lap. "Oh, sorry! I wasn't—"

I laughed, "It's fine. I realized scholar Declan had come out when I saw your reaction to the name Donaloo. I swear, it's like you have a separate personality."

Declan wasn't listening to me. He was already combing through a pile of books near his bed.

"I don't know that I looked back far enough in *Evaness Treasury History*," Declan muttered aloud. I leaned against his desk and watched bemused, as he paced the room, flipping pages in the book. "Here!" He smacked a page triumphantly with his pointer finger. "I found it!"

I went over to him and peered down at the page. On it was the profile of the woman from the gold coin. "Queen Aubrina." I looked down at the date. "She lived nearly two hundred years ago."

"Exactly! I hadn't found her yet, but I did go through the tax payments from last year. The payment from Aiden and his province was made almost entirely in these coins. They're in our vault."

"What does that mean? I can't punish anyone for their ancestors stealing from the crown," I shook my head. "Or digging up buried treasure or whatnot."

Declan bit his lip. "I know. The question becomes, where did he get all these old coins? Doesn't it seem unlikely that he'd stumble over buried treasure? I mean, his land is smack in the middle of the country... pirates aren't likely to go there." Declan started pacing, book in his hands.

Blue fluttered over to me and settled on my shoulder. I patted his wings. "Sunken treasure or a pirate ship seem far more reasonable for the coastal provinces."

"Sunken treasure!" Declan's eyes lit up. "That's an idea."

"But how would Aiden, or whoever he's working with, get it?"

Declan shrugged. "If it was in the shallows, a diver could get it. Or magic it up, obviously. They'd need to know the exact location, so divers might still need to be involved. The sea between Sedara and Rasle used to have horrid storms. I did a research project on it for Tutor Mathers once. One of every six or so ships would end up sunk. Quite nasty. I bet there's a ton of coins down there." He tapped his lip and paced again.

"But," I tilted my head and said, "let's say you're an incredibly magical person who could control a djinni and a dragon. Wouldn't you be powerful enough to just create coins? Modern coins?"

"Dammit!" Declan slammed a hand into his bedpost and marched over to his desk. He put a tic mark on the edge of the parchment. But then he ripped the parchment and handed the sliver with the mark to me. "Keep that. Sarding hell! Your version makes more sense. Why the hell would someone powerful use old coins that weren't just lying around? It would be stupid. Too much work. Harder than minting them."

"Sorry," I shrugged, worrying the little parchment into a twist. "I just ... I feel like we're missing something big. And I don't know what it is."

"I feel it too," Declan said. His look was pure anguish. "I hate that I'm missing something because whatever it is, Avia's the one who ends up hurt."

I knew he'd been close to Avia when we were growing up. The sad brokenness of his tone mirrored how I felt inside, shredded at the thought of Avia getting hurt. Of Avia being tormented. Even if mother had stolen Avia from her family whoever had taken her ... they hadn't taken my sister gently. They'd sent a dragon to terrorize her.

I slid my arm around Declan's waist, flicked my hand to send Blue flying off, and then I hugged my knight. "We'll find her," I promised.

"We better," Declan's voice grew bitter. "I don't want my damned mother barging in on this."

"Connor told you?"

"We always tell Quinn everything, so he can spread the word quickly," Declan said. "I just … I need to figure this out, Bloss. We need to get her back. We're Avia's family. Blood or not, kidnapping or not, you and I …" he leaned away and met my eyes as he whispered, "you and I are her family."

I nodded, fighting tears. My stomach felt sick with the thought that it had been days since she'd been taken. "I know."

The problem was … we were at an impasse. "Everything about Avia's kidnapping just doesn't make sense. I mean, who in the seven kingdoms would want to steal her?"

Declan pulled me in harder. "Her family would. Whoever Queen Gela took Avia from. The problem is, we don't know who that is."

And that was the question we needed to answer.

CHAPTER SIXTEEN

*C*onnor collected me from Declan's room when his meeting was done.

Declan and I had sunk into his books, flipping pages, listless and desperate for answers at the same time.

When Connor saw us, he said, "Enough! Declan, Ryan wants to go over some unusual activity near the border with you so get your figures for troops from the last flyover together. Bloss, come on, I want to show you something and then I need to update you on the rest of today's meeting."

I stood woodenly and followed Connor, who waved Blue backward, shooing the bird until he stayed in Declan's room.

"Nope. No birds."

ANN DENTON

Instead of leading me to his room across the hall, he led me to a secret passage, waving off the guard who tried to follow us.

"Subterfuge, sorry," he told the guard. Then he leaned in and whispered, "We'll stay within the walls, but we're going to the north wing where the duchesses and duke are staying. You can alert the guards in that area."

Then Connor led me through the passage, shut the door behind us, and shoved me against the wall.

"Connor! What's going—"

His mouth was on mine in a second, no preamble. He kissed me hard.

Gradually, my shock turned to willingness but the second my tongue moved against his, Connor pulled away.

"I need to show you something," he whispered.

"Okay." I was a bit confused by his rapid changes of pace. "A good something?"

"We'll see. Duchess Malia felt off today. And I want to check on Aiden, obviously," he ran a hand through his curls, suddenly looking nervous. "I didn't hit your head when I pushed you against the wall, did I? I've just … I've always dreamt about doing that."

A grin lit my face. He was so sarding cute and concerned, running his fingers over the back of my head. The alpha move was definitely out of character.

I grabbed his hand and placed it on my breast, giving him a saucy wink. His playful smile back was adorable.

"You didn't hit my head. You wanna do it again?"

Bam. My shoulders smacked the side of the passageway. Connor's eyes narrowed and heat filled his gaze. This time I knew what was coming and I wrapped my legs around Connor's waist. We kissed until we were breathless.

He nipped at my lip and groaned. "Gah, I don't want to stop."

"You don't have to," I whispered. "We don't have to hide any more either. You could do this to me in the hallway and the guards would have to go around the corner and wait."

Connor trembled beneath me. "I don't want to hurt you—"

"We can be sweet for round two," I promised. "Besides, I owe you for leaving you alone with those awful Countesses all day."

"You do," he moaned as I grabbed him through his trousers, stroking the length of his bulge.

"Go ahead and be dirty for round one then," I told him, wondering what my sweet little Cee would do.

"We can't." Connor dropped my feet to the ground and backed away. "Not yet. We need to check on everyone in their rooms before the official dinner."

I was disappointed. But he was right. We could use the opportunity to check on Aiden.

Connor latched onto my hand and hauled me quickly through the passages, cutting my arguments off with short shushes.

Torches lit our way and I realized Connor must have told a guard or two ahead of time, so they could light our path. Once we got close to the north wing, the torches stopped. Connor's feet slowed. He leaned close to me and whispered, "We have to be absolutely silent now."

I nodded. Then he led me into the pitch darkness, pierced only occasionally by spy holes. He stopped and I nearly ran into his back.

He pulled me toward the wall, and I put my eye up to a small peephole. Connor stood next to me and leaned forward to peer through another opening.

The room we stared at was Malia's dressing room. Her maid was removing her day gown to replace it for the formal dinner we were set to have in a few hours. Malia was an older duchess, slightly plump, but quite curvy in a good way. She lifted her arms to let her maid pull down her overdress. Once she'd stepped out of it, she shed her chemise. And then Malia stood naked but for her thigh high white stockings and jeweled court shoes. A few glimmering blue scales ran up her backbone and on the back side of her arms, a sign of her mer heritage.

Her maid hung the dress and Malia stopped her before she grabbed another. "Can I just have my robe? And the letter again, please?"

The servant brought the requested items and then Malia shooed her away. "I just need a moment."

Once the maid had left the room, Malia slipped on the robe, sat at her dressing table and unfurled a scroll.

Her eyes scanned the contents briefly before she leaned forward onto the table, propping herself up on her elbows.

A heart wrenching sob filled the room. I pulled back from the peephole, feeling guilty.

Connor leaned back and grabbed my hand. We had just turned away when there was a knock at Malia's door.

Connor froze. Then he dragged me back to the peephole.

I touched his arm. When he looked over at me, I held my hands up in question, silently asking what we were doing.

He held up clenched fists and shivered in response. Shivering was his physical answer to me, from a secret communication style we'd developed as teens. It meant he felt fear from someone. Scared—Malia felt scared.

Malia's maid answered the door.

"Oh, I must have the wrong room!" a deep, familiar voice said.

Malia put her scroll into a drawer in her dressing table, wiped her eyes, and stood.

"Lysa, go ahead and pull my gown, will you? I'll help this gentleman."

"But—" her maid looked in askance at Malia's lack of clothing.

The duchess just waved her off and opened the door.

"You have the wrong room?" Malia asked. "We have a map of this floor of the palace from Jorad. Would you care to see it?"

"That would be so kind," the man replied, stepping inside. Donovon followed Malia over to a writing desk on the far side of the room. She picked up a large sheet of parchment and handed it to him.

"Is this what you needed?" she asked.

"It's a start," Donovon scanned the map.

"How is everything going since you arrived, Ambassador?" Malia asked.

"To plan," Donovon replied.

"Good. He's out?"

The ambassador Donovon was replacing had just packed up with Isla's entourage and would be leaving with her.

Donovon nodded.

Malia smiled, "Is everyone still on the same time line?"

"Yes. Just hours away. Just long enough to get everything and everyone in place."

They were just discussing Rasle leaving. Nothing exciting. Nothing incriminating. It made me feel a bit guilty about watching Malia's private moment before. Perhaps not all was well with her family.

I tugged on Connor's sleeve, but he didn't leave.

Malia nodded. "So, Rasle is excited for the change?"

"It's been a long time coming."

"When you're being strangled, every second feels like a lifetime," Malia agreed. "And those taxes have strangled us all."

I leaned back from the peephole, fear punching a hole in my chest. Did she mean my taxes? Our taxes? Evaness? Was Malia angry with Mother? Me?

"Sedara's been taking advantage too long," Donovon replied. "If the blighters in Lored weren't such cowards, they'd agree."

My chest loosened a bit. Sedara. They hated Sedara. Sedara taxed everything that went across the sea. It was natural to resent them and their navy.

I felt a rush of relief that I wasn't looking at a noble who was furious with me. I was almost giddy that their anger was directed at someone else. I didn't think I could handle one more problem right now.

Malia nodded at Donovon. "Lored are a bunch of cowards. No one likes getting jammed."

"Well, thank you for the map. I'll let you get ready for dinner."

Malia grabbed his arm before he left. "You said hours."

Donovon nodded and glanced over at the maid. "Thank you again."

Malia just nodded as he shut the door behind him. She gave a long sigh and went back to her maid, who silently began dressing her for dinner.

Connor tugged at me and pulled me down the passageway for a bit toward the next room and the next set of spy holes.

Aiden was just as naked as Malia. But he wasn't alone. A naked brunette sucked his length into her mouth. On the floor beneath her, another man lay on his back, his head planted between the brunette's legs. A third man stood behind Aiden, tweaking his nipples. Moans filled the air.

I started to turn away, but Connor stopped me. He moved behind me and pressed against me. And then he shifted my head to the right, so that I only had one eyehole. He stared through the left.

The man behind Aiden spit on his hand and stuck his finger in Aiden's ass.

Aiden started to moan.

Connor's shaft grew thick against my ass.

"Turn around and stay on your knees," Aiden told the woman. She complied, lifting her legs and turning away from Aiden, careful not to kick the prone man on the floor. She put herself into a sixty-nine position with the man on the floor. But Aiden smacked her ass and made her straighten her legs so he could stay standing and slam into her twat. The man from the floor sat up and started licking. He didn't seem to care whether his tongue hit her cunt or Aiden's balls.

A servant's door opened.

"I was thinking about that bet from the other night. And I think I could trounce you—" Willard cut off at the sight in front of him. "Um … umm…"

"Bet you a hundred gold pieces you aren't brave enough to join in," Aiden snarled as he thrust roughly into the moaning woman.

"Oh! Um …"

I pulled roughly away from the wall and hurried down the passageway. I had to shove down mixed feelings of horror and humor. Connor followed behind.

I waited until we hit torchlight before speaking, "I'm sorry. I know we think he let the dragon in. I just did not want to permanently have an image of Willard—"

"Shh," Connor's hand closed around my wrist. He pushed me up against the wall and slid his thigh between my legs. "Don't think about that. Think about what happened before that."

"Did you like it?" I asked him. He'd always had a weakness for watching. When we were teens, he'd dragged me along once or twice through the passageways. I'd blushed and looked away then. Not anymore.

"Sard," Connor moaned into my neck before his tongue traced a hot path up the side. I took that as a yes.

"Do you watch often?" I kissed his jaw. The thought of Connor groping himself as he stared at the nobles through the spyholes made me wet.

My hand traveled down to his trousers. His length was hard and thick and there was already a wet spot on his pants. Of course, there was. Connor could sip emotions. He could feel how turned on everyone had been. For a moment I was jealous that he might have liked watching that brunette. But all that desire was only to my benefit.

Because now his hands were roaming my body and his lips were on my neck. I asked again, "Do you watch a lot?"

"Sometimes," he whispered.

I put my lips on Connor's collarbone and sucked. He moaned, pressing into me and nibbling my earlobe as I dragged my hand up and down his shaft through his pants. I smacked my lips as I released his skin, ensuring that the hickey would mark him as mine.

"Give me details," I said, as I undid his belt.

"It's embar—"

"Details, Cee," I yanked on his belt until his trousers fell to the floor. I stepped back and made a show of licking my entire hand before reaching for Connor's hard shaft. I pumped it once, then stopped, staring up at him.

"Details," I repeated, getting breathless. My nipples grew hard where they rubbed against my dress, they hadn't settled back into the corset after I'd flashed Declan.

"Lady Alred, who lives here in the palace, is courting Lord Marshall," Declan's voice was breathy. "He's a royal guard, one of Ryan's best. She likes him to come to her after his practices. And she likes to lick every drop of sweat off his body."

I moaned, spreading my legs further and pressing myself into Connor's thigh.

"What does she wear while she does it?" I asked, sliding up and down Connor's thigh, my hand sliding along his dick in time with my body.

"A red corset and white stockings," Connor murmured as he reached for my breasts. They fell out of my dress with almost no effort and then he was kneading them, twisting them, pinching.

"Does he touch her?"

"Once she's done. Then he'll take her stockings off and tie her hands with them. He'll tease her with his cock, brushing it over and over her cunny," Connor rubbed against me as he spoke.

The thought of the lady being tied and helpless made my entire body grow flush. Connor's dick pressing up and down along my thigh made me go breathless. My lady bits pulsed. I raked my teeth gently down Connor's neck before begging, "More, tell me more. Who else do you watch?"

"There's a little kitchen maid who lets her two husbands take her at the same time," Connor rasped.

I knew that sound. He was getting close. I squeezed his shaft at the base. "Don't you dare come yet. Tell me more."

"She's got red hair and the three of them like to sneak into the parlors on the first floor. They like to play royals. The guards let them do it because they like to watch the show. One of them, the one with the skinnier dick, takes her ass and the other plows her pussy. Some nights they move in tandem and I can hear their balls slap against each other as they make her moan."

I yanked up my skirts, bunching them around my waist. And then I straddled Connor's thigh once more. I started to rub against him. The wet brush of my womanhood against his thigh and the idea of the naughty things this maid let people watch her do, things I wanted my knights to do to me, made me moan. "Tell me more. I'm gonna come soon, Cee."

Connor kept one hand on my breast but reached the other under my lifted skirts to stroke the crack of my ass. I could feel the hard bulge in his pants as he breathed in my ear. "Bloss Boss." His fingers pinched my nipple.

My mind filled with cloudy wonder, that high floating sensation that comes before a huge orgasm.

What the sard are you doing?

Quinn's voice broke my concentration.

I—I what? The 'what' came out as a moan in my head as Connor used his hand on my ass to piston me up and down against his thigh faster and faster.

You're having sex without me.

It's not sex!

Tell me someone hasn't sprayed his dick sauce all over your fleshy red beef curtains!

Ew!

Quinn sent an image of a butcher's shop, with meat dangling from hooks, thin flaps of meat swaying against one another. A butcher came into the shop and grabbed a side of beef. He tossed it on the table, grabbed a knife, spun around, then ran a knife sideways through the meat, filleting it. And then, in typical Quinn fashion, the butcher started playing with the meat. He grabbed each of the flaps and smacked them against each other, like they were lips. He ran his finger down each of their edges whispering, *"You know how I like it? I like it raw."* The butcher rubbed the slabs of beef together. *"Mmmm."*

I shuddered.

This only encouraged Connor who murmured, "Yes, Blossie, let it go," as he tweaked my nipple again.

You're ruining everything! I yelled at Quinn, when the nipple tweak didn't do a damn thing for me.

Good! Because I should be there.

I'll make it up to you.

Connor chose that moment to drop his leg. He shoved his fingers inside me instead, pumping roughly.

"Yes," I breathed. "Like that." His fingers were hard and thick, and my pussy began flutter around them.

Connor took his free hand and scratched down my chest before reaching around and squeezing my ass, hard. That pain, combined with the pleasure from the fingers inside me, sent me back up the hill, close to the peak.

The image of a large toad with a flat back punctured by row after row holes flew into my head. Then, in the most disgusting birthing display I've ever seen, baby toads popped out of the holes like pimples. *Pop. Pop. Pop-pop-pop-pop-pop.*

"Ew!" I screeched.

Connor stopped. "Did I hurt you?"

I breathed hard, scrubbing a hand over my face to erase that awful mental image. "Quinn's being an ass. He's sending me disgusting mental pictures so I can't come."

Connor's face grew dark. I smiled as I felt Quinn recede from my brain. I was certain he was getting reamed mentally.

I chimed in.

You're an evil cock block and not fair at all.

I wondered vaguely if his mind could handle both of us yelling at him at once. Part of me hoped not.

It was a minute or two before Quinn spoke to both of us. *Fine. I'll let her come. But only if she plays with me in her head.* His group-thinking echoed and made my head hurt.

Connor closed his eyes and shook his head. "Five-year-old. Can't share."

You'd make the same demand if you could.

Quinn turned off his group thinking and instead just spoke to me. *Will you, Dove?*

I dunno. You denied me two orgasms just now. I'm not feeling very generous.

Bloss, I can't be there with you. Do you know how lonely I am without you? I'm cold, in a crappy scratchy bedroll, all alone in the woods, worried about wolves. You're there surrounded by love—he sent me a mental image of what I was certain had to be him as a young boy. The boy had huge grey eyes and long lashes, and sarding pinchable cheeks. The boy jutted his lower lip and let it tremble.

I couldn't help my smile even as I rolled my eyes. *Fine. You win.*

I turned to Connor. "We're going to have to let Quinn play naughty with our minds while we screw."

Connor just crooked an elbow and tucked my hand into it. "Anything you want, Your Majesty."

"Well, I definitely want that. But who says we have to make things easy on Quinn? Let's go see whatever else you want to show me first. And then maybe do something romantic. And a snack. We might need a snack, too."

Dove! Quinn whined.

I just shot him back a mental image I had of Fuzzy taking a huge, disgusting berry-infused dump. Only I tried to imagine Fuzzy in Quinn's quarters instead of the garden.

I was grinning stupidly at Connor over my cleverness when Quinn mind-yelled at both of us.

Sarding shite!

What is it? I asked.

Soldiers. Cheryn soldiers disguised not to look like soldiers. And there's a huge group of them.

Where are you?

Camped near the shore. I've been searching for those 'ill princes' who are nowhere to be found.

Quinn sent us a mental image of thousands of armed men sneaking through the trees. Behind them, the ocean frothed and spit. A cog, sails unfurled and whipping in the wind, bobbed in the shallows. Small rowboats carried groups of men to the boat.

Quinn's perspective suddenly flew up above the trees and I realized he'd drunk a bottle of Flight. More ships came into view. In the distance, in the old hills where Rasle lay, a volcano belched steam into the cold air.

I met Connor's eyes and knew he could feel my fear.

It looked like Cheryn was preparing for war.

$\mathcal{M}$y mind wavered between fear for Quinn and utter confusion.

Connor and I turned to stare at each other. Immediately, without discussion, we made our way back to Declan's chambers.

We arrived in Declan's room just as Ryan burst in, Shiter and Fuzzy on his heels. Ryan tried to shoo the animals away, but Shiter darted under the bed. And Fuzzy just stood on his hind legs growling until Ryan relented.

"Fine!" Ryan slammed the door to Declan's room shut and Connor sealed the passageway behind us.

Blue fluttered from Declan's bed canopy down to settle on my shoulder. Fuzzy plopped down on a bear skin rug in front of the fire, oblivious to the irony of his bed choice. His snores soon rumbled lightly through the room.

I turned from the animals to stare at Ryan's dark expression.

"What the hell is going on?" Ryan asked. "Sultan Raj is moving soldiers to the shore? The ships? He must have done that quickly. Or had the ships disguised. I haven't had any reports from my scouts about this."

Quinn replied to all of us. *My people are stationed at the palace. I heard talk about a pleasure cruise. That must have been a sarding code word. I'm gonna head down the coast and let you know what I see.*

"Maybe my scouts have been paid off. There's a lot of those fake coins floating around. Maybe they're from Cheryn. Do we think they're going to attack us?" Ryan asked.

Quinn's response was instantaneous. *It looks like they're loading the boats. Not unloading from them. Besides, any attack on us would better be done via land or air.*

Declan shook his head in disbelief, "Are they suicidal? If they try anything out in the ocean against anyone, Sedara will smash them. It has three times the ships anyone else does and considers the water basically an extension of its territory." He took one of the ancient coins I'd brought him and flipped it between his fingers, watching it go end over end.

We all stood silently, trying to puzzle out who the country to the north might attack.

"Maybe Sultan Raj is trying to make a bunch of power plays?" I threw out, "He did supposedly send his sons down here and we ended up assaulted. Attacking us when my mother was ill, and I was newly returned was smart. Strategic, even. Maybe he wants to take the continent? Maybe he isn't going across the sea but down the shore to attack Rasle? Should we warn Isla?"

Quinn's answer projected to everyone. *Doubtful, Dove. I'm hitting the border of Rasle now. I can already see a pocket of supposed 'civilians' up ahead in the hills near the ocean. Looks way too organized to be actual civilians. They could be from Cheryn. But could be from Rasle, too. I'll let you know when I get closer.*

Be careful.

I took Invisibility. No one can see me.

I turned to Declan, "We heard Rasle's ambassador and Malia complain about Sedara tonight."

"One doesn't necessarily connect to the other," Declan shook his head. "My mother would destroy Sultan Raj. Isla's country is so small she'd be wiped off the map. Complaining versus doing something—"

Rasle has at least three groups of soldiers hidden in their northern hills near the shore, Quinn interrupted Declan.

I bit my lip. "I know. It doesn't make sense. Are they fighting each other? If so, why's Isla here? She needs to be focused on her own country if she and Raj are on the brink of conflict with one another."

Ryan threw out, "If they aren't fighting each other ... and they are amassing *together*—then that would be a different story."

Declan shook his head. "Both against Sedara still wouldn't stand a chance."

I had to throw out the question, "And why would she visit me? She hasn't tried to convince me to join some movement. Or uprising."

Ryan's eyes flew to Declan. "Maybe she thinks our loyalty lies with Sedara."

Declan gave a bitter laugh, "If they think that, the joke's on them isn't it?"

"Is it?" I asked, "If there wasn't some kind of secret agreement between mother and Sedara, then why would Queen Diamoni have sent that note about finding Avia?"

We were quiet for a moment as the weight of that soaked in.

Connor spoke first, "Two countries get together to complain about the big, bad monarch across the sea. Tired of taxes, tired of the navy bullying them wherever they go. They complain and whine and notice their neighbor, Evaness, gets all the good treaty terms. Evaness doesn't have to pay extra fees to trade with Lored for wine or spices, though every other nation does. The countries start to wonder why Evaness gets special treatment. Then Sedara sends their most powerful prince over, across the sea, to Evaness. And their jealousy grows."

"Bastard you mean," Declan chimed in.

"Still powerful as shite," Ryan countered, clapping Declan on the back and nodding for Connor to go on.

Connor stared out the window, thinking, before he continued, "Evaness prospers with the prince's magic. That prince becomes engaged to Evaness' crown princess, set to be a knight. And then ... the crown princess disappears."

"Dragon hunting," Declan put in wryly. "Officially, she was dragon hunting."

Connor nodded. "Yes. Officially. But ... Isla was a regular visitor here. She would have noticed that Avia was never in state meetings. Never went through the extensive trainings that Bloss did. Avia never sat in the back of the room, forced to observe every obnoxiously boring state interaction as Bloss was."

Declan picked up the thread of thought and continued to unravel the tangle. "She's not an idiot, Queen Isla. She would have started to wonder why—when dragon hunting is so dangerous—Queen Gela never prepared her second daughter for the crown."

"She guessed that Avia wasn't a second daughter," Connor concluded, turning back to us from the window.

My entire body felt tight as a wire. I hung on their every word. I knew what they'd say next, but I needed to hear it aloud.

ANN DENTON

Declan met my eyes as he said, "Isla began to wonder who Avia was ... if she wasn't a second daughter. Another bastard from Sedara? Maybe. But bastards aren't worth much in terms of treaties. We're far too common."

I went and grabbed Declan's hand. "Stop calling yourself that," I muttered. I bumped him with my hip, moving him slightly in his chair. He gave me a side smile but kept his eyes on Connor.

Connor leaned back against the window, ruffled his brown curls, and mused. "Isla began to wonder if Avia wasn't something else, some chess piece that gave Evaness power over Sedara."

Declan grimaced. "Rasle has plenty of spies and mages of their own. Cerena's newly a castle mage. Just hardly more than a hedge witch. If she could restore that old midwife's memory, imagine what Isla's people might have found."

"But how does Cheryn come into all of this? How does Sultan Raj fit in?" Ryan chimed in.

Blue suddenly started chirping madly, flying to the middle of the room and doing circles.

"If you're trying to tell us something, you're failing miserably," I told the little bird.

Blue landed on Fuzzy's back and pecked at him, tweeting more. Fuzzy just batted him away, too intent on sleeping.

Blue flew over to the bed and hopped underneath, chattering at Shiter. Shiter didn't exit the bed. Frustrated, Blue emerged and flew back to my shoulder. He perched on me and gave what could only have been a birdy sigh.

"Sorry, little fellow," I stroked his breast. "I kind of wish you could talk."

Declan snapped his fingers. "Wishes! That's it!" He stood, letting go of my hand so he could pace. "Cheryn has djinn. They make the perfect puppet soldiers because you can wish them to do whatever you want! Isla figured out who Avia is and she got Sultan Raj to send that djinni after Avia, disguised as Abbas. I bet his sons aren't even sick! That was just a ruse to keep them out of the way while he went after Avia."

"Why not use his sons?" I asked.

"His sons aren't even full djinn," Ryan dismissed. "Except for the young one."

Blue tweeted his agreement.

"And why put his heirs in danger if he had someone else?" Declan added. "He could just spread the rumor that they're ill."

Blue flew over and pecked Declan's hand.

"Ow!" Declan smacked at the bluebird and I had to rescue the poor thing.

"Sometimes his bird instincts take over," I said. "I'm guessing the same happens to Fuzzy." I jerked my head at the snoring bear. "Bears are mostly hibernating now."

I pulled Blue close to my chest and nuzzled him. "Sorry, little man. But you can't peck my knights, alright?"

Blue gave a sad little tweet.

"See, he's sorry."

Declan just glared, unconvinced.

Back to the grown-up conversation and not Bloss's menagerie obsession—Quinn's voice interrupted us.

"It's not an obsession! And it's not my fault that someone keeps cursing people."

As I said, on more adult topics, Sultan Raj's sons certainly aren't at the palace or anywhere near, Quinn thought at all of us. *So, the idea he got his heirs out of the way before he launched an attack is plausible. I've also counted twelve more groups of Raslen soldiers.*

I look around the room at each of my knights. There's still something that doesn't make sense. "So, Isla and Raj are angry at Sedara and us, by extension. They steal Avia. But, why not just renegotiate treaty terms? If they have Avia, they have the same power mother had."

Declan's lips pressed together in a thin line.

Ryan stepped forward. "You only want to negotiate if you think you'll lose, Little Dearling. In war, if you think you'll win, you press your advantage."

"That still doesn't explain why Isla's here now. And it doesn't explain how they think ... how could they possibly win against Sedara?" I asked.

I stared at three solemn faces.

"That's what we don't know," Declan admitted. "Because we still have no idea who or what Avia actually is."

CHAPTER EIGHTEEN

"*I* think it's safe to say that either she or her family are incredibly magically powerful, if Cheryn and Rasle feel confident enough to go to war with Sedara," Ryan muttered.

Connor nodded, "I agree. Evaness has gotten treated with kid gloves in comparison to the other nations."

Quinn's voice in all our heads was grim. *What if Avia's family did want her back? What if they're the missing link here?*

"That's why Sedara's worried," Connor chimed in. "That's why they care. They know Avia's family could damage them."

Declan's brow furrowed. "I can't think of anyone in recent history who could do such a thing."

I stood and moved toward him, "Maybe we shouldn't be thinking about recent history. These coins that keep showing up are centuries old. Shite! Dragons hoard coins.

Could this be from a dragon's lair? Could Avia's family be dragons?"

Declan stood. "Possible. Very possible. I need to get a book—"

The window rattled behind me and then something smashed into it. I nearly jumped out of my skin.

Blue was startled off my shoulder and had to pump his wings hard to avoid smashing into the floor.

We all turned to face Declan's balcony. There, in the window, standing on the balcony and carrying a sack on a stick over his shoulder—wearing two curl-toed shoes topped by bells—was Donaloo.

"Yoo-hoo! Peekaboo!" the wizard grinned.

I swallowed a groan. The man looked even madder than last time, if that was possible. His eye patch was a bright red, and his hair was as matted as a bush of thistles.

Connor—ever the diplomat—stepped forward, opened the door, took Donaloo's bag, and gestured for him to come in. I just assumed Quinn told Connor who'd arrived.

"Welcome, sir."

"Thank you, thank you! Out of the blue and into the stone. Seeking a dragon, never alone." Donaloo took off his jacket and a vial dropped out of his pocket onto Declan's balcony. Immediately, purple flames shot toward the sky. Connor yanked the old man inside so that he wouldn't be burnt to a crisp.

"This is the wizard?" Declan whispered skeptically to me.

Donaloo didn't seem to notice his close call. He smiled at me, "Dragons live with a flame inside, a beast that's hard to tame inside. You think you know, you think you know, but don't look up, look below."

I had no response to that. Had he heard our conversation? What the sarding hell did he even mean?

Donaloo stepped away from me and his eyes traveled around the room. "Oh, there's three! Well, that *is* a muddle, goodness me!" Donaloo stared around the room.

At first, I thought Donaloo was staring at my knights, but then he pointed at the bear. "You don't belong here, no siree. Nor does your brother, where be he?"

Shiter hopped out from under the bed. The bear and bunny lined up like school boys before the wizard, startling me. I pointed at Blue and told him. "Apparently, you need to get in line."

"He's fine, he's fine," Donaloo waved me off. "His future is set, but these two silly souls forget. They have travels ahead, ahead, through mists and miles and the undead."

That sounded ominous. And Fuzzy made the first sound I'd heard from him since he'd come to the castle (other than snoring). He moaned. It almost sounded as if a bear were complaining.

Donaloo just clucked at him. He ruffled the bear's fur like he was a dog. "Just follow me. If you do right, it'll all end well, you see!" He headed to Declan's sitting room without addressing any of us.

"Are we sure about this?" Declan whispered.

I shrugged. I wasn't certain of anything. Other than the fact that I was desperate. I'd just gotten my crown, my sister had been stolen, Sedara was threatening to seek her out—to no good end—and the two countries bordering me were gearing up for war. At the center of it all was my sister, who might be related to dragons, unless I believed the old coot.

Desperate is an understatement, you're drowning, my mind snarked at me.

And it was. We were beyond desperate.

We all stared at Donaloo. I was curious, fascinated, and a little put off all at once by his appearance. Donaloo wore tunic and tights, a horribly outdated fashion, and his tights had a massive rip near one thigh. His curly leg hair peeked out like a tuft of dead grass. It was horrifying and also impossible to ignore as he chatted with Shiter as if the bunny spoke back.

The wizard snapped his fingers and suddenly Quinn appeared in the midst of us, blinking and shaking his head. When he saw the wizard, he looked starstruck for a moment. Until he took in Donaloo's full appearance. And then he looked a little sad.

Still, he shuffled forward and gave the wizard a hug.

That set the old man chuckling as he patted Quinn's back, "Welcome home, young sailor, well met. You have a ring or four I'll bet?"

Quinn furrowed his brow. But his vest lit up with orange light. He dug into his pocket, producing four shiny rings.

"What are those?" I asked.

Took them off Abbas' hand, remember? I thought one of them might control that dragon ... remember how Abbas' had a ring that kind of glowed? I've been holding the rings. I tried them on. Wished the dragon would come back to the castle, peacefully and help protect you. Lead you to Avia. That sort of thing.

I nodded. "Well, I'm kind of pissed that didn't work."

I might have cut off the wrong hand, Quinn shrugged, undisturbed by that statement.

So ... if we take Abbas out of that stein, we might be able to find the ring that controls that dragon?

If a ring ever did control that dragon. We assumed the ring was a djinni that had shape-shifted.

Donaloo tutted at Quinn and walked over to pluck the rings out of my knight's palm. He took them and whistled for Blue.

Blue flew over and perched on the wizard's finger. Donaloo put a ring around the bluebird's leg and it magically shrunk to fit neatly against his leg, hardly visible.

I watched in fascination. The wizard didn't chant. He didn't use a huge handful of ingredients. The ring simply shrunk by power of will, or so it appeared. His magic was beyond anything I'd seen.

"What are you doing?" I asked the mage.

"Returning that which should not have been taken if morals were held and not forsaken," Donaloo sing-songed as he picked up Shiter. He didn't seem to notice that the rabbit dropped a number of pellets right onto his shoe.

"So, do these rings belong to them? Are they djinn?"

"Not in whole, they're broken souls."

I resisted the urge to grab Donaloo's ear and shake him until he gave me a straight answer.

Declan saw my frustration and came over. He put his hand on my neck and gently massaged. "I think he means they're part-djinn. That's my guess anyway."

Donaloo patted his nose and pointed at Declan.

I tilted my head, deep in thought. "We already believe Sultan Raj is involved in all of this."

Declan's fingers dug further into my neck as he caught my train of thought. He stared at the animals. "His sons are missing."

"And there are three animals here."

"He's got five sons," Ryan interjected.

Quinn added to all of us, *There are four rings and only three animals here. The fourth ring could belong to the dragon. We could still be right.*

"If the full djinn brother came disguised as Abbas … theoretically he'd know enough about his brother that he could act like him and the servants wouldn't be able to tell the difference." Declan moved his hands to rub my shoulders. I wasn't certain if it was to help him think or for my comfort. But I didn't argue. I was tense. And his hands were warm, smoothing out the knots in my shoulders until they were butter-soft. I leaned back into him.

"Did your brother do this to you?" I asked Blue.

Abbas was a shite piece of work. I didn't put it past him to find someone to put an irreversible spell on his brothers and make himself the only heir.

Blue shook his head, side to side, a very definitive 'no.'

"Your father?"

Blue stared straight at me. His head didn't move. And I recognized the tell-tale signs of a geas. Under one myself, I knew exactly what it felt like.

"The sultan had a spell put on his own sons," I breathed, "But not to hide them. He had them cursed. In a way that's impossible to break."

I crushed Blue to my chest, smothering him in a hug. No matter what my mother had done, she'd have never done that to me. My anger at Raj flared.

Declan's voice was thoughtful. "Could Avia be part dragon? If the dragon isn't the fourth brother ... if the ring didn't recall him ... is the dragon we fought actually her mother or father?"

My chest tightened. Dragons had vicious instincts. Lady Agatha hadn't been wrong when she'd suggested it was unusual that a dragon let Avia live.

Sarding hell. Is my baby sister a dragon? I wondered. I'd always considered dragons to be monsters. They'd stolen my birth father from me.

Donaloo burst into laughter. "Don't be ridiculous! Dragons are *so* conspicuous! The evil you seek has lost its name and has no power over fire or flame."

The wizard wove through us, dismissing our serious conversation with a wave of his hand as he carried Shiter toward Fuzzy. He waved a finger at the two animals. "You two have far to go. You should not be here, no, no no. Say goodbye, goodbye and without a cry."

He enlarged a ring and put it on Shiter's paw, then thinned it until it disappeared under the purple-grey fur. He put a black ring on Furry's claw and did the same. "Twenty-four hours and no more, for you to find what fate has in store." He patted Fuzzy on the rump and walked to the hall door.

"Wait!" I called. Donaloo turned to look back at me.

"If all these men are half-djinn, can't they just wish themselves back to human?"

Declan spoke as he wrapped his arms around my waist. "No. Djinn can't make wishes for themselves."

I looked at Blue, "I could wish for you!"

Blue gave a sad little tweet and nipped my finger in thanks. At least I assumed it was thanks.

"A wish itself wouldn't be enough to undo the powerful magic surrounding you," Donaloo shook his head sadly at little Blue before he continued, "Only a true heart will do."

"And isn't there an awful price every time a half-djinn gives out a wish?" Declan asked. "I thought I read somewhere that every wish granted cost a living nightmare. It's why it's so hard to get half djinn to give out their wishes."

I turned to the bluebird for confirmation. Blue gave a single nod of his head.

A wish wouldn't save him.

My poor little feathered friend. I stroked his belly. It looked like this prince would be stuck as a bird forever.

CHAPTER NINETEEN

*D*onaloo ruined the contemplative moment by shouting, "Now, to the Mage's tower! Like the bloom of a flower!" Donaloo disappeared with an "Oop—" that got cut off.

"Sard!" My heart fell. I didn't think he meant to do that.

We all exchanged a concerned glance.

"I think we need to reconsider whether we're going to have him help—" Declan's sentence was cut off as an earthquake shook the castle.

"Shite!" Ryan yelled, coming forward to protect me as furniture toppled over.

When the waves had settled, and the earth stopped undulating, we all shared a look.

Donaloo, Quinn thought.

That sarding wizard better not have just destroyed my castle, I seethed.

We ran, jostling one another. We hurried through the castle toward Cerena's tower, the menagerie bounding along behind us, guards trailing them. I ignored the stares of the courtiers we passed. They were all shaken by the earthquake anyway.

When we reached the base of the mage's spire, we could immediately tell what was wrong. The entire tower had turned into a giant mass of vines. Flowering plants had erupted through the stone floor. Bright pink coral honey-suckle, drooping purple wisteria blossoms, orange trum-pets, flowers every color of the rainbow bloomed on the tower. In midwinter.

Cerena came down the newly moss-covered steps, her eyes wide. She forgot to hide her limp as she stared in shock at the walls. Her hand pulsed with an orb of fire, that she wielded like a weapon.

One of the orange trumpet flowers suddenly shot off the vine and swallowed the flame in her hand. It glowed, expanding until the flame was a bright ball inside its petals. Then it belched out a puff of smoke and fell to the ground with a sigh.

"What the sard—" Connor whispered next to me. It was a sign of shock that he was cursing in public. Connor never cursed in public. I grabbed his hand.

"Fire eaters," Declan peered closer at the orange flowers. "Interesting." Of course, he would find a damned magical flower interesting after everything that happened.

"What in the sard is going on? Who in the sarding hell is this?" Cerena yelled when she saw me.

She jerked her head toward Donaloo, who was following her, a bit of a bewildered grin on his face as his hand traced over some yellow flowers.

I took a deep breath and reminded myself not to sigh in public. Guards surrounded us and no doubt courtiers were running this way. Isla's entourage was still packing to leave. Every single one of my provinces had a duchess or duke here.

"He volunteered to be your new assistant."

Cerena's nostrils flared and I could sense a fit of rage coming on. I let go of Connor and quickly walked over.

I grabbed Cerena's hands, guiding her around several haphazard stones in the floor that had been displaced by the quake. I led her away from Donaloo toward a window.

"He's a wizard," I whispered. "A true wizard. We found him living in the clouds—"

"His head's certainly there."

"Literally. His house was levitated into the clouds and he's three hundred, or so we believe—"

"Ew! Three hundred! He pinched my ass," Cerena looked horrified.

"I'm not joking."

"Neither am I."

I tilted my head and stared, silently reproaching her. "He can help. He offered to help us with the dragon that took my sister."

"You honestly trust this witless fool?" she gestured at the wizard.

Donaloo was fingering the yellow blooms and the vine started glowing. A crowd gathered behind him. Suddenly, the vine shivered and let out an ear-piercing shriek. We all covered our ears.

Donaloo shushed the flower, but I had to blast it with peace before it settled down.

When I did that, Donaloo accidentally stepped into the green light. That made him go limp, which made him trip. That meant he fell right into a magenta flower that started to smolder. As did Donaloo's sleeve. He yelped and jumped, and the smolder on his arm was fed with air, turning into a bright flame.

Declan held out his hand, lighting the room up in a blaze of yellow. Water splashed down on all of us, soaking our clothes. As usual, Declan overdid it with his power. We stood in a good two inches of water afterward. My slippers were soaked.

Cerena turned to look at me, pushing her sodden hair out of her face. "Are you sure you want him here?"

I rubbed the water from my eyes. "No. But, we need the help."

She gritted her teeth. "He asked me about the prisoner."

I widened my eyes. "We hadn't mentioned that."

She glanced behind me and suddenly Quinn was next to me.

I looked at Quinn. *He knows about Abbas. I told him we had a problem with a djinni. But I didn't tell him we had one imprisoned.*

Quinn put a comforting hand on my back and thought, *He can be trusted.*

My eyes wandered toward the flood and the Donaloo's burnt sleeve meaningfully.

Quinn shook his head. *I promise. His thoughts are all good. Ask Connor.*

I waved Connor over.

"Have you sensed any deception from Donaloo?" I whispered.

Connor shook his head. "No. But are we worried about deception or competence here?"

I sighed.

Quinn reiterated, *His thoughts are clear. Not muddled like his actions.*

You're sure?

259

I'm sure.

You trust him?

Yes.

I stared at Quinn a long moment, but his eyes didn't waver. He meant it.

"Quinn says you can trust him," I told Cerena.

I wasn't so sure. I didn't think the old man meant any harm. He was powerful. But at the same time … he'd just turned my tower into a flower pot. And then set himself on fire. I didn't think he was incredibly reliable. But Quinn was my knight. And he and Connor had powers I didn't.

And what was love if not trust? I trusted them.

Cerena thought differently. She shook her head and rolled her eyes but marched back up the stairs, grumbling the whole way.

Donaloo followed and Quinn held out his arm to escort me up.

Where is she going? I asked Quinn.

I had her seal the djinni in the container we captured him in. Then she hid it in her tower. Hopefully Donaloo knows how to extract more information from him.

The stairs underneath our feet suddenly become covered in bright green clover. A deer appeared out of nowhere and bounded down the steps, forcing Quinn and I to push apart and hug the wall so we wouldn't be trampled.

This might be a bad idea. He's turning the palace into a wood-land forest.

First off, the animals showed up before he came. You can't say that's on him. That Raj's fault. And secondly ... he fixed me, Quinn's mental voice was tight, tense. *He's incredibly powerful.*

I don't doubt that. I mean, feel this. I ran my hand over the flowers. They felt completely real. Until I touched a purple one and the petals suddenly shuddered. The petals moved and rearranged themselves and a tiny pixie popped up, fluttering purple flower petal wings. She reached back and unsheathed a sword that had looked like a yellow stamen on her back. "Do not touch!" she growled.

I held up my hands in surrender. "I'm sorry. I didn't know."

She narrowed her eyes but sheathed the sword and returned to her place on the vine, her wings settling back again until she looked like nothing more than a flower again.

I widened my eyes and shared a look with Quinn.

He just raised an eyebrow. *Built in tower defense,* he thought, smugly, defending his hero.

Built in tower insanity, I thought, but tried hard not to project that thought to him.

I simply kept walking up the stairs, all my knights following behind.

We entered Cerena's chamber, me doubting the sanity of one of the magicians. Walking into her room only made me begin to doubt them both.

Donaloo stood to the side of the room, unconcerned. Cerena was throwing things, pulling her room apart at the seams. "It was here!" she shouted. "I had it!" She threw aside a large chameleon skin, an animal paw, and a bronze contraption that looked suspiciously like a penis.

Cerena whirled around, limped toward me, her eyes livid. "He's gone!"

She held up an empty beer stein.

"The slave defies his master only to find a new one. Rebellions require obedience and expedience, ingredients for deviance."

I didn't even listen to Donaloo's drivel. The sight of the empty stein was a lance to my gut. The djinn, fake Abbas, whoever he was, had escaped.

I met Quinn's eyes. His were blazing.

There's no sarding way he got out of that himself! Declan and I checked the spells and watch her seal him in.

What's that mean?

Someone freed him.

CHAPTER TWENTY

*I*t hit me. Isla. That's why she was here. Why she'd come so quickly and suddenly. Why she'd broken protocol. She'd come to free the djinni.

I wanted to use her crown to smack her across the face. That bitch. That sarding clever bitch made me waste away in meetings with her … I tried to think past my anger and put the pieces together.

I'd survived and captured Abbas. She and Raj hadn't planned on that. Maybe they'd planned to plunder Evaness for resources or just take over. But either way, a powerful magical slave wasn't something they'd want to lose.

I turned to Cerena and demanded, "Has Isla been here? Any of her people?"

"Just your friend and her father."

Ember. Donovon. Ember had already gone. My heart constricted at the thought that she might have done it.

I looked at Connor. "Didn't you say Sedara executed her family?"

He nodded gravely, "For smuggling."

Ice ran through my veins. It was her. It had to be her.

"Get her father locked up."

Ryan nodded. "I can have his quarters searched."

I knotted my fingers. "We should search all of her people. One of them might have it on their person." I said it, even though my gut told me Ember had taken it. We couldn't chance that. We couldn't let them get Abbas back in their clutches. He'd already nearly killed me twice. I didn't know if I'd get lucky a third time.

Connor grabbed my shoulder. "Bloss Boss, think carefully. I don't think we can do that. If we publicly accuse Rasle and don't find proof, we're offending a country already prepared for war."

"Their soldiers are on the shores, away from us! Preparing to go across the ocean," I threw my hands out in frustration. I wanted nothing more than to tear apart Isla's gowns and find that evil, sharp-toothed djinni.

Isla's not stupid. She came here to take your measure, distract you, and free that djinni. It doesn't mean she won't attack you. She has back up plans in place, I'm certain.

I turned to Donaloo. "Rasle and Cheryn have amassed troops on the beach. Who are they going to fight?"

"Why ask a question, when the answer's already known? Those who seek power always seek to topple the one who sits on the highest throne." Donaloo's answer confirmed everything we'd suspected.

They were going to attack Sedara. But sarding hell, Quinn was right. I couldn't jump into accusing other monarchs when I didn't have proof in-hand. I'd look crazy. Unfit. I needed to know more. I needed to know what they thought their trump card was.

I stared again at the wizard, "Who are Avia's real parents?"

"What creature's unseen in the deep, deep dark? What creatures have black minds but the voices of larks?"

Could he mean dragons? They live in caves? Fairies? I asked Quinn.

Declan will have to—

Yes. I know. Look it up. Wait! I have an idea!

I touched Donaloo's unburnt sleeve. "My mother was supposed to have left documents for me. Confidential documents left in the care of her mage. He passed before I got them. I understand they were concealed with magic. Possibly in this tower. Do you think you could retrieve them?"

Donaloo gave a happy grin and dance. "Mother to daughter, secrets revealed. Knowledge unlocked and scrolls unsealed."

Scrolls and papers fell from the ceiling of the mage's tower, twirling and falling lightly like snow.

I snatched one out of thin air.

Answers! We'll finally get sarding answers! I thought.

But no sooner did Cerena reach out to grab a page than the entire mass of parchment transformed into a swarm of bees.

I screamed and covered my head as buzzing filled my ears.

Quinn swatted one away and was immediately stung. He grabbed his sore hand.

The rest of my knights flung their hands out to protect their faces. The bees grew angry at the intrusion. They attacked.

Stings rained down on my head and neck. I swatted the bees, screeching at them. I lashed out, blasting the room with so much peace power that everyone swayed. The bees clattered to the floor, turning back into pages once they hit the stones. I swooped down, grabbing several, ignoring the gashes in my wrists and the pain from a wound deep in my thigh. Declan did the same, albeit slowly. He was dazed from the peace magic.

Ryan scooped me up and started healing me despite my protests.

"You're getting blood all over the pages!" he scolded.

I forced myself to be still and take deep breaths. My heart calmed down as my wounds closed.

We're close to answers, I told myself. The closest we've been.

But the moment Donaloo bent and picked up a page, they turned into ants. The little black insects scurried around the room, slipping into cracks, crawling onto the vines, disappearing into the flowers and disturbing the purple pixies.

"A very thorough protection spell," Cerena looked appreciative. Not angry. Like she should have. As I felt.

Sarding shite.

Our answers were getting lost in the flower petals and leaves. I lunged out of Ryan's arms, only half-healed from my gashes, eyes locked on an ant. I squished it against a vine in the wall. It turned back into a page under my fingers. "Squish them!" I cried.

Everyone fell to stomping and smacking—everyone but Donaloo and Cerena who froze after Declan yelled, "Not you! The pages are protected from you!"

I was somewhat surprised they listened. But I didn't have time to analyze. I was too busy smacking ants on the floor.

Declan tried to shake a purple vine, and that sent a whole group of pixies flying at him. His shirt was shredded in seconds by their tiny yellow swords and he released the vine, backing away. Donaloo tried to get out of his way and backed into a blue and green vine, which sprayed mist out over us. A mist which smelled very much like skunk.

The door swung open. Jorad appeared. His lip curled when he smelled us. It curled further when he had the opportunity to look around the room and saw us. "The party from Rasle are ready to take their leave. I suppose I should have them wait, while you all get ... as clean as might be possible."

Sard it all. Of course. Rasle was leaving. I had a dinner with my duchesses to attend. And I smelled like a chamber pot. I pressed my lips together and took a deep breath through my nose. I had to decide if I wanted to offend Isla by making her wait or offend her by appearing like this.

I looked down at the two tiny bits of parchment in my hand. They were all I'd retrieved. My knights had similar results. Most of the pages had been lost.

My eyes scanned one of the scraps I held. I wasn't ready to decide yet what the hell I was going to do with Isla. All I really wanted was proof she was going to war. Proof she'd ordered that djinni to attack. Proof enough so I could lock her in my dungeon.

The pages didn't provide proof. The couple sentences were vague. Until one phrase caught my eye.

"She oversteps. There will never be eight kingdoms—"

The parchment cut off.

Eight kingdoms. I glanced up at Donaloo. He'd mentioned eight kingdoms before. And I'd mentally dismissed him as foolish. I wanted to ask. But I wasn't certain I'd get a straight answer.

Jorad interrupted my thoughts. "What way would you like to offend Rasle, Your Majesty? With your smell or your tardiness?"

Gods, I needed to smack that butler again.

"Bloss," Cerena called softly. "If you don't mind, could I try to help?"

I turned to her, where she shifted from foot to foot, a small smile on her face, as though the old woman was excited.

"Help?"

"With you … your gown," she gave an embarrassed shrug. "Isn't it every little hedge-witch's dream to be a fairy godmother?"

Relief and warmth coursed through me. I gave a single nod toward Cerena. "Of course."

She balled her hands into fists and waved them excitedly, before giving a miniature clap. "Yes. One princess-to-the-ball spell coming up!"

She scuttled around the room, yanking ingredients out of the vines that drooped leaves over her shelves. She pulled out salt, rosemary, her mortar and pestle, and the wing of a butterfly. She tried to climb to reach a high shelf but couldn't.

Donaloo snapped his fingers and whatever ingredient Cerena wanted floated down in its box.

"Thank you," she gave a sharp nod as she set everything out on her work table. Immediately, she set to mixing and muttering.

Every so often Donaloo would mutter some advice.

Cerena mixed every ingredient in the pestle and spit in it, making a paste. Then she opened the box and said excitedly, "Last thing we need!"

To my horror, she pulled out a human eyeball, complete with an optic nerve trailing off it.

I swallowed my disgust. "Is that really necessary?"

Both Cerena and Donaloo looked up at me.

"It's an essential ingredient. It ensures all eyes are on you."

With that, she took the pestle and smashed the eye into the mix. Then, a look of triumph on her face, she handed the mortar to me and said, "Eat."

For a fleeting moment I wished Wyle was back in the castle. He'd never have made this for me.

But Cerena looked so proud. And Jorad looked so impatient. And I had a foreign queen waiting.

So, I tried very hard not to think about what I was doing as I stared at Connor, swiped my finger in the bowl, then put it between my lips.

The change was instantaneous. It was as if a small whirlwind surrounded me and then disappeared.

My hair was suddenly up. I couldn't see it, but I could feel the massive jewels set into the crown I wore. Curls fell neatly down onto my neck. My dress was a deep wine color with tiny rubies lining a plunging neckline.

I sniffed. I didn't smell skunk.

I smiled. If it weren't for eating the eyeball, this would be a wonderful way to get ready each morning. "Thank you."

Cerena glowed.

I swept past my men to take Jorad's extended arm.

"Wait, can we eat that too?" Ryan asked. "I don't want her going down there alone."

He scooped a bit onto his finger, and I yanked Jorad to a stop to wait for him.

Cerena shook her head frantically but Ryan had already brought the mixture to his lips. He didn't eat a full scoop like I did, or else the magic wasn't as effective on his enor-

ANN DENTON

mous size. But a wind whipped around him and a jeweled
crown appeared on his head, inset with yellow topaz.
Rouge appeared on his cheeks. And a bright yellow gown
ripped right up the back seam as it tried to encase him.
My general was left half-dressed in woman's clothes.

I exploded in laughter. "I wish I had a court painter here
to capture you in all your glory!"

Ryan bit his thumb at me.

I simply wiggled my fingers in a parting wave and left him
to deal with the fallout of his choice. How he'd sneak all
the way back across the castle without anyone seeing him
in his current state was his problem.

My own problems were far far worse.

I had to look the woman who'd arranged to have my sister
kidnapped, who'd sent a djinni that had tried to kill me. I
had to face the woman who'd stolen my prisoner and
might even now, have him. I had to face her, lie to her,
and let her walk away.

Because I couldn't prove a sarding thing.

My crown felt as sharp a knife. It cleaved me in two.

What I wanted to do and what I had to do had never been
further apart.

CHAPTER TWENTY-ONE

I strolled into the winter courtyard without a cloak, letting the cold air cool my rage.

The moonlight fell on the cobblestones and painted them a soft chalky white until a cloud passed overhead. I glanced up to see more clouds gathering. The sky looked dark in the distance.

Isla and her entourage were gathered, their winged bears were lined up and saddled in the background.

I strode up to her and grasped her outstretched hand. I gave the warmest smile I could manage.

"Thank you so much for being the first to welcome me to my throne. I look forward to working together for years to come."

"I think you will settle into your new role nicely," Isla patted the back of my hand. "Next time we see one another, I hope things will be vastly different."

I caught the double meaning in her words but kept my face pleasantly neutral. She didn't know I was aware of anything. It was best not to give away that small advantage.

I gestured behind me. "I want to apologize for my knights. They wanted to come say goodbye, but they ran afoul of the wrong end of a skunk."

Isla pressed her lips together, smothering either a laugh or whatever she really wanted to say. "You do seem to have a bit of an animal infestation."

I nodded. "Yes. We do. Perhaps they can sense that I'll protect them."

"From what?"

"From those who use magic to hurt others," I replied, studying her features.

She simply raised her brow.

I didn't have my knights here to hold me back, so I pushed further. "The animals who come to me are people who've been transformed and trapped by magic."

Isla's eyes darkened. "How interesting."

"Isn't it?" I smiled.

"Trapping and transforming others is a very, very *unfortunate* practice," Isla responded.

She meant Avia. I knew she did.

My voice was thin and tight as I responded, "One I would never approve of."

Isla's face tilted as she studied me. "I almost believe that."

"My mother used enough magic to bind me that I could not abide such methods."

Isla raised an eyebrow. Then she leaned forward. "Never say never. When people are starving and revolting … a queen will do whatever it takes."

"So, I should forgive my mother then?"

She smiled and pulled her fur-lined cloak tighter around her neck. "Bloss, I have so enjoyed our visit."

Back to formalities and trivial lies? I thought. Fine. Two can play at that.

"As have I. Perhaps next time your daughter could accompany you," I said.

Isla's lip stiffened. That was her only tell.

I leaned toward her. "Isla?"

"Yes, that would be lovely," Isla's wide grin was back in place.

But I didn't buy it. Isla was worried about her daughter. She should be. Unless their magical accomplice was able to wipe out an entire navy, Isla and Raj were probably in for horrific losses against Sedara. If Isla was killed, Queen Diamoni wouldn't think twice about punishing her daughter. Taking away the throne would be the least of those punishments.

"Are you certain you want to leave things this way?" I asked.

A long silence stretched out as Isla studied me.

"Whatever do you mean?" she finally asked lightly.

I opened my mouth to speak but a huge bolt of lightning zagged across the sky, drawing our gazes up. It was low enough that I could smell the charge in the air. Thunder followed shortly after.

Isla pulled her hand back. "We'd better hurry."

"In such a storm? Surely, you can stay the night? For your own safety, of course."

I could have Quinn's people search your things, I thought as I smiled brightly and continued, "My duchesses would love to have the chance to visit—"

"It's not a long flight. If we hurry, we can stay ahead of the storm."

The storm was coming from the west. From Rasle. But Isla was clearly determined to leave.

"Isla, I look forward to working with you for many years to come. And I promise, I'll work with Declan and his schedule, to help you in the most expedient manner possible."

Isla's eyes gleamed as another flash of lightning charged across the sky. I could see the jagged bolt reflected in her eyes. And for a second, I felt I got a glimpse inside. Not at the composed queen, but a glimpse at the raw, angry energy that fueled her. Isla was volatile. On edge. She thought she'd win. But she wasn't quite certain. That made her desperate.

The realization sent a chill down my spine. I shivered.

"You really shouldn't step out without a cloak, Bloss," Isla's maid handed her a pair of riding gloves and she pulled them on. "The cold can kill you."

I felt the threat all the way down to my bones. My hackles rose and before I could think through the consequences my mouth spit out, "Not if you do so first, Isla."

Her lips quirked, "What a sense of humor."

Behind me I heard a noise.

Donaloo shuffled down the steps of the palace, Shiter cuddled in his arms.

"Your Majesty!" he called. "Your Majesty, wait!"

"Yes?" I turned, wondering what the befuddled wizard could possibly want.

Donaloo held up the bunny. "Queen Isla, a parting gift."

"You can't give her Shiter!" I said. The loon wizard was trying to give away a person!

Shiter shited. I thought that meant he agreed with me.

Donaloo shook his head. "This is not a rabbit. This is a heart in search of a match. I believe your daughter's heart could use a protector?"

Isla took a step back, "My daughter is married, sir!"

I just stared at Donaloo in shock. Where had his ridiculous rhyming gone?

Donaloo straightened, fixing his one good eye on Isla. The lightning crackled again, and the wind whipped up. For a moment, I didn't see the fool wizard. I saw a man who radiated power, a dark glow surrounding him. "Do you want to refuse my gift, Isla?" his voice boomed across the courtyard and one of Isla's bears let out a whine.

The elder queen slowly stepped forward and took the rabbit from Donaloo's hands.

Then she whipped around, marching swiftly to her bears.

I watched her mount. The bears wings extended. Then, with military precision, her entire entourage rose as one into the lightning-riddled sky.

"What the hell happened to your rhyming?" I asked Donaloo.

"There's a time for rhyme and a time to speak clear. Time's running out, have to face what you fear."

"You do it to annoy me, don't you?" I narrowed my eyes at the old wizard. "This whole senile bit is a ploy to amuse yourself."

His eyes glittered with mirth, but Donaloo didn't answer me. The wizard just straightened his red eye patch, clicked his tongue, and walked in a zigzag up the stairs.

I stared after him.

Gods, I hope the senility is a ploy, I thought.

I stepped into the main hall, glad to be rid of one enemy, only to be confronted by another.

Jorad sneered at me. "Your Majesty, I need a moment."

The butler turned without waiting for me to answer, assumed I would follow, and strode down the main hall. He opened the door to the rose parlor.

I took a deep breath and stomped down on my inclination to smack him. Then followed him.

When Jorad had shut the door behind me, he turned on me in a fury. "You told him to sleep with Aiden!"

"What?"

Jorad pointed. Over in the corner of the room, Willard cowered. The sweating, fat, pig-of-a-noble spy widened his eyes and stared hard at me, willing me to back him up.

Oh, no he didn't try to throw me to the wolves. My eyes widened in rage.

Willard pleaded silently.

I turned to Jorad and said, "I told him to keep an eye on Aiden. To stick with him. I didn't tell him to stick the duke."

Willard's wobbly cheeks grew red with fury.

"You'd better have something useful for me," I glared. I was furious Willard would try to use me to justify his cheating.

Jorad slammed the door as he went back into the main hall.

Willard, turned to me, red in the face.

I held up a hand. "Don't. That's your problem to deal with. Tell me what you know."

Willard clenched his hands. He tried to calm his own temper. The entitled shite had expected me to fall on the sword for him.

"Donovon's been snooping in the halls," Willard said. "Even wandered toward the royal wing."

"He's been taken care of." With any luck, Ryan's men had already locked him in the dungeon. "Anything else?"

"Malia has plans to go out this evening," Willard stuttered. "I-I-I … she said that the weather change was giving her a headache." Willard swallowed and leaned closer, his foul breath far too close to my face. "Mother offered her a compress. She suggested mother feel the same shortly after the meal."

"You were in the room?"

He shook his head. "Mother's dressing room. I was selecting her dress for dinner."

"Did she say anything else?"

"She said a bit of fresh air always helps her clear her head."

Malia was a sympathizer at the very least. She could be more. She could be recruiting for Rasle and Cheryn. For this shite rebellion against Sedara and their navy.

I nodded at Willard, "Well done, Willard."

Willard's eyes widened at the praise. It must have been rare for the bumbling idiot.

I walked off wondering what the hell Malia was playing at. I turned to one of the guards that always followed me like a shadow.

"Everyone knows that Willard's playing spy for me, don't they?"

The young man nodded solemnly. "Yes, Your Majesty."

"The nobles, too?"

My guard nodded. "He's not exactly subtle."

"No, he's not."

I thanked the guard and turned back toward the stairs. As I climbed, I pondered what Malia was trying to tell me. Because she wasn't an idiot. She knew Willard was his mother's lapdog. And unless she lived under a rock, she'd heard by now that Willard was my informant. That meant her message wasn't intended for Lady Agatha. It was intended for me.

She wanted me out of the castle shortly after dinner.

The question was, why?

The only way to know the answer was to go. Whether or not I went for an obvious stroll or took an Invisibility potion was the question. I thought about that as I ascended the stairs.

I met my knights in my chamber. They had all cleaned up and gotten dressed for the formal dinner with the duchesses and Duke Aiden.

But Quinn looked stormy and the rest of the knights were arguing when I walked in.

"We can't go! We're expected to make an appearance," Connor growled.

Quinn mind-yelled, *I wasn't saying all of us need to go. I can go.*

"Where do you want to go?"

Quinn turned to me, his grey eyes flashing. *One of my men says there's a gathering in a pub down in the capital. He's heard talk against Sedara. I think it's related to whatever Isla and Raj are doing. Gathering the troops. I think they're recruiting even in Evaness.*

"Then you definitely need to go. I want to go, too," I responded.

That caused an uproar.

"No," Ryan flat-out denied me.

"There's no real reason for you to go," Declan argued.

"You have to stay for the dinner," Connor's face was shocked. "I can't just explain your absence."

Sard. Sard, sard, sard, I thought.

My gut twisted. They were good arguments. Logical arguments. But Isla and Raj were trying to start a rebellion and trying to drag my people into it. Once they attacked, Sedara was certain to drag the seven kingdoms of Kenmare into the fight.

I couldn't stand by. I couldn't just let them actively recruit my people into what might be a death trap. What would be a death trap for so many. War always was.

And I'd been fighting my instincts since Avia had been taken. I'd stayed and met with Isla when I'd wanted to hunt for my sister. I'd sat through an idiotic meeting with my nobles that was a shite waste of time. I'd sat on my hands and followed the rules long enough.

The world was going to shite even.

And I was done doing what I was told.

"I'm going. We'll have to figure it out." My tone brooked no argument.

My knights ignored my tone.

"You're not going!" Ryan marched forward and stared me down.

But I wasn't going to cave on this.

Declan came to stand beside Ryan. And watching the two of them, side by side, I realized how I could go with Quinn and get them off my back.

A smile stretched across my face.

"I'm going with Quinn. But I'm going to the dinner, too."

"You can't be in two places at once!" Connor cried.

My eyes fell on Declan and he swallowed hard as he realized what I was about to say.

"Oh, yes, I can."

CHAPTER TWENTY-TWO

"*Y*ou look amazing," I gushed.

Declan pouted and my lower lip jutted out. A crease formed between my eyebrows. I was staring at a very, very unhappy version of myself. Apparently, taking a disguise spell to transform into me for sex was one thing. Dressing as me and pretending to be me in public did not have the same appeal. Declan was pissed.

"You're the only one who can do it," I soothed, stroking his arm, which looked exactly like my arm. It was thin and soft, a few freckles dotting the lower half.

Declan stood in a chemise in my chambers. We had kicked all servants—even Ginnifer—out while we had him take the potion.

But now I had to convince him to stop frowning and follow through. I stared into Declan's eyes. "The royal exclusion for spells only applies to you." Only the royal family could use spells with ease inside the castle. Otherwise, the counter spells set by the castle mages throughout the centuries would activate and strip the magic. Human magics at least.

"Ryan could do it," Declan huffed in my pouty voice. I sounded awful. Whiny, like a child. "I was gonna look through those papers from your mom. Make Ryan do it."

I turned to Connor. "I don't actually sound like that, do I?"

"That's what you're worried about?" Declan screeched.

"Calm down," I reached out and put my hands on either cheek. I waited until his eyes focused on me. "Declan, you know me. You've known me since we were fourteen. I'm awkward at these dinners. I used to be awkward because I was shy. Now I'm awkward because I don't say the right things at the right times. If it weren't for this damned crown, I'd have been chucked from the court ages ago." I stared into hazel eyes. "There's no way you can mess up. They all hate me in there anyway."

"They don't."

"They find me annoying."

"Well, that's just a fact of—"

I punched him in the tit.

"Hey!" he grabbed his chest.

"Don't call me annoying and you won't get hit." I narrowed my eyes at him, but I wrapped my arms around his neck. I pulled him forehead to forehead. "I need you, Dec. You're the only one."

He sighed. He was caving, I could feel it. I lingered, forehead to forehead for a moment before I pulled back to look into his eyes—my eyes.

"Your blue eyes are so much prettier," I told him.

"Not true," his hands came around my waist.

"Dec, I can't let our people get involved in this. It seems like Malia might be already. That's her choice and she'll be stripped of her title for it. Aiden might get the ax. But civilians? These people are farmers and bakers. Not fighters. And there's no way they'll understand or be told everything that's really going on. I have to hear how Isla and Raj are convincing people to rebel against Sedara. I need to know so we can figure out how to counter it."

Declan gave a rough sigh, "I still think Ryan could do it."

I giggled and leaned closer. "Everyone will expect him to shadow me. With that many other nobles around, they'll expect him and the rest of my guards to be watching like hawks for assassination attempts."

"Assassination attempts. *That* makes me feel better."

"Would it make you feel better if I promised I'd go pearl diving later?" I whispered.

A flush crept over Declan's cheeks. My cheeks. I slid my hands down from his neck, toward the breasts that started heaving as my fingers got close. My fingertips grazed the nipples. Back and forth, I teased him. I waited for the buds to harden under my fingers. When I could feel the little nipples protruding, I grabbed the left one and twisted slightly. "I need to protect our people. And I need your help." I leaned in and kissed the sensitive pulse at his neck.

Behind me, Connor groaned.

Ryan urged, "Kiss each other."

Mirth and lust bubbled in my stomach as I stepped closer to Declan. The other knights were clearly enjoying watching two of me.

"Will you do this for me, Dec?" I crooned.

"Sard it all," he cursed. And then he grabbed me and pulled me into a deep kiss.

I'd never kissed a woman before. I had no idea what to expect. The hands that held me weren't huge. They didn't cover my entire ass like I was used to. I wasn't leaning up, only forward. I didn't feel dominated or protected as I did with a man. It was different. I felt ... adored. The soft swipes of his tongue against mine. The plush, soft body pressing into me. The hand that traced down my spine knew exactly where to go in order to elicit shivers of the best kind. I felt myself grow wet and pressed closer. I loved the way our breasts mashed together, my nipples scratching against the fabric of my dress. A warm, fiery sensation filled my stomach as the kiss grew from tender to fierce.

Declan grabbed my hands and pinned them behind my back, making my breasts press forward and my back arch.

Then those lips left mine and a blazing hot trail of kisses went down my neck.

A knock at the door had us jumping apart.

"Sarding hell!" Ryan cursed, stuffing his dick back into his pants.

Connor took a second to finish himself, spurting all over the floor. He didn't bother to clean it up before he tucked himself away, wiped his hand on a handkerchief in his pocket, and made his way to answer the door.

Only Quinn wasn't touching himself. His eyes burned with heat, but his hands were firmly fisted by his sides.

I looked back at Declan sheepishly. "You'll do it, love?"

Declan sighed, "I'll do it. But our first time is not gonna be like this," he gestured at the girl body he was wearing.

"Deal," I grinned. "I love your body more anyway."

That earned me a small smile.

Connor pulled the door open to reveal Jorad.

"Dinner is—" Jorad saw Declan and me, his eyes doing a double take. He didn't even ask. His lips merely thinned. "Dinner is served."

"We'll be right there," Connor told him. He shut the door right in Jorad's face.

Ryan looked at me, "Bloss, are you sure—"

"Yes," I pulled off my red dress and tossed it to Declan. I did the same with my crown. And then I drank one of the disguise spells I'd had Cerena and Donaloo whip up. He'd shown her a trick or two. And the potion tasted like strawberries and cream, which was a vast improvement over the potions I'd bought from her in the past.

I turned into a portly young man. So portly that I got stuck in my chemise.

"Dammit, I need help getting this off."

Ryan came over to yank the garment off me. "This isn't nearly as fun when you look like that."

"Good. Or I'd be worried," I retorted. Then I pawed through the stash of clothes Quinn had brought for me. I found some breeches and a shirt and pulled them on. When my breeches were up, I had to adjust myself. Having a penis was rather uncomfortable.

I nodded toward Declan, who looked like a rather disheveled version of me. "You might let Ginnifer fix your hair once I'm gone."

Declan just scowled.

Ryan came forward and pushed something into my fat hand. "Take this."

"What is it?" I looked down to find the sharpened hair pin. "What? I can't get a real dagger even in a man's body?"

"This is still more stealthy. No one will expect it. I'll have some guards out of uniform trailing you. But still, I'd feel better if you had it."

I sighed and let him strap the weapon onto my arm underneath my sleeve. There was no arguing with my half-giant protector. I went to move away, but Ryan wouldn't let me.

"If someone grabs you from behind, show me how you're gonna get away," he said. Then he grabbed me and held me fast, his muscles bulging and tense against me.

I struggled, but Ryan wouldn't let go. Not even when I kicked his shins. He forced me to go for the weapon. I had to stab backward into his belly before he released me.

"Good," Ryan gasped.

"I hate when you make me do that," I complained, wiping the blood onto a spare shirt as pink light filled the room and he healed himself.

"Too sarding bad," Ryan growled, "I don't want you antsy about actually using a weapon." He pulled me into a hug that turned into an awkward back pat due to my man body. That made me smile.

Ryan grumbled, "Now, I need to go beat someone's head in downstairs. Then I'll set some guards on your tail."

He stomped off, the rage from his healing power consuming him.

Declan wandered to the dressing room and called for Ginnifer.

I made eye contact with Connor and jerked my head toward Declan. "Don't let him make too big a fool of me."

"No promises," Connor replied.

I rolled my eyes but grabbed Quinn's hand. Then I realized I was a boy. "Whoops. Sorry."

Quinn laughed silently. He opened his bottle of the disguise spell and rubbed a bit of it on his face and teeth. His nose grew bulbous and he lost a tooth. The others grew yellow. His pores enlarged where he'd rubbed the potion, making his face into a series of craters.

You'll have to resist me tonight, Dove. At least for a bit.

I laughed. *I didn't know you could rub on a disguise spell.*

Spies have all kinds of tricks. Learned that one from your old man when I was his apprentice. He'd have me practice doing a quick rub on my face on a lot of missions. It's a quick way to stretch out the magic and to change your appearance when you leave a building and hit the alley.

Quinn led the way to a secret passage and pressed the seam along the wall to magically release the hidden door. He stepped aside like a gentleman so I could enter first. I turned and looked at him before he grabbed a torch and followed.

Speaking of resisting, I thought at him, *you were the least affected by the show Declan and I put on.*

Oh, I was affected, Dove.

Didn't seem like it.

I'm just saving myself for later.

Later?

You and I are about to have some alone time.

Ummm ... I'm a guy right now. I was confused.

Quinn chuckled in my head. *I brought a reversal spell for both of us. For after.*

Quinn sent an image. It was he and I (in our normal forms) behind a tavern and under the stars. He bent me against a wall in an alley, plunging into me from behind. I braced myself on the stone and my cheek rasped against it as he rode me hard. He held my breasts as he took me where anyone might see.

His fantasy gave me half a hardon. I had to adjust the damned dick.

I smacked him.

Knock that off. Or I won't be able to focus tonight.

Don't tell me that. Now, I'll be tempted to tease you.

Knock that off or I'll bugger you.

That sent Quinn's eyes wide. *No thanks. I'll be good. Promise.*

I laughed. Now I had a trick up my sleeve to keep my spy master in line.

Apparently, he didn't like it in the moon.

CHAPTER TWENTY-THREE

The Roasted Goose was our destination. Quinn and I took bottles of Flight to save time and cut down on interaction throughout the capital.

We landed in the woods and made our way toward the tavern lights. The stone tavern on the outskirts of Marscha was rowdy.

Inside, a minstrel strummed a lute in the corner. People chatted and danced and yelled. The smells of ale and bread filled the air as people drank and sopped up their drunkenness with thin stew in bread trenchers.

The entire scene made me slightly nostalgic for Kylee's tavern. This group didn't seem to have barrel fever quite as bad as the miners' used to, but that was a good thing. Fewer fisticuffs from blind drunk fools.

Quinn had no qualms about cutting through the crowd. I followed the best I could, but my frame was much thicker and shorter than his. People didn't naturally part for me. I fell behind and there were a few people between us.

A prostitute was taking bids for her evening. When she looked at me questioningly, I shook my head and she said, "You sure? We're playing three to one tonight. You look like you could use a pump, sugar."

She winked and plumped up her breasts for my perusal.

I shook my head again and she rolled her eyes. "Browneyes are in the back, then."

I just pressed my lips together and nodded. I wasn't here for sex. With men or women.

I pushed through the crowd, tapping one man's arm and asking to get past.

When I touched him, I noticed something unusual. He had a white armband on his shirt.

After I'd moved past him, I looked around. I hadn't noticed at first, because most people wore white shirts. Dye was expensive.

The tavern was full of people with white bands on their arms. My gut tightened. My intuition rang like the castle's alarm bell. I searched my memory for whatever might have triggered my response. Someone started clapping along with the music. And that's when I knew. Clapping. Arm bands. The plow races. The most popular man at the plows had worn a white arm band. The group cheering for him had been the largest. The most organized.

My stomach dropped like a stone in a well. I felt sick.

I'd come here hoping to learn what lies Isla and Raj were about to feed my people. I'd come in the hope I could prevent the rebellion from spreading to Evaness.

But if Quinn had brought me here … if this tavern was where the rebels were meeting … I was already too late. I looked around. I was walking through a sea of white armbands.

Someone had already sewn and distributed the bands. That took money, time, dedication.

Shite, I thought. Shite. The rebellion against Sedara is already here.

I didn't get to Quinn before a man started talking near me. "This is all long overdue. We should be able to travel without using their sarded up, piss-poor old boats."

"Yeah, last time I went 'cross the channel, there were fish guts on the floor. They hadn't even sprayed it down none 'afore they took on passengers!"

"They charged me double when our delivery was delayed by a rain storm. As if it were my damned fault the sky opened up."

Another man sipped his flagon. "So, when's that group gettin' here with our rally instructions?"

I sucked in a breath. They were already awaiting instructions? Something was already planned? They weren't just casual supporters?

Sard.

I searched the room for weapons. Other than the normal short knives men carried at their waists, I saw only a few swords. That was good. At least they weren't getting ready for a full-on attack. What then? A raid? A trip to the harbor to protest Sedara? Hell, I hoped it was merely a demonstration. Or a rally to discuss another rally—

I made it to Quinn, who had managed to get a tankard and was drinking.

Quinn, they're waiting for instruc—

I know, he cut me off. He took a final swig and set his empty cup on the bar. When his eyes met mine, they were dark with malice. *I'm listening. There's no way my people missed this. Someone in my network must support the rebellion. My network must be sarded to hell. Compromised. The thoughts around us are all about action. They're excited, not grumbling. They're ready to do something.*

But what something?

Quinn scratched his bulbous, disguised nose. *It doesn't seem like any of them know. From what I can tell, these are mostly sailors. Couple a' merchants.*

I guess that makes sense. They'd have the most interaction with Sedara. The most resentment. Who do you think they're waiting for?

Quinn shrugged. *I'm gonna go toward the back and see if I can hear anything else. The two men behind you are Ryan's. Stick with them.*

298

I glanced up to see two very tall men eyeing me curiously. I hadn't even noticed them before. I gave a friendly shrug.

One nodded back and the other simply kept scanning the room. But both moved closer.

The front door swung open. A gust of winter wind blew in, ruffling hair and making people blink.

I turned. And paled. Goosebumps rose on my arms, and they weren't from the chill.

In strode two women with long flaxen hair. They had lean, tan bodies. Seaweed was woven into their braids and starfish clung to their hair. They hardly wore more than chemises despite the cold night. Their thin dresses clung to every curve. Gold scales lined the backs of their arms and the sides of their necks. Appreciative wolf-whistles went up all around.

I pushed passed a man and tried to get to Quinn. My shadows followed.

"Watch it!" growled the man I'd knocked forward.

"Sorry. Got to piss," I answered.

The man let me pass and I pushed around someone else. Urgency drove me forward. Quinn and I needed to get out of here before those women spoke. Or worse, sang. Because sirens had just entered the rebel's tavern. And if I knew one thing from the brothel I'd worked at, it was that sirens (even half-sirens) loved to cause trouble.

I stuffed my handkerchief in one ear and used my hand to cover the other.

Did you see the sirens? I mentally yelled to Quinn.

Hard to miss 'em. I've got wax in my ears already.

I made it to him. *Well, share, you oaf.*

He handed me a bit of wax from his palm.

You think we should get out of sight? I asked. *We're about the only ones here without a white band on our arms.*

Quinn shrugged. *Not yet. I want to hear what everyone thinks.*

I kept an eye on the sirens as they made their way through the crowd. I wondered how Isla had recruited them. She did have a lot of partial mer-people. But these women were straight from the sea. Full sirens typically stuck to themselves, other than to seek out bedwarmers. Not these sirens. They greeted several people by name. One even took a sip from a man's flagon.

They stood next to the musicians. And then one of them spoke. "Quiet."

The reaction was immediate. Everyone in the room stopped talking. Respectful silence ensued. The siren's voice was far more effective than mine was even from the throne. Heads turned toward the beautiful woman with the light green eyes.

She smiled, "For far too long, Sedara has kept us all chained. They've ruled the seas with a heavy hand. And we haven't had the power to stop them. Until now."

"Hear hear!" Several men clanked their steins together and downed their ale.

"We will not stand by and be used any longer. We won't be the playthings of a selfish queen. A greedy one who bleeds us dry. The time has come. Sedara has been weakened. Our power has increased. And we need to move, now."

"How's Sedara weak?" one man called out. "I haven't heard nothin' about no ships being blowed up."

"They've lost their chess piece. The one thing that held back the sea does so no longer."

My heart tightened. She could only mean Avia. I was disgusted she'd referred to my sister as a chess piece. My heart ached for Avia. I bit my lip and felt like a dunce.

Eight kingdoms. The sea was the eighth kingdom. Sedara ruled the seas. The mer creatures didn't want Queen Diamoni to rule them anymore—

The siren cut off my thoughts as she continued, "Rasle and Cheryn are leading the charge against the tyrant. They're gathering near the shore. They're ready to move soon. We seek those who wish to join."

"What about Evaness? Why aren't we leading this? Those fools outta Rasle don't know nothing!" a curly-haired man shouted from the far corner of the room.

The siren's eyes flashed a bright yellow in her anger. She said, "Evaness has *no* respect for the sea. No respect for others. Their house is full of thieves. The queen here is allied with Sedara. She only supports Sedara's oppression."

The magical sea community was angry at Sedara's control. And furious at my house for mother's thievery.

Shite, the gears clicked in my head. My mother was a fool. She'd stolen a siren? That's why these women raged. That's why they'd left the ocean and come all this way. That's why they recruited my own people under my very nose.

I gulped as I realized how awful the situation really was. The magical sea races were tight knit. If Avia was a siren, we weren't facing just the fury of women who could lure sailors to drown. We faced all kinds of creatures from the deep.

While I processed that revelation, mutters and mumbles spread through the crowd as quick as fire.

"I heard the queen enslaved that prince from Cheryn," one man called out.

The siren nodded.

Molten anger filled my core. That was a lie.

I bristled, my mouth opened, but then I snapped it closed. I was here to observe. Here to gain knowledge. I doubted I'd be able to change the minds or hearts in this tavern.

Quinn watched me closely, and when he realized I had my reactions under control, he nodded, turning back to the room.

The conversation only grew worse. Complaints about the crown, taxes—name it, and I was blamed for it.

One man even blamed his wife's inability to conceive on a curse I'd brought upon the nation.

The sirens waited patiently until the din quieted. They like their audiences seething, it appeared.

I certainly was.

Until the second siren stood and walked to stand next to her companion. She opened her mouth. And started to sing. Her voice was like a warm summer wind and a beam of sunshine.

Quinn grabbed my arm and hustled me out the back door into the alley. Ryan's guards didn't make it after us. They were caught in the golden web her voice.

Even so, the few notes I heard had me dizzy and giddy.

We ran down the alley and around a corner. My chubby male body was gasping by then, so Quinn stopped, and we took the reversal potion.

I could run much better as myself than the pudgy man from my disguise. I watched Quinn's bulbous nose recede and his handsome smile restore itself. His half elf ears became more pointed. He pulled bottles of Flight from inside his vest. We drank them. Then we jumped into the frigid night air.

The cold made me squint my eyes and I bit my teeth together to stop them from chattering.

Isla and Raj had a dragon. They had djinn. They had sirens, and by extension most of the magical sea folk. Things weren't looking good for Sedara. Or me, if they thought I was in league with Queen Diamoni.

Quinn grabbed me and pulled me into him. I clung to his body heat.

Those sirens were angry, Quinn said. *Inside, they were furious. Incensed.*

Over Sedara. And me.

No, Dove. They pictured your mother. They were angry at her more than anyone. They pictured Avia. They were disgusted by her human form. By the thought that she'd been taken.

I know. Avia's a siren. Mother stole a siren.

No, Dove. She didn't. A siren doesn't have the power Isla and Raj are betting on. Their range extends to a roomful at most. That's why there were two.

But—I swallowed, and the winter cold seemed to invade my insides. The chill spread right to my heart. *If not a siren, what type of creature did mother steal?*

I saw a picture in their heads. He showed it to me. The dark black of the ocean depths crept around the creature. She was a lithe woman with white hair that floated behind her. Her body had an elongated human shape. She was lined in iridescent scales on either side from foot to neck, on the undersides of her breasts, and around her eyes. The woman's fingers were webbed and tipped with claws. Huge body-length fins, like those from a beta fish, fluttered from her back like wings. Her eyes were huge—and completely black. The picture she made was utterly beautiful. And utterly terrifying.

I'm not certain what this creature is. Some kind of sea fairy. Do you know?

It definitely wasn't a siren. I shook my head. *Is that ... Avia?*

No, here's the next part of their mental picture. It's not Avia.

The creature shot out a jet of power that created a whirlpool next to her. The swirling vortex rose up, up, up. And then, with a swirl of her hand, the sea woman reversed the rotation. A ship flew down toward her, smashing into the ocean floor at her side. Bodies and cargo burst from the ship like bubbles. The woman moved forward and broke open a chest that had floated to the ocean floor from the wreckage. It was full of coins. She picked up the chest and grinned.

My eyes widened as I watched the sea witch open her wings and flap them to swim carelessly away.

The coins we've been seeing. They're old because they're—

Sunken treasure, Quinn finished my sentence for me.

This creature—whatever she was—was no siren.

She was something worse.

CHAPTER TWENTY-FOUR

*I*nstead of flying straight to the castle, Quinn flew us north toward the Cerulean forest. Most of the blue leaves now littered the forest floor and the trees were merely angry hands scratching at the sky.

My head was dazed but my heart was anxious even as he held me in his arms.

Where are we going? We have to find out what that sea woman ... sea fairy ... monster ... we need to know what powers she—

Quinn's mouth latched onto mine. His lips were ice cold from flying but his breath was warm. He pulled me to him and wrapped his arms around my waist.

I have to kiss you.

But the rebellion—

Can wait five minutes.

Only five?

He grinned. *Or five hours. Whichever you prefer.*

But ... those sirens came to get those people to act.

For tonight, they're only trying to get them to enlist. Probably on a magically binding scroll. And they might have a harder time of it than they expect. As soon as the one started singing, I planted an image of a witch—Quinn sent me a mental picture of a gnarled old witch—*in the heads of the half-dozen most violent men in the place. They'll think they're being tricked. It's why I pulled you out. I fully expect a riot to start down there.*

Sure enough, I heard yelling in the distance. I looked back to see torches leaving the tavern.

I sighed in relief and turned back to Quinn. *Thank you.*

He grinned.

I smiled at the mischief in his grey eyes. I thought: *You wanted five hours? Well, then, I'm not arguing with you.*

Because I wanted release. I craved it. All this tension, all this nervous energy weighed on me. This fear threatened to eat me whole. I needed a momentary escape.

Quinn grinned against my mouth and kissed me again when he felt me acquiesce. Slowly, his tongue began plundering deeper. He spun us slightly in midair. Without gravity to stop us, we kept languidly spinning in the moonlight, our feet dangling above the treetops.

I've loved you from the day I saw you, Quinn's mind whispered even as his mouth traced a hot path down my neck, setting my icy skin alight.

You were so hot that day, I thought in return. *Your eyes—I* pictured him in Kylee's tavern and sent the image to him.

Not that day. Quinn sent me an image of a market. I'd been in a disguise spell, selling eggs. I'd given a little beggar boy a loaf of bread.

I pulled back to study his face, astonished. That had been a least a year before he'd caught me. *How did you know that was me?*

He shrugged. *I could see you in your actions. You've always been a pure heart. A wild, wicked mouth—which I love—once the real you was unleashed.* He kissed the corner of my lip. *But a pure heart.*

My mind spun dizzily at the revelation. *But ... you didn't bring me in.* I'd been at that market a year before he caught me and brought me back to claim the throne.

His fingers fumbled with the ties at the front of my shirt. The cold was making us stiff and movement hard. Quinn directed us lower, out of the winter wind.

You were happy, he shrugged and caressed my cheek before going back to the ties. *If you were happy and weren't ready for the crown, I wasn't ready to force you back.*

But—

Happiness matters. Don't forget that. Duty is good. Selflessness great. But happiness matters, too.

Whose happiness though? We're about to get put in the crosshairs of a war and if I can do anything to stop it ... it's my duty. To sacrifice for Evaness. It's what mother would have done. She did do. She stole a child to protect this country. She magicked that baby and raised it as her own, knowing that she'd be a target—

He stroked my cheek. *Your mother's way isn't the only way.*

How else can you be queen?

He gave a shrug. *You muddle through, day by day.*

I'm pretty certain muddling through won't stop any wars.

You can plan as much as you want ... but sometimes, you just know when things aren't right. It's why I couldn't take you that day at the market. It wasn't right.

What was different at Kylee's Tavern?

You were furious. Gods, the vixen in you was out that day. You weren't happy anymore. You were frustrated. Lost. And your anger was so ...

Off-putting? I laughed.

Hot.

Quinn's lips smashed into mine and he angled us down through the trees quickly until my feet landed on a pile of dead leaves.

"Wait! We don't have any more Flight!"

Quinn didn't answer my protest.

Before I could blink, my pants were off. I was in only the oversized male shirt I wore, which was entirely too thin.

Quinn let go of me up for a moment to lay his vest out sideways as a makeshift blanket. Then his eyes locked onto mine and his hands snaked around my waist. Slowly, he lowered me down onto the vest.

He lay down next to me and propped his head up on his hand so he could stare down at me. *I love you, Bloss.*

I fell into the grey depths of his eyes and warmth lit my heart, like a candle flame. The world might be crashing down around us. But we'd sink together. Together was the important part.

"I love you, too," I whispered.

I wish I could give you your dreams.

You mean you'd help me find someone to take this damn crown off my hands?

He chuckled. *If there was anyone else fit to wear it.*

He lifted his free hand and his fingers skimmed the seam of my lips lightly.

I fought a shiver. The winter night was closing in.

Quinn noticed and pulled me closer so that I was flush against him. He brought my hands to his mouth and blew on them to warm them. *I have an idea, Dove. Close your eyes for a moment.*

I let my eyelids flutter closed and I focused on the feel of his chest against mine.

I'm a simple fisherman and you're my wife. We live in a little cottage by the wharf that smells of brine when the wind blows the right way.

The smell of the ocean touched my nose and my eyes popped open.

Not yet, Dove. Keep them closed. Quinn's grey eyes scolded me.

I closed my eyes and shoved my top leg between his, cuddling closer and stealing his body heat. I smiled as I listened to him weave a fantasy for me. A fantasy where we were simple people who fished and made homemade bread in the hearth, except on the days I burnt it.

A burnt smell wafted over us and my eyes popped open again.

If this is a fantasy, why am I incompet—my thought trailed off as I gazed beyond Quinn in wonder. I didn't see the trees of the forest. I didn't see the pile of dull blue leaves where we lay. I didn't see Quinn's vest underneath us. Quinn and I were in a cozy little cottage bedroom, laying on a lumpy mattress. The walls were a roughhewn pine. A fire crackled merrily in the hearth and I could nearly feel the heat of the flames. A loaf of bread sat on the edge of the hearth, one half black as charcoal.

Don't worry about the bread, Dove. I'll eat the burnt half, Quinn thought as he nuzzled my neck.

I can't believe—I was going to say I couldn't believe Quinn's magic. The illusion was so beautiful. So detailed. But Quinn cut me off with a kiss.

Quick. Before the others get home. Quinn gave me a naughty wink. *I love to make the cottage reek of sex before your other husbands walk in.*

I grinned and shook my head. Even in fantasy, Quinn couldn't stop his playful, childish side.

Well, if that's what you want, you'd better get to work. I raised my eyebrows.

Quinn's smile doubled and he rolled on top of me.

Yes, ma'am. His hand came up and cupped my jaw briefly before he leaned in for a full kiss, brushing his tongue lightly over mine.

After a minute, I deepened the kiss, reaching up and pulling him down by the neck so that I could feel the entire length of his strong, hard body against me. His shoulders were wide, and his hips fit perfectly between my thighs when they parted. His shaft pressed down against my thigh. It was hard and thick.

Quinn shifted his weight to one hand and brought his other up to graze my lips. Then he pushed his thumb slowly into my mouth. I used my tongue to tease out circles on the pad of his digit. When I released his thumb with a pop, he brought it slowly down my body, pulled up the hem of my shirt, and traced that wet thumb up along my inner thigh. He edged closer and closer to my core.

But as soon as he saw my breath catch, he slid away. Then he slid closer. When I arched my back, he slid his thumb away again.

Quinn! I scolded. *I thought you wanted this cabin reeking of sex! Quit teasing.*

Oh, it's starting to, wife. I can smell you. But I don't just want this cabin to reek of plain old sex. I want your other husbands to hear you screaming as they walk up from the shore. I want them to drop the fish they've caught and sprint up here, thinking their sweet wife is being attacked, only to find you impaled on my cock, shrieking in ecstasy.

His words left me panting. But I couldn't let his ego know that. *I think you have a very high opinion of your abilities.*

He raised an eyebrow. *Oh, do I?*

I traced my fingers down over his ribs, yanking impatiently at his shirt. He sat up and pulled it off, obliging me. When he leaned back down and returned his thumb to teasing me, I started outlining the ship tattooed on his stomach.

I smiled up at Quinn, determined to push his buttons. *Honestly, I don't believe you can make me scream. I just don't see that happening.*

We'll see about that.

His thumb near my core traveled upward, tracing around my clit. Around and around. My hips lifted, seeking out his touch. But he pushed me down with his own hips. His lips sank onto my right nipple and he licked it through the shirt, lapping at it with slow steady strokes of his tongue. Then his thumb slowly skimmed my folds. They were already slick. So slick that when he pushed lightly, his thumb had an easy entrance.

So wet. So hot, Quinn growled. He kept his thumb just inside me, spreading me open as his fingers strummed along my lips and clit, like he was playing an instrument.

My body grew tighter, the tension rising as the irregular thump of his fingers just served to tease me further. I started to get desperate as my pussy lips and clit grew swollen, ready for more attention. I wanted direct contact. But every time I swiveled my hips to get it, Quinn moved away.

You'd better hurry, or you'll miss your chance. The other men are already walking home. I can hear them, I added to our little cottage fantasy as I stroked his pointed elf ears in the way I knew he liked.

Suddenly, I heard Ryan boom out a laugh. Quinn's illusions were perfection.

So, you want to turn on the pressure, Dove. Fine. I'll let you come. But only if you scream out that I'm your favorite.

You shite! That's not fair. It'll hurt them.

Quinn's smile grew wide. *There's that good heart. Overruling even a fantasy.*

I turned toward him, suddenly serious. I stared into his eyes, willing him to know the truth. *You know I love you. I love you all. With everything. Right? That there's no such thing as favorites. You're all so different. And special. And I couldn't imagine my life without you.*

Quinn pulled his fingers out of me and leaned back. His belt was off, and pants were down in seconds. I only saw his hard shaft for a moment before he pushed roughly into me.

Say it again, he grunted, halfway inside me. His grey eyes were fierce.

I love you. With everything.

Again. He thrust into me deeper, his hard, hot dick sliding against my wetness. My pussy lips pulsed.

I love you.

Again.

I love you!

Quinn bottomed out, his huge mushroom tip pressed against my cervix. He reached down with his thumb and circled my clit, offsetting the pain. He thrust lightly back and forth. I could feel his cock already pulsing inside me, threatening to come. Teasing me had built him up to a frenzy.

His thrusts grew rougher and I lifted my ass from the ground, planting my feet. That made his cock slide deliciously over my insides, rubbing the perfect spot. He rutted me harder, gasping.

The cottage around us vanished and the trees returned. But I hardly saw them. I was panting, moaning, writhing at the tendrils of sensation his thumb was wringing from my clit. My entire core was alight as the head of his cock created intense sensations inside me. Tingles traveled up my backbone. I closed my eyes as the feeling grew in intensity. Bigger. Larger.

"Yes!" I screamed into the night. My orgasm was an orange flame. Wild and unpredictable and full of heat. It traveled up my spine into my head. The sensation was so intense I couldn't breathe for a moment.

He kept his finger on me, drawing out the aftershocks until I had to smack his hand away because it was too much. I was seeing black spots.

I sank back down, and Quinn collapsed on top of me. He'd come. I hadn't even noticed, I'd been so blinded by my own release.

We lay in contented silence for a minute in the dark. But gradually, the cold started to bite at me. So, we stood, casting small smiles at one another as he brushed leaves off the back of my shirt. I'd just reached down to grab another leaf when I saw a pair of eyes glowing in the woods.

I stiffened and Quinn whirled around to face the danger, swiping the image from my thoughts.

A wolf stepped out of the shadows. It was long and lean and grey. Its hair stood on end.

Quinn reached for the knife in his belt where it lay on forest floor, but I held out a hand to stop him.

I don't want a repeat of the Fuzzy debacle, I thought at him. *There's still one ring left, isn't there?*

Quinn shook his head. *No. It's the dragon's.*

Liar. Wouldn't he have come by now? Just give me a moment.

I looked the wolf straight in the eye and asked, "Are you under a spell?"

The wolf growled. His lips pulled back, showing a sharp, sinister line of fangs.

The hair rose on my neck.

I don't think he's spelled, Dove, Quinn snarked, *Permission to kill him now?*

I nodded, stepping closer to Quinn.

That drew the wolf forward. And out of the shadows stepped several of his friends.

Quinn and I were surrounded.

And we were out of Flight.

CHAPTER TWENTY-FIVE

"*S*ard!" I ran through the woods barefoot, in only a man's white shirt. Quinn ran completely naked, taking up position behind me to guard our rear. We were too far from the capital, too far from the castle.

Shite, shite, shite! My brain couldn't think anything useful with the sound of wolves growling all around me.

One leapt out of the forest in front of me.

I unsheathed Ryan's hairpin weapon from the leather band on my arm. I only had a second to wonder if I'd have to use it when a huge shadow dropped from the sky, landing on the wolf.

A horrid roar filled the air.

I skidded to a halt. Quinn stopped just behind me. He threw his hands around my waist, ready to fling me behind him.

Because in front of me, diving out of the sky, was a winged bear.

The bear smacked another wolf as it tried to attack, sending the creature flying.

The bear dropped to all fours and ran straight at us. Quinn pulled me aside just as the bear batted away a wolf that had tried to sneak up on us from behind.

After that, the wolves seem to forsake us as prey. The darted back off into the shadows.

I was breathing hard. My blood was pumping so fast I could hear it in my ears.

The bear turned toward us. I walked backward and tripped over the body of the wolf that had been smashed upon the bear's landing.

Quinn scooped me up, eyes on the bear. I had to move the hairpin to my other hand to avoid stabbing my knight. He started to slowly back us further away.

The bear eyed us for a moment. And I felt certain it was going to lunge. Felt certain that my life wasn't going to end with rebellion or my head on a chopping block. I felt sure I was about to be assassinated by a foreign queen.

Until a bluebird dive bombed the bear.

The bird smacked the bear directly on the nose and then fluttered its wings. Its claws settled into the fur on the bear's head and it pecked at the bear's ear.

The bear sat back on its ass and with a thump. He swatted at the bird, which came fluttering over to land on my shoulder.

"Blue?" I asked, incredulous. My hand went over my heart and my head tried to tell it to slow down. But it took a bit.

I squinted at the bear. "Fuzzy?"

The bear made a whining sound and covered its face with its paw.

I gasped in relief and sheathed my pathetic weapon. Next time, I was insisting on a sarding sword.

"How the hell did you get wings?" I asked.

A titter had me looking upward. Donaloo floated down from the sky. He landed next to the squashed wolf and *tsked* at Fuzzy. "Instincts are good, but we must be careful. Or we could all soon be despairful. Only the force that must be had should be used, otherwise force will use us, and we won't get to choose."

I tilted my head as I studied the wizard. "Why did you give Fuzzy wings?"

"Why—how else would he fly? Wings are best to get from here to there. And when you've got to go west, wings are better than a ship's fare."

I closed my eyes, feeling somewhat sorry I'd asked.

Can you ask him to get us back to the palace, Dove? And maybe magic us up some clothes so we don't walk in ... like this? He gestured at the very thin white shirt that ended at my thighs and his own nude state.

You look great but I ... yes, I'll ask. I sighed. I'd probably get twelve annoying rhymes as answers. But hopefully Donaloo could magic up a fur-lined cloak. I took a step closer to the wizard, "Donaloo, do you think you could make some magical cloaks or something so that Quinn and I aren't so ... exposed to the cold? And maybe, possibly ... help us fly back to the palace? We ran out of Flight potion."

Donaloo gave me a tongue click and finger point, which I assumed meant yes. At least it wasn't a rhyme.

He waved his hands, and immediately I felt as if a soft rabbit's fur cloak was brushing against my arms. But when I looked down, the cloak was invisible. My ice-cold nipples were still on full display through the thin shirt I wore. I felt quite certain if I leaned over and looked, my love triangle would also show. I closed my eyes and breathed through my nose, telling myself that the wizard had not done that on purpose.

His magic is wonky, I talked myself down. He's not a dirty old man.

I took a deep breath and made eye contact with Donaloo, who was—very clearly—smirking.

Nix that. Completely a dirty old man. And an ass.

"Donaloo, could you please ensure that no one can see my body?" I asked with a smile through gritted teeth. "This would be inappropriate." I gestured at myself. My court tone needed a lot of work, because my fury slipped through in my voice.

"Oh, not just exposure to the cold, exposure to eyes that might wander and behold," he winked.

"Yes, please." It felt like agony to have to respond. To not just grab him by the throat and shake him.

I think I like him even more now, Quinn laughed internally.

You would.

Quick as a wink, orange magic flared out and wrapped around my cloak and I felt relieved when the cloak didn't burst into flames, just settled against me, feeling slightly heavier than before.

When the sparkling orange mist dissipated, I looked down again. Now, none of my body from the shoulders down was visible. I looked over. Quinn now had a nice, normal outfit. I was a sarding head floating in midair.

Donaloo couldn't control his giggles. Even Fuzzy let out a snuffle. Quinn howled inside my head, tears dripping from his eyes. Only Blue looked at me with any pity at all.

He gave you exactly what you asked for, Dove!

I stroked my bluebird's chest, fighting down the anger that made me feel crazy enough to attack a bear, a powerful wizard, and my husband.

"Sard it," I said and turned away from the men, stomping off in the direction of the palace.

Wait! You're supposed to ask him to fly us home! Quinn called out.

I'm not sarding asking that fool for anything else! I mind-yelled, *Ask him yourself.*

My mind and the forest rang out with laughter as Donaloo and Quinn watched my floating head drift away.

✿

*W*hen Donaloo recovered from his fit of laughter over his own hilarity, he volunteered Fuzzy to fly us back. He and Quinn rode the bear through the forest until they caught up with me and Blue.

I begrudgingly accepted their ride since the castle was probably a two-day walk away. I climbed onto the bear's wide back. I ended up sandwiched between Donaloo, who navigated, and Quinn who rode behind me and kept me from tumbling backward by hooking his feet over the front of Fuzzy's wing bones. Blue flew beside us.

We were starting our descent to the castle when—*Boom!* A fireball the size of a wagon erupted from the formal wing of the palace. The wing where I would have been at dinner. Smoke billowed upward. And I heard a series of shrieks begin.

"What the sard?" My heart thundered.

My brain reeled. Those rebels were still planning. They weren't supposed to attack! They were after Sedara! Why—

A second *boom*. Closer to the main hall. Another fireball launched into the sky.

My mind shut down.

Shock.

Just utter shock overcame me for a moment.

And then fear slithered in.

Holy sarding hell. My home. My husbands! My people.

A sheen of tears coated my eyes automatically and I tried to blink them back.

I had to force my brain to turn back on. It wanted to curl into a ball as I had when I was a child during the Fire Wars.

No, I reproached myself. Think.

I grabbed at Donaloo's shirt. "Can you help? Please?"

I heard Quinn start to mind-yell to groups, unconsciously including me on some of them. Words like —*evacuate, Declan, water*—

Donaloo raised a hand in front of me and the mage's tower began to glow. The flowers on the vines lit up as if they were candles encased in colored glass.

Purple fairies rose in the night sky and unsheathed their bright yellow swords. Then they plunged, screaming, down into the courtyard. To fight what, I couldn't tell.

Orange trumpet flowers shot off the mage's tower and opened, floating in midair until they reached the flames from the explosion. Then they swallowed. They expanded after they ate the flames and then looked like bloated orange lanterns as they drifted through the air, belching smoke.

My heart was tight as a drum. *Quinn, where are the others?* I asked quietly. I feared his answer.

Quinn shook his head. I looked back at him. His eyes were scanning frantically back and forth as if he were reading quickly. I don't think he saw the scene below at all. I felt certain a hundred people's thoughts filled him at once. A million different micro-expressions crossed his face. Everyone who had a bead was probably yelling at him all at once. Only one sentence came from him. *We have a leak. Someone's turned.*

I turned to Donaloo. "Do you know where my knights are? Can you help them? Can you protect them? Please?"

I looked below, where all the inhabitants of the castle scurried around, as chaotic as the bugs underneath a lifted rock.

All I could think of were Declan, Ryan, and Connor. Their faces flashed on repeat in my mind: Declan's blond hair and piercing blue eyes, Ryan's gorgeous curled lashes and the way he towered over me, Connor's sweetly mussed curls. My heart pumped so fast that my body grew hot. I was sweltering inside even though the cold made my breath fog.

Nothing can happen to them, I thought. Nothing.

There was an endless moment as Donaloo surveyed the chaos below. He spotted Cerena running across the moat and pointed. "There!" He pushed Fuzzy into a dive. We landed on the bank of the far side of the moat, outside the castle walls.

We dismounted. Fuzzy didn't like the chaos and so with a roar, he took off into the night sky, disappearing.

Blue settled on the ground near my feet, hiding between my legs so he wouldn't get trampled. Donaloo strode immediately toward Cerena, who limped toward him.

I looked at Quinn. His face was still a somber mask and he did not make eye contact with me. That only made my hands begin to shake.

Sard. Sard. Sard. What could I do? Peace magic couldn't fight fire. This wasn't a beast. These were explosives.

I shot a stream of green magic at those who fled across the drawbridge, hoping that at least I could stop someone from getting trampled, keep the evacuation under control. I scanned every face that went past, looking for my knights.

There were maids in tears, guards fully armed, cooks, and courtiers hurrying out side by side. I didn't see the nobles.

When one young boy saw my floating head and started to scream, I pulled the cloak over my hair, hiding myself, peering through the parted material. I kept up the trail of green magic, though my arms ripped open to the elbow. I pulsed the green, trying to touch each person as they fled. My blood flowed freely, and my arms began to ache.

Donaloo and Cerena faced the castle. They linked hands. They lifted their arms toward the sky.

Donaloo uttered one word, "Stop."

And everyone froze.

CHAPTER TWENTY-SIX

I stopped pulsing magic, because everyone who had not crossed the drawbridge was suddenly still as a statue. They were frozen mid-step, mid-blink.

I didn't wait, I ran toward the drawbridge, letting my cloak fall around my shoulders once more. It took Quinn a couple seconds to realize what had happened, what I was doing.

Bloss, wait! He mentally yelled after me.

But I didn't listen. I ducked and dodged around frozen people as quickly as I could. My eyes were searching, always searching, for my knights.

I made it to the castle steps before Donaloo materialized in front of me. "Don't go in, not yet, the clock has started, and your plan's not set. Seventy-two solid hours, the castle will stay frozen under these powers. But after that, to melt the spell, you must go through the gates of hell."

"STOP! Just stop!" I screamed at him. I reached for his arm to push the wizard aside. I was done with rhymes and riddles. "I need to find my knights!"

Bloss—Quinn's hands wrapped around my waist, yanking me backward. *They aren't here.*

What? I whirled to face him. His grey eyes stared back at me. It was the first time since the explosion that he'd looked directly at me.

They followed the Countess Malia after dinner. Remember?

So, Malia's not working with the rebellion?

Quinn shrugged. *If she is, at least she doesn't seem to want you dead.*

I ran my hands through my hair, yanking on it. My legs felt like butter. My stomach churned. Relief coursed through me and it felt awful. I needed to puke. But more than that, I needed to see my knights. I needed to know they were alive.

Quinn led me out of the courtyard, toward the orchard. Cerena and Donaloo followed slowly, at the pace her limp would allow.

Blue flew ahead, scouting through the trees. He looped back toward us, flying fast, faster than I'd ever seen. He didn't stop to perch on me but started dive bombing, blocking my path.

"What the sard?" I held up my hands to cover my head. Blue smashed against them. Then he flew lower and I felt him pluck at my coat with his beak.

Declan's still disguised as you, Quinn thought. *He's telling you to cover up. Just in case.*

I sighed in relief and annoyance. "One day, I'm gonna ask Donaloo to make you into a speaking bird," I muttered as I pulled the cloak over my head and hid my face.

Quinn jogged back to tell Cerena and Donaloo to stay back and accompany me while he went on ahead.

I followed him slowly through the clearing. Blue flew near me, as if he were a tiny blue bodyguard. Whichever prince of Cheryn he was, he clearly didn't have his father's famous disdain for others.

I peered around the trees as I walked, eager to get my eyes on my men.

When I slid behind and oak and peered at them standing in a clearing, my chest loosened. I hadn't realized how tight it had been until it unwound. Ryan stood near the disguise-spelled version of me. Connor was arguing with Malia.

"We need to move!"

"Where is everyone? You need Quinn. Declan. You can't move without them—" she whispered furiously.

Quinn tromped into view and waved.

Duchess Malia leaned and peered around him. "Declan?"

Quinn tilted his head. Then he shook it side to side for Malia. As he did, he mind-spoke to all of us. *She's awfully interested in Declan. Her thoughts are completely focused on seeing him.*

Declan? Why would she be thinking about him? I wondered.

Connor says he feels desperation coming from her. Need, Quinn responded. *Stay out of sight. I don't trust her.*

Of course, we don't trust her. We don't trust anyone. Someone just blew up the castl—

Countess Malia interrupted my thought by stepping closer to Declan, who looked highly uncomfortable as me. His hands fidgeted with my dress.

"Your Majesty, please, shouldn't we go back and make sure no one's hurt?" Malia crooned.

"No one would be hurt if you'd sarding just told us there was a bomb!" Declan snarled.

"I didn't know where it was! I was just told to take a walk!" Malia replied.

And then, she did something unprecedented. She grabbed Declan—me—by the wrist and yanked forward.

Ryan unsheathed his sword, but Malia brandished a glowing orange vial.

"Don't!" she screamed. "Don't or I'll have to kill the queen!" She pressed the vial against Declan's throat.

She might as well have been pressing that vial against my own. My pulse sped. My chest constricted painfully around my heart. Fear chained me, linked me to Declan. Every tiny breath he took, the shadow of a shiver in his fingertips, I felt it as if it were mine.

"I need Declan. I'm taking the queen as ransom. I'll come back in three hours. You have Declan for me then or—honestly, I don't know what they'll do," she finished on a whisper.

My eyes moved past Declan to Malia. Tears streamed down her face as she held him. Clearly, she was being coerced. But I didn't care. She had threatened my knight. Her fate was a tomb. A cold, lonely trip to the earth.

I can hit her with peace, I told Quinn. *Give Ryan time to get to her.*

NO! Quinn shouted, shocking me.

What? My feet ignored him even as I asked the question. I took a step out from the tree I was hidden behind. But someone grabbed my arm and stopped me from walking forward. I turned to see Cerena crouching behind the tree. I peeked at her from inside my cloak. She shook her head at me and leaned close. "Let her go," she whispered.

My eyes widened, screaming 'what' and 'you're a sarding idiot' simultaneously.

I turned back to the scene at hand and I saw Donaloo behind Malia, gesturing at Quinn, holding out his hands in a 'stop' motion.

Why the sarding hell do we want to put Declan in danger?

Because if we follow her, she can lead us right to them, Dove, Quinn responded gravely.

But then Dec will be in the middle of them! The very person she wants! How the hell will we get him out?

Quinn didn't answer me. Because there was no good answer.

Malia kept one arm around Declan's neck, the orange vial tilted precariously as she whistled.

Seconds later, three winged bears dropped from the sky. This time, none of them were Fuzzy. They were Isla's.

That shite Raslen queen, I raged. *I'll smite her and obliterate her country—*

Calm, Dove, Quinn said. *We have to keep our thoughts clear. For Declan.*

I wanted to smash him in the mouth. I wanted to hit everyone. It felt like I could go through an entire nation, hitting every single person until their face splashed into the mud. And that still might not be enough to quell my rage.

Two of the bears formed a barrier blocking Ryan and Connor from reaching Malia.

Malia shoved Declan toward the third bear, who got on its belly so they could mount easily.

"You don't have to do this," Declan spoke quietly as she pushed him toward the bear.

"It's your family or mine," Malia said coldly, prodding his back.

"I could protect your family," Declan offered.

"You have no power there. Soon, you'll have no power at all."

"I know djinn who can help. I could get you a wish," Declan promised recklessly, lying through his teeth to push her into more revelations.

"She's already killed one of my fathers," Malia snarled, "And you can't wish for what you've once had. Your djinn could do *nothing* for me."

She pushed Declan up onto the beast roughly. They settled onto the bear's back as everyone else stayed still and silent. The bear's black wings flapped, rustling the leaves and creating a miniature wind. And then they were airborne, the other two bears lifting off just after.

I watched them rise into the sky. My heart flew off with them.

CHAPTER TWENTY-SEVEN

Once they were gone, I dropped my invisible cloak from my face and stormed into the moonlit clearing. "That's the stupidest idea you all have ever had! We could have taken her. We could have turned her! Bribed her! We could have used a disguise spell and posed as her—"

"Not fast enough," Connor shook his head. He tilted his head, studying me in my bodiless state. "What the hell happened to you?"

I ignored him. I didn't have time for stupid questions. And Connor was wrong. Sarding wrong. I looked at Ryan. My soldier would agree with me. He'd hate this. "And you?"

Ryan bit his lip but shrugged. "We need an advantage. They don't know that's Dec. He's got power. He can protect himself."

"Not good enough!" I stomped my foot. "We don't sacrifice each other!"

"Remember, failure is the toll we pay to cross the bridge to success. You must pay the toll or forego your goal." Donaloo sing-songed at me.

If Quinn hadn't grabbed onto my invisible waist and held me back, I would have decked the old wizard. Which would have been a mistake. Because we needed him still. The other side had a dragon, some fairy-looking sea-monster bitch, and djinn. And now they had my Declan in their clutches.

"Why the sard aren't we in the air already?" I growled.

"Just having Quinn tell my men to guard the palace," Ryan responded.

When Quinn gave a nod that the order had been received, Donaloo clapped his hands and our feet rose, as if we'd each just taken a bottle of Flight.

We rose into the air and scanned the sky. Ryan spotted them first. "There," he pointed. The bears were flying toward Rasle. Of course.

Blue fluttered next to me as we all turned that direction.

I eyed him. "It might be a long flight, little man. Why don't you stay behind? No one can hurt you. The castle's frozen." I'd deal with that problem later. I'd add it to the ever-growing list of world-ending problems I faced.

Blue shook his head side to side, vehemently protesting my suggestion.

I sighed. But at least one person seemed to understand the concept of sticking together. Of not hanging their fellow knight out to dry.

He'll be fine, Dove, Quinn said. *Dec is tougher than you think.*

He's a scholar! I mind-yelled as I held out a finger for Blue to perch on. Once his claws were wrapped around my index finger, I brought my other hand up out of my cloak to grab him gently. Both my hands curled around him and pulled him into my chest.

Quinn must have decided it wasn't worth fighting with me, because he simply kicked his legs and started flying after the bears. Everyone else followed, except Ryan.

"What are you doing?" I asked him.

"I'm covering us from behind."

I bit my tongue. I didn't ask how the sard he was going to stop anything from attacking us midair. Yes, he had a sword. But they had a dragon. And bombs. And every sarding weapon known to man apparently. And spies. In our network. And nobles they'd bribed or threatened.

Countess Malia was part mermaid. I assumed Isla or Raj or their mystery sea fairy threatened the mermaid side of her family. How or when they'd killed one of her fathers, I had no idea.

My mind raced as I tried to work out what the hell we could do when we caught up with her.

"Donaloo, if the dragon's there, do you have a plan?" I asked the wizard.

He grinned at me and patted his green vest. He pulled a ring with a dark band and blue stone out of his pocket. So the dragon was a djinni!

Donaloo said, "A djinni and his ring are inseparable things. Not to fret, not to fret, I've—"

He dropped the ring.

He dropped the sarding ring!

I dove. I didn't blink. My eyes roamed everywhere. But I didn't see it anywhere. The moonlight wasn't bright enough. The ring wasn't glinting.

Tears of frustration came into my eyes.

Fear.

Utter fear.

It hammered at my insides, turning them to mush.

Declan. If they took my knight anywhere near the dragon, we'd just lost the ring that might stop it.

Ryan's arms enveloped me. He pulled me upward in the sky, away from the lost ring. Away from hope.

I turned into him. I needed his comfort. I needed reassurance that things were going to be okay. Ryan pulled me in tight. Blue got squashed between us and let out a squawk of protest. Ryan loosened his grip slightly, so my bird friend could breathe.

"We'll find another way," Ryan reassured me.

Quinn thought, *They can always freeze the dragon like they did everyone at the castle.*

The ache in my heart eased. I nodded, then rested my cheek against Ryan's solid chest. I took a few breaths to calm myself.

Then I forced myself to turn on queen mode. The mode my mother had tried to beat into me year after year. I tried to evaluate our enemies' weaknesses.

"Malia's part mermaid. If she stays out of the water, she can't access her powers." Even as I said it, more of my childhood made sense. Avia had never gone abroad. She'd never gone to the christening of a new ship. Mother never even had her taught to swim. She'd always said my swimming lessons had been so disastrous she couldn't stand to repeat the experience. Lies. All moves to keep my sister away from water. Where she might be discovered. Might be found.

I shook off my anger at mother. Now wasn't the time. I had to focus. Declan's life was at stake.

"What are the chances Malia goes underwater?" I worried.

Ryan shrugged. "Dec can turn water to sand. Quinn can give him a signal. Keep faith."

I nodded. My heart unclenched the tiniest bit. "That's right." I tried to stay analytical. "Opponents: Dragon, to the wizards. Water creatures to Dec. What about soldiers?

And we need to expect winged bears. How are we going to fight them?"

Ryan grumbled, "I can take one on. But hopefully we can freeze the rest? Or you can stun them with peace?"

I'd forgotten the wounds on my arms and legs. Adrenaline had kept me from thinking about them. With the cloak, Ryan and the other knights couldn't see them and fuss over me. But I was battered. The wolves and then the exodus at the castle had taken a lot of blood. My arms still throbbed. "Um … about that. I used my power at the castle." I didn't mention the wolves. It didn't seem like Ryan needed any more stress right now. Not with what we were about to face.

Ryan ground his teeth together. "How bad is it?"

I bit my lip. "Not so bad," I lied. It was probably worse than I'd ever been, minus the fight with the dragon.

"Show me," he commanded.

I held Blue in my left hand and lifted my right. It was a shredded mess. Ryan exhaled through his teeth, his square jaw clenched in fury.

My heart melted a little at that. My wounds brought out the protector in him. The giant ready to smash trees and destroy the world in order to keep me safe.

He carefully put one of his hands near my arm and pink light glimmered softly. My skin healed over in seconds.

"You're getting faster at that."

"You give me too much sarding practice. Give me the other one."

I transferred Blue again and let Ryan heal my arm and then my legs. By the time I was healed, he was breathing hard.

"I'm sorry. Was that too much?" I caressed Ryan's neck.

His chocolate eyes smoldered down at me. "No. I'm pissed. Gods, I hope there's a fight when we get there. I hope she's not just taking Declan to some wayward cabin in the woods." His fingers clenched slightly as he held me, but he didn't hurt me. He'd never hurt me.

In the distance, near the shore, was a volcano, belching into the night sky. Three tiny specks descended toward it.

I took a deep breath to steady my nerves. But the rebellion was prepared. We weren't. "I love you, Ryan," I whispered.

"Don't you sarding talk some goodbye shite to me! None of that!" he snapped. The general came out. "Look ahead, I think we'll get our fight."

"Why do you say that?" I asked.

"Where there's smoke, there's usually a dragon," Ryan's smile wasn't kind. It was the smile a warrior got when the bloodlust took over.

We flew closer, and I realized I was wrong. There was no volcano. There was a mountain with steep sides that dropped straight into the sea. As we flew closer, the sides became easier to see. Black basalt columns lined with moss and mold rose up out of the water. There had once been a volcano here and its flows had cooled into hexagonal columns, making the mountain look more like a fortress or a towering cathedral than a regular mountain. A cave opening gaped, creating a path for the frothing ocean water to snake into the mountain's heart. Smoke drifted out of the cave opening. The smoke I'd mistaken for a volcano's was dragon smoke.

"Freeze the dragon, hit the bears with peace," I repeated to myself.

"Quinn, you tell Dec we're behind him?" Ryan asked. "Let him know we'll move in on his signal. Get us a damned good mental map of the place, okay?"

Up ahead, Quinn's black head of hair dipped in a nod.

Quinn shared Declan's thoughts in a direct feed with all of us.

Once they dismounted from the winged bear, Countess Malia grabbed Declan and dragged him to the mouth of the cave.

Our group landed in the wooded hills to the east of the cave. We set down amongst tall pine trees and I released Blue so he could stretch his wings. He fluttered up to a pine branch just above me. All of us kept eyeing the entrance even as we watched Declan's thoughts inside our minds.

He entered the cave. Inside, the front cavern was gigantic. It looked as though the entire center of the mountain had been hollowed out. There were smooth black slabs of volcanic rock along the floor. The columns along the wall formed a rough geometric pattern of edges and corners, like children's blocks lined up corner to corner. There was no smooth wall, only edged columns that stretched toward the moss-covered ceiling.

At the back of the cave, the blue dragon was chained to the wall, smoke curling up from his nostrils and scenting the cave. The chain explained why he'd never come to us when summoned.

His orange-red eyes flashed. He did not look happy to be there. Neither did the soldiers that paced nervously through the place, giving the dragon wide berth. They were a mix of Rasle and Cheryn's soldiers.

"That's good," Ryan muttered, "They won't be well equipped to fight together. Confusion will help us out. And the dragon might throw fire, but he'll have limited range."

I did not point out that the sheer numbers they had might overcome any advantage that confusion gave us.

Malia dragged Declan past the soldiers, past the dragon, down a tunnel to a smaller chamber. They rounded a gigantic hexagonal column.

I wasn't prepared for who they saw. I'd known she'd turned. But seeing Ember in the cave still felt like a blow to the head. The fairy that I'd considered my childhood Raslen friend was part of this rebellion.

Ember was naked, her black wings stretched wide. Her breasts dangled like ripe fruit as a man pumped her from behind, his face hidden by her wings. Ember moaned as she leaned forward over a broken column, her pale skin the brightest thing in the cave. Her fingers gripped the stone tightly, a black ring on her finger pinging as she scratched at the boulder.

My eyes zeroed in on that ring. That ring either controlled the dragon or Abbas. I'd have bet my life on it.

Malia cleared her throat uncomfortably.

But whoever was *doing the story* with Ember failed to care. He must have been too close to firing off. He started pumping more rapidly, even as Ember spotted Malia and leaned up to say something. Her wings lowered and a man's hand reached down to slam her torso into the pedestal.

"I'm not finished," Abbas growled, coming into view. His black curls fell to his shoulders and his beard looked bigger and rougher than the last time I'd seen him. His tan skin and defined body showed no signs of the abuse that had been wrought in my dungeons. He had both hands. He'd been magically healed. The tattoos on his biceps flexed as he held Ember down and continued to pump into her.

My entire body twitched with anticipation. Instead of fear, determination filled me. I was going to rip that sarding wicked excuse for a—

"I wish you would stop," Ember commanded.

Her black ring sparked with gold for a second. A cloud of twinkling yellow specks filled the air. And then Abbas froze. Ember pushed herself up off the column. She lifted her leg and slid Abbas' hard, thick cock out of her as she walked around him. His hands clenched in fury. His cock was still red and swollen, begging for attention.

Good. Let him suffer.

Ember didn't give him a second glance. She lazily tossed on a silky black wrap that she scooped off the cave floor. She pulled the material tight around herself and knotted it behind her neck. Then she strode over to Malia, her lavender eyes scanning Declan—scanning me—dismissively. "I told you to bring Declan."

"He never showed. I took her and told the rest to find him and bring him or I'd off her."

Ember's eyes closed in fury. Her lips pressed together. I could almost hear her counting in her head. She turned back to Abbas. "You can finish in one of them."

Malia's eyes widened, and she scrambled backward, tripping over a broken column of rock. "I did what you—"

"You failed."

"You can't just let him—" she didn't finish her sentence. Because just then, Abbas slammed Declan into the angular wall columns. Our vision of the scene went red, as Declan struggled to see. Abbas' fist reared back and connected with Declan's face, smashing it into the columns again.

"Shite! We need to move!" I stepped toward the edge of the tree line.

"No!" Ryan yanked me back. "We aren't just going to be able to get in there past all those soldiers. We need a diversion first."

Cerena rubbed her hands together and looked at Donaloo. "Ideas?"

Donaloo sighed and shook his head, "Ideas need time to germinate. To take root and grow. They need time to culminate in a magic show." He clapped his hands and immediately all the evergreen trees around us yanked their roots out of the ground and stood on those roots as if they were legs. Their needles shook and changed shape, transforming into long, thin green arrows, their sharp-ened points facing outward, glinting in the moonlight.

The pine soldiers started to march on the mountain. The ground shook beneath them. Loud thunks announced each of their steps.

Cerena stared at Donaloo with wide eyes. Her jaw went slack.

Isla and Raj's soldiers heard the racket and poured out of the mountain to confront the threat. The trees spit arrows at them en masse. The soldiers didn't have time to react. They simply fell down, bodies as riddled with spikes as any porcupine.

I didn't have time to be impressed. I ran over to Quinn and grabbed his arm.

Show me what's happening to Declan! I demanded.

Quinn shook his head. I shook him roughly. *That's a damned royal order! You show me.*

Quinn showed me Declan—still in my body. He was doubled over, clenching his arm. Abbas waved a severed hand in front of Declan. My hand. The hand he'd chopped off my knight. The sick shite was still naked.

"Oh, I wish you'd use that to pleasure yourself," Ember murmured.

Gold sparkles ensued. Abbas took the severed hand and used it to stroke himself. His dick hadn't even gone soft.

My heart tripled its beat. Panic soaked my thoughts. I was suddenly drenched in sweat.

Declan's vision flickered.

I took off running, sliding my cloak up over myself so that I was completely invisible.

"Wait!" Connor yelled at me. "The trees are still—"

I ignored him, grabbing the sharpened hairpin from the strap on my arm and wielding it.

Blue swooped down near my head. But he couldn't tell exactly where I was. Only where I was going.

I hurried toward the mouth of the cave.

I could still see Declan's thoughts as Quinn projected them to us; Declan's vision grew hazier as Abbas stabbed him in the thigh.

Sard. Sard.

I did not allow tears to fill my eyes. I shut that shite down. Only rage, I breathed to myself. Only rage.

My feet kept moving.

Suddenly, Declan looked up. There, rising from the water at the far side of the cave was the sea fairy. The one who'd sucked down a ship without a second glance.

Her white, accordion-style wings fluttered in the air, sending droplets of water splattering across the stone floor. Her body glimmered in the light of the lantern Ember had set on a desk at the far end of the cave. There were scales edging every feminine curve and they glowed, pearlescent.

A giant wave rose out of the subterranean river. It splashed across the floor, supporting her and surrounding her as she floated forward.

"A sea sprite," Declan whispered in disbelief.

I tripped over a body on the side of the mountain. I had been too focused on Declan's vision. I pulled myself up, still stumbling toward the cave entrance, still ignoring

Ryan and Quinn and Connor as they fruitlessly chased after me.

In Declan's vision, Ember bowed, going to her knees when she saw the sea sprite. She muttered, "I wish you'd bow," before a golden mist full of sparkles forced Abbas abandoned his sadistic play with the severed hand and do the same.

The sprite's black eyes took in Declan—in my body. "This one wears a crown."

Ember nodded. "She's the daughter of the thief who stole your Avia."

That caused the sea sprite's head to jerk as she took a second look at Declan. Her eyes narrowed.

Beneath the sea sprite, the water rose higher, as high as a castle wall. It moved her closer to Declan. His gaze lifted to track her.

That's why he only noticed the water freezing from the bottom to the top at the last minute. Declan's gaze went down just in time to see a dozen ice spears fly straight at him.

I love—

Declan's vision faded to black. Quinn's voice in my head cut off.

Numb disbelief filled me. My feet slowed, then stopped as I heard distinctive thumps behind me.

I turned away from the cave and ran back down the mountain.

I came upon Ryan first. He was face down in the dirt. I sheathed my weapon and dropped my cloak. I shoved and shoved his huge shoulder until I could turn him over. His curled eyelashes framed empty chocolate eyes. My giant. My protector.

A battering ram slammed into my chest.

No! I thought. This isn't real.

I stumbled to my feet and ran back further. Quinn was laid out on his side, his dark hair hiding his grey eyes. I pushed his hair away and reached out with my mind. Nothing. There was nothing in his eyes. Nothing in his naughty mind to respond to me.

A tornado opened and howled in my ears, battering me with thoughts and emotions as jumbled and sharp as debris.

Connor was only steps behind Quinn. By the time I reached him, his body had already paled. He was already cold. My sweet, childhood love … was gone.

Donaloo and Cerena walked over to me, where I crouched.

"They had a bonding spell?" Cerena asked.

I nodded.

My husbands were dead. All four of them.

CHAPTER TWENTY-EIGHT

*M*y heart cracked like a glacier. My soul fell into the sea. I drowned.

My mind spun. I wanted to die. But I hadn't yet, and it didn't make sense that I hadn't. It was like I had jumped from a cliff. But I couldn't hit the bottom. I was simply falling, endlessly. I was stuck in midair in the moment between existence and non-existence.

There was nothing left for me. They were gone.

My Ryan wouldn't keep me safe anymore. He wouldn't sweep me into his arms and surround me with his strength or pin me down and make me feel like the most desired woman in the world.

My sweet Declan's face flashed before me. I'd never get to rub my fingers over that little crease in his brow and smooth it down again. I'd never get to kiss the corner of his lips and tease him into admitting things that made him blush or have him rub my worries away.

I'd never get to joke with Quinn, never get to stare into his grey eyes and have my core grow slick with just a look. I'd never get to play commoner with him again.

I'd never learn every single one of Connor's secrets. I'd only just started to fall back in love with him. And now, we'd never run through the secret passages. Never peek naughtily at the other nobles again. Never kiss sweetly over a midnight snack.

Because they were gone.

When I finally stood, I felt as if I was floating. Nothing felt real. I blinked when Blue settled on my shoulder. It took me a moment to remember who he was.

I swayed on my feet.

Donaloo somehow appeared in front of me. He put a hand on my shoulder. "I gave Cerena control of the trees. I'll take the dragon. You go do what you need to do."

I blinked. It was a full minute before my tongue seemed to work. "Your rhymes?"

He gave me a sad smile. "This doesn't feel like the time to play the fool."

I nodded, my head still fuzzy. I felt as if someone might have taken my head and stuffed it full of feathers. Because my thoughts were fluff and emptiness.

But my heart, it hurt. I opened my mouth and a wail began.

Cerena grabbed my hands and shook me hard. "No! You do not get to feel right now! Shut it off!" She leaned in, her wild white hair a tangle behind her. "You go and you kill. That's all. You *kill*."

I stared into her eyes and let her energy pour into me.

The lightheaded feeling faded as I recited. "Kill them. I'll kill them."

I pulled the cloak back up, restoring my invisibility and dislodging Blue. He'd have to fend for himself.

I unsheathed my sharpened hairpin and marched toward the cave. I wove around soldiers still trying to escape the trees. I walked lightly past the dragon as he flamed a pine tree that had made it into the cavern. He made a mistake, as he roasted six soldiers in the process and another couple were killed by the fallen tree.

I went down the tunnel, adjusting my grip on my weapon.

Why didn't I grab a sword? I thought. But, two steps later, I was in the second cavern. It was too late.

The sea sprite was gone. The only thing left of her was a puddle. She must have left after she thought she'd killed me.

I saw the shadow of Declan's body, where he'd fallen. The disguise spell was slowly wearing off in death. But he was faced away from the shites who'd murdered him.

And they hadn't noticed yet that they'd killed the weapon they'd wanted. Because I was certain they'd wanted

Declan's powers. Multiply arrows. Decrease enemy shields. Who wouldn't want that power in a war?

My anger increased as I realized what an idiot I'd been. Isla had wanted him. When she hadn't gotten him easily enough, they'd sent Malia to get him.

Where was Malia?

I looked into the shadows and saw a body lying there. Her skirts were ripped and bloody. Her bodice was open. It looked like Abbas had been forced to have his fun with her once the sea sprite killed Declan. If she wasn't dead, I was certain the Duchess wished she was.

I couldn't be bothered to care. My emotions were at bay right now. A sea wall held back the flood.

My eyes narrowed on Ember and Abbas. He'd dressed and they had unrolled a scroll and were talking quietly, standing by the desk, the sole piece of furniture in the cave. I walked silently over to them, waiting until one turned toward me, and I had an open shot.

As I waited, I fought pain in all its glory as it smashed against my defenses. Waiting let my anger build. I struggled not to let sorrow take me over. Not yet. It could have me soon. Death could have me soon. But not yet.

Ember moved first.

Quick as lightning, I shoved the hairpin up under her ribs. Her look of shock and disbelief was worth it.

"Ah!" she gasped.

I yanked out the hairpin and struck again. This time I twisted, trying to rip her black heart right out of her traitor body.

"Ember?" Abbas bumped into me as he reached for her. His eyes widened when he felt me.

I yanked the hairpin out and backed away quickly so he couldn't grab me.

Abbas' mouth opened in shock when he saw Ember grab at her stomach and her hands came away covered in blood.

Abbas shifted into black smoke. The sarding bastard.

The cloud of smoke flew at me as Ember fell to her knees. I ducked down to avoid the darting smoke and crawled over to her, struggling to hold the invisible cloak on me the entire way.

I yanked the black ring from her bloody fingers and slipped it onto my own.

Abbas wanted to play djinni. Then that's what we'd play.

Then I stood, letting the cloak fall from my face as I screamed, "I wish you were dead!"

The swirling black smoke froze. But no golden sparkles appeared. No Abbas fell at my feet.

Sard, I realized. I can't wish for death. But I can level the playing field.

I growled, "I wish you were a powerless human without any magic."

Gold sparkles lit up the room and the smoke coalesced into a boy who looked like Abbas but was frail and weak. He looked younger, like a teenager. Not fully developed. He lay on the floor, chest rising and falling rapidly.

When I took a step toward him, the boy cringed and scrambled to his knees, backing away from me.

A ragged breath echoed in the cavern, distracting me.

I glanced from the dark-haired boy to Ember. She was already still.

It was Malia gasping.

"I wish you couldn't run away," I said to halt Abbas as I stalked toward the duchess.

When she saw me, Malia stiffened, "I'm sorry—"

I cut her off. "He do this to you?" I jerked my head in Abbas' direction.

"She ordered him every step of the way," Malia said.

"You defending him?"

She coughed up blood. "I know what it's like to be coerced."

I tilted my head. I'd been too lenient with Ember's death.

I knelt next to Malia and pulled out my bloody weapon. "You're sentenced to death, for betraying Evaness."

She coughed, "Don't."

I shook my head. "It's done."

"No. Don't kill me. I don't deserve mercy. I deserve …"

I smiled down at her coldly. "I wasn't going to show mercy. I wanted to give you hope, for a moment, and then rip it away. Just as you gave me hope when you fed Willard information. Hope that you might not be irredeemable. But you tried to take my—" I couldn't say Declan's name.

I didn't bother to finish. I didn't owe her explanations. I had a djinni to kill.

I walked over to Abbas, who was trembling in his human form, tears streaking down his cheeks.

I stared at him, my lip curled in disgust. How could he cry after all he'd done? He didn't get to cry. Monsters shouldn't cry.

But then I remembered what my knights had told me about the djinn. Quinn's words echoed in my head. *Djinn are slaves to wishes. Any wish short of death is fair game. If a djinn grants you a wish, he has to fulfill it. He has to do anything to see it fulfilled.*

Full djinn had to grant wishes to anyone who wore the ring. Abbas had no choice. I curled my fingers into a fist and stared at the cave ceiling.

Why in the sarding name of the gods did I have to realize that now? I asked myself. I didn't want to pity him. I wanted to kill him.

I looked down at the boy, who wiped a line of sob snot with his forearm.

My mother would have killed him.

I was not my mother.

I took a deep breath and said, "I wish you were fully human. I wish you'd forget everything you'd ever done or been before this moment. I wish this ring was broken."

I strode toward Abbas, but something midair smacked me hard in the side of the face. I fell backward, hitting my head on the cave floor as gold light erupted from the ring.

My vision went black.

When I opened my eyes, I grabbed at my cheek, where I'd been hit.

It almost felt as though my bird had flown into me in the dark. "Blue?" I asked. My vision flickered as I rose to my elbows.

I didn't see Blue crumpled on the ground beside me. A man leaned over me, naked.

Abbas stared down at me.

Sarding hell! The wish didn't work! It was a trick. Somehow, it was a trick.

My stomach churned and I scrambled backwards.

Above me, Abbas smiled.

He was sarding with my mind.

Rage was a fireball. And my hands flew forward like flames. I struck out.

I hit him with enough peace magic to light the entire cavern an eerie green. If I bled out, so much the better.

Abbas eyes went wide, and his body swayed.

My hairpin hit its target. He gasped.

Good. The sarding demon deserved it. He'd tricked me. He'd made me pity him. See a boy who wasn't there. A vision. Like—I pushed away any thought of Quinn. I twisted the hairpin.

"Wait," his voice came out a gnarled scratch. "Bloss."

I stabbed a second time and then scrambled backward before he fell onto me. I had no delusions. Abbas would kill me. But then I'd join my knights.

I just needed him to hasten my death. I needed him angry.

"I've killed every one of your brothers," I lied. "I have soldiers marching right now to Cheryn. Your entire family will be dead in an hour."

Abbas just clutched at his stomach, still crouched. Playing the victim. Trying to catch me off guard. I'd already fallen for that once.

"Bloss, I just want—I'm Blue. Can't you tell? I'm Blue!" Blood bubbled on his lips.

Fury shot like lava through me. I stood and screamed. "Liar!"

"I just … wanted to give you a wish."

The cruelty of it. The irony. He was toying with me. He'd heard me with Malia. Now he was giving me hope just so he could snatch it away.

My lips couldn't resist the temptation—even though my head screamed that a djinni couldn't give me back what I'd already had. "A wish! A wish! I wish my knights were alive and well, you sarding shite!"

I ran at him and tackled him to the ground, landing on top of him.

I expected him to grab me, choke me, bite me. But he didn't as I scrambled backward.

Abbas' breath grew jagged, ragged, he spit blood.

Abbas gasped out, "Granted."

I waited for him to transform himself back into black smoke. Waited for him to transform into a snake or a monster and attack me. End me. I waited for him to show he was toying with me yet again.

But his eyelids only fluttered.

And then a golden haze surrounded us.

CHAPTER TWENTY-NINE

*T*he entire cavern lit up with a cloud of sparkling golden light.

The cloud moved past us, obscuring my view of the rest of the cavern with its bright glow.

Then, a guttural cough disrupted my train of thought. Abbas was still gasping for breath. I slid closer, careful to stay out of reach, looking down at him.

But the sound wasn't coming from him. He was still, lying on his stomach, one cheek on the stone floor; just a slight twitch came from his limbs as blood dripped from his lips.

I turned and scanned the cavern, clutching my hairpin.

The shimmering golden cloud settled over Declan's body.

I heard the cough again and then a low, familiar groan.

My heart stopped. No. It couldn't be—

I ran through the golden light, to Declan, and dropped to my knees. My hand sought out his. When I squeezed ... he squeezed back.

My head exploded. Stars. Colors. Confusion. Hope. Delight. Awe.

"Dec! Declan?" I dropped his hand and shook him, until I saw his eyelids flutter.

I watched, in wonder, as the golden sparkles melded to his body. They reformed his hand in a shimmering glittering haze of magic. And suddenly his real hand was back, fingers stretching and bending. I ripped at the scraps of my gown where they still clung to him, checking Declan's torso for wounds that stitched themselves up before my eyes.

I clutched at Declan, peppering his blond head with kisses. His ears. His face.

Tears marred my vision and I had to sit up to swipe angrily at them.

"Huh ... huh?" Declan groaned and put a hand to his head. "What happened?"

I didn't answer, my thoughts were cycling so quickly: It can't be true, can it? It's supposed to be impossible.

I stood, heart in my throat and screamed internally, *QUINN! Quinn Hale, you answer me right now!*

The image of a bucking mare and a groomsman muttering, *Whoa!* flashed through my head. The thought was too random to be my own.

Is that you, you shite! Don't tease me!

Yes, it's me, Dove. Stop shouting. I've got one hell of a headache.

Connor. Ryan. Are they okay? Tell me! Now! I paced. My hands shook, my entire being seemed to vibrate with nervous energy.

They're okay. I think. We all fell to the ground. What's going on? Was there another explosion?

Sard! Sard!

My hand flew to my mouth. They were okay. They were alive. Alive. My chest felt light as air, but my throat grew tight. I wanted to dance and sob at the same moment.

My eyes landed on Abbas' body. Blue's body.

He'd told me the truth.

He was Blue.

He wasn't Abbas. I corrected myself: Blue wasn't Fake Abbas. Blue wasn't the djinni.

Blue was Abbas. The real prince. The part-djinni.

And Blue had given me a wish. He'd made my impossible wish come true. He'd brought my knights back to me.

My stomach grew hollow.

Bloss? Are you okay?

I didn't answer Quinn.

I ran out of the cavern as quick as I could. I slid as I went up the slippery stone passage that led to the bigger cavern.

Quinn, tell Ryan I need him.

My knights were already at the mouth of the larger cavern and when they saw me, they started to run.

I launched myself at them. Connor was closest.

He took a step back as I wrapped my arms and legs around him and kissed him wildly. Before he could do much more than stand there in shock, I jumped down and assaulted Quinn. He was ready for it, having seen Connor. His hands gripped my ass and his mind brought me back to our moment in the woods.

But I broke off again.

Ryan scooped me out of Quinn's arms and slammed his lips into mine. He pulled me roughly into him, before he whispered, "You know you're still a floating head, right?"

I laughed. I'd forgotten all about the cloak's magic.

But that thought reminded me. Magic.

"I need you to heal someone," I breathed to Ryan.

He started to march across the cavern with me in his arms.

But Ryan froze and I realized he was staring at the dragon. I'd completely forgotten about the beast when I'd seen my knights.

I turned to look at where the dragon was chained. My jaw dropped when I realized his chain was no longer connected to a ring bolted to the cave wall. But that wasn't the most shocking thing I saw.

At the far end of the cavern, a gigantic sphinx filled nearly half the cave. The giant lion had Donaloo's face and beard, and a blue eye patch. It pinned the dragon down and batted at it, like a kitten might bat at a lizard. The dragon wheezed in protest and shot a tiny bolt of blue flame at the sphinx. But the fire didn't burn Donaloo, he batted at it like a ball of yarn and it unraveled into a trail of smoke.

"What the sard?" I whispered. "Donaloo's a sphinx?"

Cerena appeared, coming around a set of columns in the cavern. "Dunno. He can turn into one, at any rate."

"How long has he been at this?"

"He told the dragon he won't let him go until he answers a riddle. I've already yelled at him a couple times, trying to remind him dragons don't talk."

I pressed my lips together and shook my head. Since Donaloo had the dragon covered, I needed to focus.

"Come on," I urged Ryan.

The sphinx blocked us, carrying the dragon in his mouth and dropping him, pinning the blue monster down with a giant paw. The sphinx's tail twitched back and forth, blocking the passage that led to the second cavern. That led to Blue.

"Uh-uh-uh. A riddle first before the worst. What door has no knocker, for all are welcome to enter and none to leave, because those who do are considered thieves?"

My knights stared at the Sphinx, wide-eyed.

Ryan went to grab at his sword, but I stopped him. "It's Donaloo."

I climbed down from Ryan's arms, glaring at Donaloo. Blue was hurt. He needed us. There was no time for stupid wizard tricks.

Donaloo simply glared back and repeated his question, "What door has no knocker, for all are welcome to enter—"

Can you read his thoughts? I asked Quinn.

Never could even when he was a human. Too much of a magical shield. Definitely not now that he's an animal.

Shite.

I turned to Connor. "Do you know this? Some court game?"

He shook his head.

I covered my eyes and rubbed my forehead. I had no time for stupid pointless riddles when Blue was at death's—

I pulled my hand off my head and glared at Donaloo. "Death," I snapped.

Donaloo's tail stopped flicking. "Correct," he nodded.

But the implication of what he'd asked sank in.

No. He can't die now, I thought. No!

I bolted past the sphinx, down the passage and into the second cavern.

I fell to my knees on the rocky floor next to Blue—I refused to call him Abbas—my friend was Blue. I grabbed his hand.

He was already pale. So pale. The blood was drying on his lips. It wasn't bubbling anymore.

"Sarding hell, don't die! Don't die." I pressed down on the puncture wound on his stomach.

"Bloss?" Declan came over to me. He was naked, having struggled out of the scraps of my dress.

"We need Ryan to heal him. We need to heal him," I repeated, pressing deeper.

"That's … Abbas!" Declan exclaimed.

I shook my head. "It's Blue. It's Blue and he brought you back. We need to heal him!"

I heard my other knights gather behind me.

Ryan knelt next to me and gently moved my hands. His big fingers pressed into Blue's windpipe.

"Heal him!" I screamed at my knight. "You were dead, and he saved you!"

Ryan's chocolate eyes filled with sadness as he met my gaze. "He's gone, Little Dearling. I can heal. I can't bring back the dead."

"No," I whispered. "No, I made a mistake. It was a mistake. Don't die because of my mistake." I pushed Ryan back and leaned forward, taking Blue by the shoulders. My fingers dug in. "Come on. Don't go. Stay, Blue. I believe you. If you're Blue … and you're Abbas—the real Abbas…" I was engaged to Abbas. The real Abbas.

The golden haze that had filled the cave to save Declan appeared again.

Hope bloomed in my chest.

But this time, the haze didn't shoot down and heal Blue. It hovered in midair over us, hesitantly.

"What is that?" Connor asked.

I didn't answer. I stood and yelled at the haze, pointing down at Blue's body. "I wished for my knights to be alive. All of them. That includes this cad." I bent over Blue and whispered in his ear. "You didn't know, but your brother signed an engagement contract with your name on it. You're mine. You're my knight."

Blue didn't move. Darkness licked at my stomach like black fire and I rose up, screaming at the golden haze. "Fix him! You have to fix him!"

Still, the haze hovered. It didn't move. It didn't fix him.

My pleas meant nothing.

Of course, they meant nothing.

Magic did what it wanted. Not what it should. What had that wizard said? It caused more problems than it fixed?

My thoughts and vision grew blurry as I stared down at the poor, innocent prince. The one who'd given a wish to me … even as I'd killed him.

I bent down slowly and settled beside Blue, stroking my red palm over his soft midnight hair. "I'm sorry. I'm so sorry I didn't believe you." I stroked the side of his cheek. "The djinni … he looked like you. No wonder you were pissed at him." I laughed hollowly.

"Bloss Boss," Connor gently tried to take my hand and pull me up, but I wrenched away, grabbing onto Blue.

I stared down at his empty brown eyes, smoothed his thick straight brow, "You were a friend, right from the moment we met."

I reached my fingers to close his eyes.

Donaloo's voice sounded in my head. "The spelling's in the details. And the details are in the spells."

My thoughts cleared. I saw what I'd been missing. Like I was now thinking through a magnifying glass and could see details that weren't there before.

The magic cloud of golden dust still hovered uncertainly above me as the realization hit.

Blue wasn't my knight yet. Almost. But not quite. And something inside prompted me, urged me to bind myself to him.

I had to try, to see if this was the detail that the spell needed, wanted. I desperately hoped so. But, even if it didn't work, at least my Blue would see from the afterlife that I tried, I cared, I regretted.

I leaned forward so that my lips brushed his cold ear and I whispered, "I bond myself to you. In mind. In body. In spirit. For all the days of my life."

I looked up. The haze stood, unmoving, and tears gathered in the corners of my eyes.

That wasn't the detail the spell was looking for, apparently.

My eyes closed. I was a murderer.

I'd killed my friend.

The impact of it didn't sink in. Not truly. I was in a numb state of shock. I didn't process anything emotionally. But intellectually I stood back and stared at myself.

I imagined how I looked at this moment, kneeling in a cave and covered in blood.

I looked at myself as one might look at a stranger. I felt like a stranger, like I had no idea who I was. I'd never thought of myself as a person violent enough for murder. I'd never thought of myself as a capable queen either, because I'd hated that casualties were part of that job.

Apparently, I didn't know myself very well. I had no idea what I was capable of. I'd killed many people tonight. Including someone who hadn't deserved it.

Red dappled lights flitted against my eyelids.

"Bloss!" Ryan cried out in alarm.

I opened my eyes. The golden haze surrounded me. It descended like a rain shower made of light. The droplets of gold went around and past me, as if they were magnetic, drawn to one source only. Glittering golden droplets fell onto Blue's skin and soaked in. I sat, amazed, as the drops spread like a web over his skin, linking the magic until he shone as brightly as the sun.

"What the hell …" Declan didn't finish his sentence.

I ignored him and latched onto Blue's hand, leaning forward, urging the magic to be more powerful than death once more. Urging it to fix my mistake.

I watched as the puncture I'd created in Blue's belly knitted itself back together and the skin grew smooth once more. My heart beat harder and my mouth grew dry as I waited. After that outward sign, I couldn't tell if it was working. The golden light continued to soak into his skin, but he wasn't breathing. I leaned closer, putting my ear to his mouth. Nothing.

"Come on. Come on!" I squeezed his hand. "Hurry," I whispered at the golden light, as if that would affect them. It didn't. I started to rock back and forth. "Dammit all, you shite light. Bring him back. He's my knight. You'd better be bringing him back."

Cursing the magic didn't seem to affect it either.

I dropped Blue's hand and stood.

"Bloss," Connor reached for me, but I pulled away. I was missing something. I was still missing something.

I started pacing, nervous energy wracking me.

If it it's not bringing him back to life, what is it doing? I wondered. Sard! Does it need something else? I gave the vow.

My eyes dropped to Blue, where he lay in a pool of blood.

Sarding hell. I knew what had to happen next. Of all the stereotypical bullshite magical requirements. The magic wouldn't bring him back to life until I sealed my vow … with a kiss.

I had to kiss the man I'd murdered.

My stomach roiled.

What the sard? Why did magic have to be such an asshole stickler for the rules? Why did it have to be so exact?

I closed my eyes and exhaled. This is my fault. All my fault. You have to do this, Bloss, you owe it to him, I thought.

I knelt back down next to Blue, trying to ignore the wet feel of blood soaking my cloak. I closed my eyes and mentally cleared my thoughts. The magic was healing him. He wasn't technically dead anymore.

He's … in a state of suspended animation, I told myself.

I pursed my lips and leaned forward, hands clenched inside my cloak, eyes still shut. But trying to kiss him that way meant I overshot his face. My lips only brushed his hair. Dammit!

"What is she—" Ryan started.

But Declan shushed him. My scholar had worked out what I was trying to do.

I leaned up and tried again, lining myself up better so that I closed my eyes only as I got close, making sure my lips would line up with Blue's. My face tingled as I neared the magic. I could almost hear it vibrating underneath his skin. My lips pursed, ready to touch his—

"Whoa!" a man's voice startled me. I shot up and my eyes popped open.

I looked down to see Blue staring at me, a smirk on his face as he said, "If you're into necrophilia, I'm not sure things will work out for us."

CHAPTER THIRTY

*M*y heart galloped. I put a hand over it even as tears flooded my eyes.

Then I punched Blue in the chest. "You nearly gave me a heart attack."

He coughed. "Seems only fair. You did stab me to death."

"I'm sorry … I thought you were … the Abbas I knew." I push away thoughts of the Abbas I'd fought at the castle.

"Yeah, I know. I would have stabbed me, too, if I'd been you."

"Blue, how'd you become human?"

He bit his lip, "When I saw you free my brother. I just knew—" he touched his heart but didn't finish his sentence.

Another of Donaloo's inane questions came back to me. "What is the most potent magic?"

I let the silence draw on as the answer thudded in my own heart. I cocked my head and stared at him as he laid there. I took a second to stare at him and tried to burn into my mind the reality that this was the *real* Abbas.

It wasn't until he grinned that I remembered he was naked.

"Are you feeling okay now?" I tilted my head and acted like I'd been scanning out of concern. "You spent a long time as a bird. Did everything transfer back—"

He propped an elbow behind his head, showcasing very defined triceps. "I'm fine. No pain or anything."

"How do you feel about … retaliation?" I asked weakly. I doubted he'd attack, but still, I wanted to read his face as I asked.

"Bloss, a wish always costs a living nightmare. I knew what it would cost."

I was floored. "That was a nightmare? I'm pretty sure that was worse than a nightmare."

"It was my nightmare. That you'd hate me. That my brother—being forced to take on my body—had ruined everything. That you'd just see *him* in my face. Not me."

I gulped and looked down. Guilt scratched my ribs. "That's exactly what happened."

A half-grin lit Blue's face. "Well, it's why you don't need to worry about revenge. I'm not like that. Unlike my ass of a father who forced his full djinn son to steal my body, my weapon of choice is sarcasm. So, if your plump ass can't handle that..."

My knights erupted in laughter behind me.

"Plump?" I was offended and amused at the same time. I glared into his sparkling espresso eyes.

"Yup, you're lucky I don't mind a little cushion, but we really do need to discuss the kissing dead people thing. I'm not about to make a habit out of visiting graveyards—"

Quinn sent a picture of me prying open a coffin to all of us.

"I think I might have liked you better as a bird," I narrowed my eyes at Blue.

"You don't mean that."

I definitely didn't. This man could've given Quinn a run for his money in the mockery department. I decided he didn't need further encouragement.

I glanced back over at my knights. Ryan was closest and held out a hand to help me up.

"Are you still feeling okay?" I asked Ryan, uncertain about the after-effects of this magic. It just didn't seem possible that they were all okay.

"Oh, sure, pick a favorite knight," Blue groused.

"He's not my favorite!"

"Yes, I am!" Ryan joined the banter.

Impossible, Quinn mind-shouted. He showed all of us an image of he and I rutting on the palace hall floor with me screaming, "You're my favorite!"

"That never happened," I pouted.

Yet, Dove. It will.

"What never happened?" Blue asked.

Quinn pulled a bead out of his pocket and tied it into Blue's hair.

Then I assumed he resent the image, because suddenly Blue blushed like a school girl.

I shook my head. I couldn't understand how I had continued to exist for a single second without these men.

I turned to Connor and Declan, a grin on my face. "You two aren't joining in?"

Connor shook his head and crossed his arms, "When you know you're the true favorite, it isn't seemly to brag."

Ryan tackled him. Quinn jumped on top of the dogpile.

I laughed until I cried.

Once I started crying, I couldn't stop. Sobs engulfed me.

Declan's arms went around my waist and he lowered me slowly toward the cave floor.

He cradled me in his lap and rocked me back and forth. "Shhh, Peace. It's alright. It's alright."

The others stopped wrestling once they realized my mental state.

"You died. You all died. And I was alone—"

"Bloss Boss, I'm sorry—" Connor gasped, from the floor.

Ryan stood, brushing Quinn off his back and helping Connor up. Blue stood awkwardly, nakedly, off to the side.

"Can you give us a minute?" Declan asked.

Ryan nodded and swung his arms around Connor and Quinn. He nodded toward Blue, "Let's get you some clothes, man."

They left the cavern.

Declan rocked me, using one hand to trace my spine. "Shh, Peace. It's okay."

I shook my head, "No. It's not. I watched you get tortured. I watched you die, Dec!"

He hugged me tighter and I cried until my throat was raw.

When I was quieter, he raised one hand and gripped my neck tight at the base of my skull. He pressed in then down. Then he repeated the motion, petting me. Pulling the tension out of my body. The movement gradually turned my muscles limp. I took a number of long shuddering breaths.

I swiped at my swollen eyes and met his steady blue gaze. "Why didn't you fight back?"

He gave a sad half-grin. "I was trying to give you all a chance to get there. Trying to get as much info as I could. I didn't see the ice—"

I punched his chest lightly. "That was stupid shite. You're supposed to keep yourself safe."

"No. I'm supposed to keep you safe."

I shook my head. "You should have used your power."

"And let them know it was me? That they already had exactly what they wanted?" Declan shook his head fiercely. "Sard them."

"I agree. Sard them all." I pressed my hand against his chest and realized I was covered in blood. "Oops. Sorry." I pulled my hand back and stared at it.

Declan shifted and pulled me up. "Let's get cleaned up."

He moved toward the subterranean stream. But I balked. "I'm not getting in there," I said. "That's where she came from." The nameless sea sprite who'd killed him.

"Shh," he calmed me. "We won't get in."

He brought me over to the edge, and we followed the water down, away from the cavern filled with death. We wound our way along the narrow ledge for a bit until the cave opened up again into another cavern. This cavern looked as though it belonged to fairies. It was breathtaking. The roof was full of tiny, twinkling blue lights. They looked like tiny stars or chandeliers.

I looked up to see Declan's response and saw the same awe reflected in his eyes. When he noticed me watching him, he turned toward me and smiled.

"May I?" he gestured at my invisible cloak.

I shrugged, grinning but still sniffling from my crying fit. "You don't like me as a floating head?"

"I love you—any way I can get you," Declan replied.

I smiled and the tears threatened again.

"Except for crying, Peace. No more," he scolded as he stripped the invisible cloak off me and laid the plush fur on top of the rock. The inside was visible when it was laid out and I could make out the different shades in the gray rabbit fur. When he saw I only wore a stained man's shirt beneath the cloak his eyebrows lifted.

I shook my head. "Later. I'll explain later."

Declan pulled off my shirt. Then he dipped it into the water, letting the current pull out some of the worst stains.

"Sit down," he told me.

I sat on the soft fur of the cloak.

Declan wrung out the shirt and came over to me. He cleaned me gently, wiping away all traces of blood and grime. He took care even to clean the beds of my finger-nails with small swipes. Declan moved from my hands to my torso. He dragged the makeshift rag slowly up my stomach, circled my breasts, and then back down. Goosebumps followed in his wake. He wiped my hands, held out my arms and swiped all the way to my armpits, tickling me slightly. He swiped from my feet upward, tracing lazy circles on my calves, under my knees, and then up higher.

"Shouldn't you swipe down?" I asked as he brought the cloth up my inner thighs.

"I don't know, should I?" Declan asked, his eyes burning into me. He leaned closer as he swiped the rag up over my hip and around my inner thigh. He braced himself on one hand and leaned into me as he wiped the other hip and thigh in the same, slow seductive manner.

My breathing started to become shallow. He was so close I could feel the warmth of his body. It contrasted the chill of the water that had raised goosebumps on my skin and pebbled my nipples.

Declan's eyes stared into mine as he cleaned my most intimate spot gently. One swipe then another. A small circle.

My lips opened in tiny silent moans.

He never broke eye contact. He never touched me, other than with the rag. He just softly swiped again and again until I thrust my legs open desperately.

When I did that, Declan sat back on his knees and said, "Now you do me."

I swallowed hard and took the rag from him with shaking fingers. Declan had said he wanted our first time to feel special. That he wanted me desperate for him. I'd nearly lost him. That had driven desperation to a whole new

level. Torture. And he'd sent everyone away. Did he …
was he ready?

I dipped the shirt into the seawater and my mind was
made up. I needed him. I needed to feel him, alive and
thriving and whole. I needed to warm my heart with him.
I needed to see his eyes flicker and close in ecstasy. I
needed to erase the pain. I was going to do my damned
best to show him that he meant everything to me.

I wrung out the garment and made my way back over
to him.

I started with his feet, knowing that once I got too close, I
wouldn't be able to stop myself. I tried to massage his foot
with my fingers through the cloth, working out any
soreness.

I washed his legs, using every excuse I could find to touch
him. I dragged my finger along the edge of his quadriceps.
I washed his hands, kissing each palm after it was clean. I
washed his arms. Then I rinsed the shirt and cleaned his
back. When the pale muscular expanse of Declan's back
was clean, I pressed my aching breasts against his scars. I
traced one and kissed it, before coming back around and
straddling him.

I smiled softly at him as I stroked the rag over his neck,
his pecs, down the flat plane of his stomach.

My heart filled so much I thought I might burst. The
emotions were as airy and multicolored as soap bubbles.
Adoration, affection, longing. So much tenderness.

Tears filled my eyes again and I sucked in a jagged breath.

Sard! I hadn't even finished cleaning him and I was going to melt down again.

"Bloss?" Declan's hand came up to cup my cheek.

I stared at him. "I'm sorry. I was trying. I wanted to show you how much I love—I'm just still shaken up. I can't lose you, not ever."

Declan brushed away a tear that escaped down my cheek. Then he kissed me, gently. "I know you love me. I can feel it."

My tears continued to flow but I shoved my sobs down, tossed away the shirt, and pulled him roughly into me. This was what I needed. This. A physical reassurance that he was here. That he was mine. That he still loved me. I yanked at his hair and pushed myself closer, mashing my breasts into his chest. Our kisses grew fiercer. He sucked on my tongue. Then he released it and bit my lower lip so hard I gasped.

I pushed him back on the rabbit's fur cloak and leaned over him. I skimmed my teeth along his neck and lightly over his collarbone. "You're mine, Declan," I whispered.

"Yes."

"No, say it!" I ordered. "Tell me." I bit his pec savagely, letting my teeth dig into his pale skin. I marked him. Claimed him.

"Argh! I'm yours!"

I grabbed his hand and licked it, from the base of his palm to the tip of his middle finger. "Touch me."

Declan slid his hand between our bodies as I leaned back down over him and bit his earlobe lightly. I circled the spot with my tongue and then started tracing a path up the shell of his ear.

His finger traced an oval around my opening, teasing me just right.

I leaned up on my arms and stared down into his eyes. "Tell me what my body likes best," I breathed, as he moved his finger in, spreading my lips slightly and sending a shudder up my spine.

"You like your pussy lips touched gently," Declan's eyes were blue fire. "Your clit likes to wait, to be swollen and aching first. I need to touch your nipples first."

His free hand traveled over my ribs and across my breast. His fingertips latched onto my nipple, pulling lightly in a steady motion that drove me crazy. After a minute, he started flicking my nipple with his nail. Then he pinched hard and twisted. At the same time, he dragged the finger he'd soaked in my juices up across my clit.

I clenched my teeth and mewled as my orgasm rippled up my spine. It was one of those softer, teasing orgasms. Openers. The kind that left me desperate for more.

"Again," I moaned at Declan, taking control of his mouth.

He complied, circling, circling down near my core. His fingers at my nipple went back to a light latch.

I knew what was coming. And my anticipation grew with every lazy circle. I grew so wet that I could hear his finger as it circled.

"Now," I said.

Declan shook his head. "Not yet."

I smacked his side with my hand. "Now!"

His fingers wrenched my nipple and he strummed my clit. There was nothing teasing about this orgasm. It ripped through me like a tidal wave. I bit down on a scream. I didn't want anyone running down here. I wasn't done with him.

Declan drew my orgasm out by fading from direct contact to circles that lightly stimulated my clit every few seconds. The orgasm faded gradually to a shiver.

"Gods, you're amazing," I kissed him gently. "I can return the favor, or you can—"

Declan thrust up into me without another word.

I was so wet that after a few thrusts my thighs were coated in my own slick. I sat up and ground down, riding my knight. He bent his legs behind me, planting his feet on the floor.

"Lean back," Declan murmured. I leaned a bit and he pushed me further. "Now plant your feet and ride me, Peace. Use me. Make that beautiful body come apart on top of me." I slammed down and realized what a genius Declan was. Leaning back was exquisite. My insides became molten as his shaft hit that perfect spot. Again, and again and again I moved, throwing my head back.

Declan's magic hands snaked up to my breasts and grabbed them, pushing upward, doubling their bounce. It made me feel even more wild. My eyes opened, but I couldn't see as the next orgasm surged up through my head. I was awash in bliss. I floated for endless moments, limp and unmoving until Declan yanked me back down to him.

I expected him to rut me hard, but what he said left me gasping. "Now, I'm going to show you your very favorite position."

More? My brain was dazed. I was getting more orgasms?

Declan gently lowered me to the cave floor so that I laid on my back. Then he laid down on his side with his body perpendicular to me. He moved forward and lifted my legs so he could scoot underneath my thighs. He lined up our pelvises at a ninety-degree angle. He thrust into me at that angle. Then he let go of my legs and ordered, "Plant your feet on me. One on my thigh, one on my ribs."

I followed his instructions. Once my legs were propped up and out of the way, Declan grabbed onto my hips and started to move. He stroked in and out slowly. And with every stroke, he set me on fire. Then he did something I didn't expect or anticipate. He reached his hand through my legs and started rubbing my clit. With this position, he had unfettered access.

"Hump me," Declan told me as he reached for a nipple with his free hand.

I used my feet on his side to thrust. And I nearly collapsed. I saw stars. It was perfect. The hot warm press of his member inside, the circles his hand made, the tingle that shot down my spine when he pinched my nipple—I was trapped in a constant rolling orgasm. I keened, unable to help myself. I drew it out as long as I could. But eventually, I felt like I was going to pass out. I collapsed. My body was liquid. Declan had melted me.

Declan quickly moved on top of me with a proud grin. "Now, aren't you glad I had so many years to get to know this hot body?"

I nodded lightly, still unable to focus my eyes. "So, so sarding glad! Gods, you can do anything to me. Anything. My ass if you want."

I starfished.

Declan laughed and leaned over me. "Maybe another day, Peace." He swiped a gentle hand over my cheek. "Now, is it my turn?"

I nodded again, still enjoying the afterglow.

Declan lined himself up and then he rutted me like an animal, pressing my shoulders down so hard I could feel the shapes of the stone under the rabbit's fur. Every stroke hit my cervix. He was so deep, but my insides were soft and compliant and more than willing after all the orgasms.

"Say you love me," Declan panted.

"I love you more than anything," I reached up and caressed his face. And those damned tears resurfaced. "So, so much."

Declan leaned down and kissed me as he came inside me.

He collapsed onto me, wrapping his arms and legs around me in a giant prone hug.

And then I heard a round of applause.

"Let me comfort, Bloss, she's crying. I'm using that excuse next time, you tricky bastard," Ryan teased.

Declan laughed and leaned up, still inside me as he bit his thumb at Ryan. "Sard off."

"Is that an invitation?" Connor asked.

I arched my head back and saw all four of my other knights in the cavern. I gave them an upside-down glare. "Leave him alone. He just died!"

"So did we," Connor gestured at the group.

I rolled my eyes, which was ineffective upside down. I slid away from Declan, gave him a wink, and stood. "You weren't tortured."

Blue raised his hand immediately.

I rolled my eyes, "Fine. If you're hungry …" I gestured between my legs.

Quinn and Connor ran forward, both slapping and elbowing each other.

I laughed. "You're both idiots."

"Your idiots," Connor grinned. And, like always, that grin turned my insides to mush.

"My idiots," I agreed. "I'd love nothing more than to make love to all of you right now. But we have a castle that was attacked and is under a freezing spell that lasts seventy-two hours. We have two insane nations and a sea sprite about to launch an international war. And we still haven't found Avia."

Quinn rolled his eyes and projected to everyone: *Fine. I guess we can take turns with you.*

"Is there a dance card?" Blue asked. "You know, like a sex signup sheet?"

I laughed until my ribs hurt, and my throat was raw.

Blue pouted, "Well, that would be the fair way to do it."

Connor patted him on the back. "Try it. You'll realize, you'll just be giving Quinn a schedule, so he knows exactly when to pipe up and ruin your moment."

Quinn grinned. *I like this idea. Signup sheet it is!*

I laughed. And laughed. And laughed until Ryan came over and scooped me up because I wasn't capable of standing on my own two feet.

I looped my arms around him as Declan threw me my cape.

"Ready to go take on the world?" my giant asked.

I smiled. Because with my knights back at my side, I was ready. I looked at each of them, holding each man's gaze long enough to show him what he meant to me. Then I said, "Let's go do impossible things."

EPILOGUE

e all went up to the main cavern. When we reached it, Donaloo and the dragon and Cerena were gone.

"Where'd they—"

"Outside. Apparently, after Donaloo's paw ended up wet, there were some words about dragon toilet-training," Connor shook his head and looked at me. "You realize the world's gone insane since you came back?"

"You can't blame me for that!"

Declan narrowed his eyes and studied me. "Statistically speaking—"

I hopped out of Ryan's arms and punched my scholar. "No. Statistical nothing. I didn't start this war!"

The guys looked at Blue. He shrugged. "My father tossed my full djinn brother to the sea creatures before you came back. And then Syan—that's his name—turned my other brother into a dragon to steal your sister *before* you were back—"

My knights groaned as I smirked ... until Blue added, "But ... technically, I was only turned into a bird once we heard about you. So, *my life* was technically, officially ruined because of you."

The men all cut up laughing.

I put my hands on my hips and marched over to Blue, naked except for the invisibility cloak draped over my arms. His eyes darted to my breasts.

"You wanna repeat that?" I glared up at him.

Connor doubled over. "You look exactly like your old nanny!"

I gasped and turned to glare at him. "That was low."

Declan asked Connor, "You saw your nanny naked?" which led to a round of chuckles.

Apparently, death experiences made us all a bit giddy in the aftermath.

Ryan stripped some clothes off a guard for me as he asked Blue, "So, you said your father tossed your brother to the wicked fairy. But you still haven't explained how you became a bird."

"Syan had some wizard turn us into animals so he could control us more easily."

I shook my head. "Well, thank goodness that didn't work out for him."

Blue grinned, "Thank goodness for me." His eyes roamed my figure as I pulled on a tunic that fell to mid-thigh. "At least he got me engaged to a hot queen."

I laughed. "You're married now, sir."

He bowed, "My Lady."

I rolled my eyes. "Yeah, that's never gonna work for me."

I turned the topic back to his brothers. "I guessed the dragon was your brother from the beginning," I said, glad I was right about something in this debacle. "What are the others? Who the hell was Shiter?"

Blue laughed. "Nath's the dragon. He's always been the most easy-going of us, so he was probably easiest to control. My brother Harsh was your rabbit friend. I'm pretty sure he'd be offended by that cloak you have."

I petted my rabbit fur cloak and laughed. "Harsh. Well, Shiter's name isn't too much worse then."

Blue cracked a grin. "Sedarth was the bear."

"Why animals?"

Blue's eyes twinkled. "How else do you think the Elven chain was smuggled into your palace? Sedarth carried it. Harsh burrowed under that spell your mage made. It doesn't extend underground. Then I was forced to alert him when it was ready."

My eyes grew wide. My mind flew back to the image of a bluebird attacking Abbas. "That attack, when we were walking in the garden?"

He pushed himself roughly into a sitting position. "He forced me to alert him. He just wasn't specific enough about how I had to alert him. His mistake. I like loopholes." A wry grin hit his face.

"Good thing," Declan said darkly.

That was all it took for my throat to tighten up as I looked back at my blond knight.

"Yes. Very good thing."

We all were quiet for a moment.

Blue shrugged. "Unfortunately, I couldn't do much to the bastard in bird form."

"But he didn't keep controlling you, did he? I mean, the past few weeks, you've been with us …" Ryan let the question trail off.

Blue jerked his head at Quinn. "He pulled those rings off and asked us to come protect Bloss."

I glanced at Quinn. *Thank you, my love.*

He quirked a grin at me. *Anytime.*

We had another quiet moment, standing in a circle and we all just breathed one another in. Our little family.

Then Connor said, "Dec, can you get dressed? I'm kinda sick of seeing your roly poly."

Declan waggled his hips, letting his penis slap his thighs, "You mean this broomstick?"

"Tiny nob," Ryan corrected.

"Staff of life," my scholar argued as he pulled on trousers.

"Mouse," Blue contributed to the male anatomy argument.

Tickle-tail. Fireplace poker. Stallion. Quinn sent us all mental images to accompany his penis-names.

"Shaft of delight," Declan laughed. "The *peace*maker."

Everyone groaned at that pun.

I rolled my eyes. It looked like the giddiness was back in full force. Good. We needed the humor to fortify us. Because I had a feeling the days ahead would be dark.

"I'll let you boys argue about the proper names for your cocks while I go make a grown-up plan with Cerena." I pulled on a dead soldier's pants and boots as they continued to toss out every term they'd ever learned. There were far too many. Men spend entirely too much time thinking about their own dicks.

I found Cerena outside the cave. But no Donaloo and no dragon.

I walked over and stood beside her as she watched the pine trees stomp back to their homes in the forest and rebury their roots in the soil.

"Where's our wizard?" I asked.

"Said he had to take care of something. Took off with the dragon and some kid."

We stared at the trees until I heard the jostling and joking of my knights behind me.

I rolled my eyes at Cerena and said, "Here they come, the hope of the realm."

When they reached the cave entrance and spotted us, they all moved forward. All except Quinn, who froze, stock-still, staring at Cerena and myself.

Are you okay?

Quinn rubbed his face. He squinted at us.

The other knights noticed and turned to watch him.

Slowly Quinn's eyes widened. He thought at all of us: *I can't tell what Cerena's thinking.*

I turned to Cerena. "Did you use a spell to protect your thoughts?"

"No. Why?"

"Did Donaloo?"

"I don't think so."

I turned back to Quinn. *Maybe ... after coming back to life ... maybe your powers are just a bit slower?*

Quinn shook his head; his breathing came more rapidly.

"Declan, can you multiply something for me?" I asked, thinking that maybe my other knight might struggle a bit and that would help Quinn relax.

He's just too tense, I thought.

Declan raised his hand at a shield held by a dead Rasle soldier.

Nothing happened.

His light blue eyes met mine in a panic.

My heart started to beat faster. I turned to Ryan. I ran a fingernail over one of my old scars, scratching myself. "Ryan, heal my scratch."

Ryan came over. His hand closed over my wrist. But there was no pink light. My scratch didn't heal.

I turned and stared hard at Blue. "Do you know what the hell is going on?"

Blue swallowed hard, his Adam's apple bobbing. Everything about his body language was uncertain. He fidgeted with his hands. "You can't wish for what you've already had."

"What?" I asked the question even though black dread filled my stomach. Because I thought I knew the answer.

"A wish can't make things exactly the same as they were. The magic doesn't allow it. Whenever a wish touches something or someone, it changes them."

My stomach tightened. "Changes them how?"

Blue shrugged. "I had to use that loophole. I had to wish for them to come back, but not exactly as they were before."

Understanding poured over me like a waterfall. I turned back to stare at my knights.

"Connor, what am I feeling?" I turned to my best friend, hoping against hope that he was unscathed.

Connor walked over to me, eyes focused on mine. His easygoing facade fell as he reached me. He grabbed my hands and squeezed my fingers tight. That squeeze told me all I needed to know. He couldn't feel a thing.

I turned to Quinn. *How can you still hear thoughts?*

I can hear yours because you have a bead. From Donaloo. I can hear and talk to the five of you. To my spies. But I still can't hear Cerena.

I turned and stared at Blue as hope collapsed and fear chomped my stomach to bits.

"Say it. Just say it," I commanded my newest knight.

"I think the wish brought us all back … as full humans."

KNIGHT'S END: TANGLED CROWNS
BOOK 3

Knight's End - Tangled Crowns Book 3

Now Available at Amazon.com

ACKNOWLEDGMENTS

A huge thanks to Rob, Raven, Ivy and Makayla. Thanks to my cover designer, Carol at Marques Designs, and my amazing ARC readers.

And thanks to you…my amazing readers. Without you, these ramblings of mine would be confined to my computer. You and your encouragement make me brave enough to put my imaginings out into the open and let them roam free. I'm eternally grateful to be able to do what I do.

Made in United States
North Haven, CT
31 May 2024

53149894R00232